AMOUNTING TO NOTHING

Visit us at www.boldstrokesbooks.com

By the Author

Harmony

Worth the Risk

Sea Glass Inn

Improvisation

Mounting Danger

Wingspan

Blindsided

Mounting Evidence

Love on Tap

Tales from Sea Glass Inn

Amounting to Nothing

AMOUNTING TO NOTHING

by
Karis Walsh

2017

AMOUNTING TO NOTHING

ISBN 13: 978-1-62639-728-6

This Trade Paperback Original Is Published By
Bold Strokes Books, Inc.
P.O. Box 249
Valley Falls, NY 12185

First Edition: February 2017

Credits
Editor: Ruth Sternglantz
Production Design: Susan Ramundo
Cover Design By Sheri (graphicartist2020@hotmail.com)

CHAPTER ONE

Merissa Karr dropped a handful of index cards on the floor of the car when Dennis Morgan accelerated to pass a semi on I-5. She kept her head up and her eyes fixed on the sun setting on the horizon as she groped for the cards, fighting off a wave of nausea. Her stomach lurched along with the sporty little BMW as he slid back into the right lane.

"Sorry," Dennis said with a rueful grin in her direction. "I'm trying to tone it down for you."

She waved off his apology. She'd driven with her boss and mentor often enough to know that he really was making an effort to smooth out his driving for her. She'd experienced his speed and sharp turns plenty of times before she'd been comfortable enough to tell him she was prone to motion sickness. She had been queasy during most of her internship with his firm. Damned inconvenient affliction. She focused on the city sprawled on her right and kept her breathing deep and even until she felt her stomach settle.

The view of the city wasn't attractive enough to distract her mind, but her vision of its future was. The approach to Tacoma from Interstate 5 wasn't pretty from either direction. From the south, the town snuck up on you in an increasing jumble of strip malls and cheap hotels, culminating in a large indoor mall. From the north, driving down from Seattle like she and Dennis were doing today, the city's innards seemed exposed to view. The industrial Tideflats, with its pulp and paper mill and oil refineries, sprawled along the edge of

Commencement Bay, spewing steam and God knew what else into the air and contributing to what was called—indulgently by locals and sneeringly by everyone else—the Aroma of Tacoma.

The nickname was a call to action for Merissa, and she wanted nothing more than to replace it with something more positive and beautiful. She stared at the downtown area where it climbed the hill rising steeply from the bay. From here, she could see buildings and houses, but the details weren't obvious, especially as night descended and the streetlights were bright. The city's efforts at improvement—from the museums and boutique shops to the Chihuly Bridge of Glass—blended in with the vacant, graffiti-covered buildings and run-down homes. The possibilities seemed endless from this vantage point.

"It looks like a blank slate from here, doesn't it?" Dennis asked, as if reading her mind. He took the City Center exit and braked suddenly to avoid hitting the cars stopped at the light in front of him.

Merissa braced her hand on the dash. "Sometimes I wish we could wipe it clean and start from scratch," she said. The idea of reinventing her city and making it a place more citizens would be proud to call home filled her with a sense of purpose she'd never felt before she came to the Morgan Consulting Group. She'd grown up in a world of big business and big money, but it had always seemed pointless to her. Her first tentative forays into urban planning after graduate school had been fulfilling, but she hadn't even dreamed of the epic possibilities for change she now saw.

Of course, business always required compromise. She was slowly learning how to deal with investors and builders by watching Dennis whenever she got a chance. He had a natural ability to adapt and change his vision during negotiations, and she doubted she'd ever be as flexible. She'd have to figure out how to stay true to her vision while acknowledging the ideas proposed by other people who were involved in her renovation projects. She hadn't seen his bargaining skills in action since he usually pitched ideas on his own, but she'd pieced together some sense of the concessions he'd made by comparing the ideas he seemed to particularly like during the firm's weekly brainstorming meetings with the finalized specs he created before he met with his contractor. In her mind, the two versions of the same plan—what she and the other employees contributed and what he eventually created—were often very different, and she hadn't been with the firm long enough to see the actualized concept after the third draft, when the contractor and investors gave their input. She figured the more money involved, the more say the investors had, but even when she factored in the necessary compromises, the potential for growth and positive change with this firm was still astounding and exciting to her. She had toured plenty of the spaces D.M. had designed and built before she came to work with him, and she was thrilled to be part of the firm's future.

"It'd be amazing to begin with an empty space and create a city with intention and good planning, but who will ever have a chance like that? We have to work with what we have and take it one block at a time," Dennis said, as if they were trying to cure the city of an addiction to unattractiveness.

Merissa took advantage of another stoplight and sorted through her index cards. She and Dennis had spent the afternoon in Seattle, driving around neighborhoods as they searched for ideas for their next renovation project. Sometimes she felt as if she learned more from a day with Dennis—slowly traveling up and down city streets while they talked about the different design elements they noticed—than she had in the two years spent pursuing her master's degree. McGill's program had been challenging, but Dennis had knowledge and insight she soaked up like a sponge. Many of their discussions seemed more theoretical than real, because few of the design elements they appreciated in common actually made it onto the plans for residential and business complexes the Morgan Group produced, but she lovingly filed away every structural form and general impression they observed and deliberated over. Once she had proved herself in the lower levels of the company, she hoped she'd be able to put her own flair on the proposals she presented. Until she had that sort of autonomy, she was determined to at least vocalize her ideas, whether or not they were used.

She looked away from her notes and out the window once they started moving again and pointed at a cement staircase leading up the hillside.

"I want an entrance like that in the new neighborhood," she said. The Tacoma branch of the University of Washington was bisected by several series of wide steps and shrub-filled plateaus. Old-fashioned lampposts illuminated the ascending courtyards with a soft yellow glow, inviting pedestrians to walk through the campus instead of bypassing it. "We can line it with boutiques and open-air cafés. Maybe a small park."

She imagined the families living in condos she had designed and gathering in the common areas she envisioned, exchanging conversation and sharing stories. "And how about a dog park? There aren't any nearby, and the local residents could come and bring their pets. It'd be a wonderful way to draw families and people from nearby neighborhoods into the courtyard. They'd likely stay for a cup of coffee or something to eat at one of the cafés, and then window shop while they pass by the stores. They'll return if they need something from one of the shops…"

Dennis pulled her out of her daydreams. She was good at picturing ideal neighborhoods and giving them shape in her mind. Dennis was more experienced at giving concepts a physical substance.

"Where will the condos go if you have so many elements in the center of the block?" he asked. "Will they be in a narrow strip around the outside? You'll be giving up too much rentable space that way." The argument was good-natured and familiar to Merissa. Dennis wanted to isolate the blocks they designed, and she wanted to welcome everyone inside. His tendencies were naturally more prevalent in the Group's projects because he was the boss and sole head of design. Merissa and the other employees were on equal footing with each other, but far below him. She'd noticed his increased interest in the trajectory of her career lately, though, at least on a personal level. He took her on these trips and seemed to enjoy their discussions, and he even had her join him and his wife Karen for dinner at their home. She hoped an opportunity to experiment with her personal designs would follow someday.

Already, he had been incorporating more of her input than that of any of her peers. Those elements were small, but recognizably hers, and she hoped she was seeing a pattern emerge. Just like she rebuilt Tacoma in her mind, she also rebuilt her position at the firm, picturing a new future and more chances to create real-life versions of what she saw in her imagination.

"We can add a small central garden in the middle, for the surrounding tenants to use," he continued. "With a big gate to keep everyone else outside."

Merissa laughed. She'd long since learned that even if Dennis didn't accept one of her ideas, he never minded when she offered suggestions, even if she was blunt. She couldn't resist being forthright now. "You're too shortsighted, D.M. People will come here to shop and eat in a relaxing environment. They'll love it so much that they'll be waiting in line to buy the next complex we build. Restricting access will limit exposure."

"Shortsighted," he repeated with a snort. "Yeah, that's the reason we're the number one consulting firm in the city. Because I can't see past the nose on my face."

Merissa glanced at Dennis before answering. He was grinning, the wrinkles around his light blue eyes proving he spent more time smiling than not, and he looked perfectly at ease in his beige cashmere turtleneck and brown suede jacket. He was prone to understatement in his words as well as his clothes, making his point more effectively because of it. Morgan Consulting was more than the top firm in Tacoma. It was the highest grossing one in the Northwest, and growing every year. Most of the credit for its success was due to the handsome gray-haired man sitting next to her, but for more reasons than his personal talent and drive. He oozed charisma and the promise of wealth through his bearing and his outward appearance, and he had the skill and instincts to back up his promises. Merissa doubted those traits alone would have made the Morgan Group what it was today if he hadn't been the type to hire and encourage employees who saw the world in different ways than he did. He rewarded original thinking, even if—especially if, Merissa amended in her mind—the thinker didn't agree with him. Merissa had grown up around the yes-men and sycophants her grandfather had hired, as well as the groupies who followed her globe-trotting parents wherever their whims took them. She'd never known a world where original thought and dissension were seen in a positive way. Right now most of her positive feedback from him was in the form of praise and validation, not necessarily in concrete buildings and blocks, but she was patient. She'd wait and learn and store away her designs in her mind. Once she had paid her dues and had moved up in the company, she would be ready to make the real changes she wanted to see.

Until then, she was thriving in her relationship with Dennis. She'd learned long ago to be suspicious of people who blindly agreed with anything she said. He spoke his mind and expected her to do the same, and she never had to look for hidden agendas or subtle manipulation in his interactions with her. She trusted Dennis more than anyone else, and he seemed more like family to her than her own.

She looked forward again, mentally cataloging the ages and styles of the houses they passed. Postwar Craftsmans, stately Victorians, early twentieth-century brick homes. Even though she wanted to revitalize the city, her visions were often based on older styles, and she liked the idea of keeping some of the higher quality and well-structured original homes and buildings. Yet another difference between her and Dennis. Restored and preserved, those old homes would make stunning shops and restaurants. Residential space, packed tight in the downtown area, would expand upward to newly constructed condos and apartments. "The city is changing," she said. "The more blocks we transform, the more we'll want to encourage movement and a flow of commerce between them. If we close them off now, they'll be too isolated. We'll have designed a series of tiny neighborhoods instead of a connected city."

Dennis didn't respond right away, and when she looked at him expectantly he was staring in his rearview mirror with a slight frown. "What's wrong?" she asked.

"Hm, nothing. I just thought I recognized someone, but I must have been mistaken," he said, turning left and heading up the hill, away from busy Pacific Avenue and toward their target block. He continued their conversation, a smile back on his face. "You'll eventually learn, dear Merissa, that exclusion, not inclusion, is the key to making people line up for a chance to live in the neighborhoods you create. The more you look like you're trying to keep people out, the more desperately they want in."

"Cynic," she said with a shake of her head.

"Idealist," he countered.

Merissa smiled and pushed her dark blond hair behind her ear. They were each a little of both, she thought. Maybe that's why they got along so well. He had been born and raised in Tacoma and he had seen both growth and decline over six decades here. She had been raised mostly in Europe with her jet-setting parents, and she still carried a slightly idealized image in her mind of beautiful cities where life was lived on the sidewalks and in the cafés. Places where it didn't matter if you felt lonely behind closed doors, because once you stepped outside, everyone was family and friend. Her years in Montreal for university and grad school had cemented her belief that public spaces where citizens congregated and shared information, beliefs, and philosophies made for stronger communities in a general sense, and less isolation and loneliness on a personal level.

She wouldn't let Dennis talk her out of her vision of the city as a walking-friendly one where neighbors and consumers lived more on the streets and less hidden away inside buildings. He, likewise, wouldn't likely give up his goal of self-contained, exclusive— and expensive—complexes where select people lived and worked together. Their shared goal was a beautiful and safe Tacoma.

Dennis turned again and slowed even more. In some ways, the area around their target neighborhood didn't look either safe or beautiful right now. Most of the stores had bars on their windows, and a lot of the cars looked like they needed to be towed if they were going anywhere besides where they were parked at the moment. Dennis gestured around them.

"You can see why insular is the way to go," he said. "Tenants want to feel secure, and an enclosed environment is the only way to make them feel at home here."

Merissa shook her head with emphasis and had to tuck her hair back again. "If we only look at what's here before us, I'd have to agree with you. But we have to look into the future and see what this city can become."

"Here we are," Dennis said instead of commenting on her words as he started to circle the block they wanted to develop. Merissa watched through the passenger window as they passed a variety of structures. A derelict strip of medical offices, most vacant and for rent. Three short and squat apartment buildings, complete with peeling paint, balconies crowded with toys and plastic furniture, and weedy parking lots. A miniscule grocery store with displays of fruit and cases of beer in front. A smattering of single-family homes, including two that were abandoned and had graffiti-covered plywood over their doors and windows. Like stop-motion photography, in Merissa's mind she saw all of it torn down piece by piece and her new vision erected in its place.

She noticed a family gathered on one of the tiny lawns that separated an apartment building from the sidewalk, and her mental construction project paused. A woman with gray hair pulled back in a tight bun sat on a chair in the center of the space, near a table with some balloons and a cake. She was surrounded by adults ranging in age from twenties to eighties. Little kids, some shirtless and some shoeless, ran and played around the group of adults, while a cluster of teens leaned on the brick wall between the apartment entrance and the grass. As she and Dennis cruised by, a pedestrian waved and called out to the woman, and then he was pulled in and assimilated into the group. A few of the younger adults moved away to join the teenagers. Flux and movement, a blurring of lines between families and strangers. There was no sign of wealth or prosperity here, except for the unity and friendliness she could see even from a distance.

"Where would you put the entrance to your town square?" Dennis asked, bringing her back inside the car.

"On the north side of the block," Merissa replied without hesitation. She had the site fully developed in her head and on paper in her office. She pointed toward the east, where Mount Rainier would be visible from the hillside in daylight. "That way, we maximize the number of condos with a view of the mountain. The block on the north side is a prime location for our next renovation project, and we could eventually connect the two. Maybe even put an elevated walkway between them…"

She faded to a stop as she started to imagine the next block and the types of stores and services they could provide to the local residents. Like a cascade of dominoes, the rest of Tacoma's city blocks were emptied of the old and refilled with new homes and shops. A new thought came to mind after watching the celebrating family, and she easily added it to her list of renovations.

"What if each block had an apartment building on the non-view side with less expensive units? If we use standard materials and go with a simpler design, we could offer a more affordable option right next to the luxury condos. That would give people more options for buying or renting, instead of limiting our potential residents to the wealthy ones who want to live downtown. We'd expand our market, and—"

"Whoa," Dennis said with a laugh as he drove along the north side of the block. "Keep focused on this block for now, and on the style and quality of housing the Morgan Group is known for. Always keep this in mind, Merissa. Investors need to be able to imagine themselves living and working in the buildings they're funding. Even if they never set foot in any of them, they will expect to see a certain level of security, privacy, and comfort in your designs."

Merissa frowned. "How many people can afford the kinds of communities we've been bringing to Tacoma? There are so many new waterfront and view condos popping up, and not enough people to fill them. Doesn't it make sense to diversify, especially on the west side of each block? No one will pay the amount we need to make if all they can see from their windows is another neighborhood that needs renovations."

"Good point, Merissa, but for now I want you to focus on what we do best. Align your vision with the other Morgan Group projects just this once, so you're confident and prepared when you pitch your ideas to Kensington."

Merissa was busy trying to rein in her expanding plans, and she nearly missed the meaning of Dennis's words. "When I…you mean I'm doing the proposal? With my own design?"

Dennis patted her on the knee. "It's a big step, but you're ready to take point on a project this size. We'll work together to get a mock-up done by Thursday, and we'll meet with him next week."

"I'd hug you if we weren't driving," Merissa said. She figured the smile on her face must be goofy and huge because she felt it all the way from her toes to her head. She was one step closer to making the dreams she had for her city a reality.

"Of course you would. You'll make a fortune if this deal goes through."

Merissa shrugged. She'd grown up having a fortune, but she hadn't discovered a real purpose until this job. Even if she had to learn how to compromise before she'd even stepped into the meeting room, by altering her elaborate plans, she was willing to do what it took to make Dennis proud. He hadn't steered her wrong yet, and she'd known she would have to get better at letting go of some of the elements she held dear in her visions. She hadn't expected him to move her forward in this way so soon, and she wouldn't let her ego get in the way.

She hadn't processed much of Dennis's earlier statement after hearing that they were going to use her design, but she finally turned her thoughts to the second thing he'd said. "Why Kensington and not Edwin Lemaine?"

"It might be time for a change. See what some new blood can do," he said, with a casual shrug. Merissa wasn't fooled. Dennis never did anything on a whim. He had a calculated reason for pitching to a developer other than the one they usually used. She wondered if he'd tell her his reasons before the meeting or after. "Based on the other projects Jeff has done, I'll bet he'll be inspired by your vision. We'll see how it goes Monday, and if we don't feel he's right for the job, we can pitch to Lemaine."

Merissa filed away a mental note to research Jeff Kensington's career before the weekend was over, to get tips on presenting her proposal and to help her decide if he was the best person for the project. She shuffled through her index cards again, looking for one with a sketch she'd made of some decorative stonework. "Remember the cornice on that building we saw today in Pioneer Square? I'd like something similar on the condos, to keep them from looking too modern and boxy."

She saw the edge of a white card under her seat. As she bent down to get it, she heard the dull thwack of a rock or something hitting the car and felt Dennis weave a little out of his lane. Her stomach twisted at the movement and she sat up quickly.

"Oof." She held up the missing card. "I might get sick after that maneuver, but it was worth it because I found the drawing."

Dennis didn't answer, and Merissa looked over at him. He was staring ahead, with a surprised expression on his face. He slowly pulled over to the curb and put the car in park with what looked like a tremendous effort.

"Dennis? What's wrong?" Merissa struggled to figure out what she was seeing, what had gone wrong in the seconds she'd been looking away. "What happened?"

"Karen," he whispered, still staring straight ahead, his eyes wide and vacant. "Tell Karen I…"

"Tell Karen what?" Merissa's confusion was steadily rising as panic fueled the already queasy feeling she had. She saw blood slowly begin to drip from his chin and onto his neatly pressed khakis. "Dennis? Dennis? *Dennis!*"

Her voice got louder with each repetition of his name, and she reached for his chin to make him look at her and explain what was happening. The fourth time she called his name was a scream.

CHAPTER TWO

*B*illie Mitchell sat on her heels in the dusty alleyway between
abandoned shops. Her back was pressed so hard against
the comfortingly solid wall behind her, that she knew she'd have
bumps and creases in her skin from the irregularly shaped bricks.
Sweat gathered between and under her breasts, and her leg muscles
ached from the miles of crouching, crawling progress they'd made
to get here, to the center of an enemy-filled town. She sat perfectly
still, not shifting to flex her cramping calves or reaching up to wipe
away a drop of sweat caught on her long eyelashes. She held her M4
against her chest as if she was cradling a teddy bear.

Someone had been out here for a cigarette recently. Her nose
and throat burned with the scent of cheap smoke, probably laced
with more than nicotine. She kept her breathing shallow. Weak,
sore, burning. On the outside, she was calm and untouched by the
swirling dust and the stench of the trash-filled alley.

"Hey, Beast," Mike whispered. She turned and looked at his
grinning face. The sun was behind him, creating a halo of light
around his head. Regulations meant little out here, and he hadn't
shaved for days. "I'll bet you dessert that the cockroach over there
makes it to the street corner before we do."

A large roach scuttled along on the other side of the alley,
traveling over rocks and twigs with purpose. Their point man,
Hamilton, was either the most cautious person alive or just the
most closely related to the sloth. Smart money was on the bug,

and dessert—even though it was probably only a tiny package of cookies—was a hot commodity these days. Still...

"You're on," Billie said, unable to resist a bet. She raised her voice slightly. "Yo, Hamill. We've got to be at the LZ before dawn. Let's move."

"No fair," Mike protested. He stood up and walked over to the roach. "Hurry up!"

"Mike!" Billie yelled, suddenly terrified. She ran toward him and caught one last look at his relaxed smile and cheerful blue eyes before the cockroach exploded and he disappeared.

"Aunt Billie! Aunt Billie!"

The children's shouts were accompanied by a stomach-crushing leap onto the bed. Billie gasped, pressing her palms into the mattress as she struggled to figure out where she was and whether she was in danger. As the weirdly combined fragments of truth and fiction making up her dream shattered, she managed to see what was in front of her open eyes. She was in her apartment. The small weights currently holding her down were Mike's children. She was safe.

Mere seconds passed before she felt her reflexes relax enough for her to tickle the kids until they writhed and giggled on her bed. Another few moments and her heart rate and breathing slowed and she was laughing along with them. Even though she tried not to sleep deeply enough to lose herself when the children were at her house, the wrenching moments between waking and settling back into her present surroundings were always a little frightening, especially when her two human alarm clocks kept her from easing slowly and carefully into the wakeful world.

The three of them collapsed back on the bed, and Billie's gaze moved to the photo on her dresser of her and Mike sitting outside a canvas tent. A wicked dust storm made the sky behind them look threatening and dark, but they wore shorts and bright smiles as they posed for the picture. They were a contrasting pair—Mike was tall and blond with the handsome and healthy look of a Tommy Hilfiger model, while Billie was shorter and dark-haired. She was private, both in expression and personality, while he was as open as anyone she'd ever met. They were an unlikely combination, but they'd become best friends from the first moment they met. And now he was gone...

Billie refused to get sad while his kids were here. "Who wants pancakes?" she asked, getting out of bed and pulling a sweatshirt on over the T-shirt and sweats she was wearing.

"I do! I do!" Ryan and Callie were only a year apart in age, at six and seven, and most of their conversation seemed to be in the form of a chorus. Words and phrases were echoed between them, proving how close they were as siblings, not just in years.

Billie walked to the kitchen like a monster in a horror film, lurching and dragging her feet since one child was wrapped around each calf. Their infectious smiles and obvious delight at staying with her helped her maintain her happy mood—they were as good for her as she seemed to be for them. They sat on stools at the chipped laminate counter while she cooked, chattering on about friends at school and the vacation they were taking with Mike's parents later in the summer. Billie cracked eggs and poured milk while she listened. She'd spent months in therapy after she'd returned from her deployment, minus Mike forever, but the sessions had never been as helpful as times like this were for her. The failure had been partly due to the mission's level of security—how could any therapist really help her when the most she could say was some version of *I was somewhere, and something happened, and now I'm sad.* No specifics meant no real understanding or sympathy. Billie was so accustomed to keeping classified information out of her conversations that she even omitted it in her own mind. She never thought of the place names or the specifics of her missions, especially the final one. Everything was vague. Mike had been there, and she had been whole. Then he was gone and she was bleeding and in pain.

She was healed on the outside, now. And her occasional weekends with Mike's kids healed her insides a little more every time. They anchored her in the present as few other things and people were able to do. They reminded her of the past and of Mike, but led her into the future as well, with their conversations and anticipation and the glimpses they showed of the teens and adults they'd eventually become. She was able to settle somewhere in the middle while she was talking to them. She was *here*, the same way she was when riding a horse or patrolling with her mounted police unit.

Billie ladled the first batch of pancake batter onto an electric griddle and got syrup and butter out of the fridge while the discs browned. She flipped them and smashed them with her spatula, preferring thin, crepe-like pancakes to the fluffy thick ones she got in restaurants. A throwback to the breakfasts her dad used to cook when he was at home and not at sea on the fishing boats. Old habits.

Billie piled the finished pancakes onto plates and started another batch while Ryan and Callie ate. She gave them the second batch as well before making a plateful for herself and dousing it with sugary syrup that had probably never seen the inside of an actual maple tree. The three of them were hungrily demolishing the remaining pancakes when someone knocked on the door.

"Mom's here!" Ryan yelled, hopping off the stool and running to answer the door. Beth Grant came in and dropped some bags on the floor before grabbing Ryan in a hug.

"I missed you," she said, putting him down and hugging Callie next. She picked up the bags again and brought them into the kitchen. She gave Billie a kiss on the cheek. "I missed you, too. I brought you some grown-up food to thank you for watching Ryan and Callie again."

Billie had been watching Beth's entrance with a feeling of relief. The years following Mike's death had been hard on her—Beth had seemed to age twice as fast as normal, and the blond good looks that had meshed so well with her husband's had been overlaid with dark circles and frown lines. Lately, Beth had been smiling more and her skin color was brighter and healthier. Billie had a suspicion there was someone behind those changes, but she was waiting for Beth to bring up the topic first. She peered into one of the bags and saw a bottle of red wine and a six-pack of beer. "Grown-up food? All I see in here are grown-up drinks."

Beth started emptying the other bags. "I brought steaks for that silly little grill you have on your patio, and fruits and vegetables. Real food."

"I eat real—" Billie started to defend her eating habits, but Beth waved her off.

"When I was here on Friday, I noticed that your fridge was full of the kids' favorite foods and old takeout containers. You only buy groceries for them."

Billie wanted to protest, but she decided to let Beth believe her statement was true, and that Billie only cooked on the rare weekends when the kids were with her and the rest of the time either grabbed a bite in a nearby bar or brought home dinner in a fast-food sack. In reality, Billie rarely ate takeout, and the cartons Beth had seen were her coworker's leftovers from when he had visited her earlier in the week. Don Lindstrom's wife didn't approve of him eating fried food and burgers, so he came to Billie's once or twice a week with a contraband meal. Billie gave him safe haven, with the warning that if Marie ever asked her what he was eating at her place she wouldn't lie for him.

Billie didn't want to admit she had a fridge full of children's food because she ate the same way herself. Chicken nuggets, fish sticks, peanut butter and jelly sandwiches on soft white bread. As much as she tried to break away from the past, Billie couldn't keep herself from craving the foods she'd eaten as a child. She put up with the teasing she got from the other members of her team, and at least when the kids were here, she had an excuse for eating the way she did.

Billie put a large bag of broccoli in the vegetable crisper while Ryan and Callie rinsed their breakfast dishes. "How was your weekend?" she asked after Beth had sent the children to the spare bedroom to pack their things.

"It was fine. I learned a lot, and the keynote speaker was one of my favorite professors back when I was getting my teaching certificate." Beth put the breakfast plates into the sink and ran the tap water while she talked, keeping her face averted from Billie. "I feel guilty leaving the kids with you while I travel so much."

"You don't need to feel guilty. Not at all," Billie said. She kept herself busy rearranging the groceries in the fridge and giving Beth some space. Beth's job as a school administrator meant she had to travel to seminars and symposiums on a regular basis. And Beth knew how much Billie loved having Mike's kids be part of her life. She figured Beth's concerns were stemming from a different source.

"There's this guy…"

Billie kept her face neutral even though she wanted to smile. *Of course there's a guy* she wanted to say. She'd suspected as much for several months now. "Who is he?" she asked.

"He's a principal in the Ferndale school district. We've been to most of the same seminars over the past year and we talk a lot. About work. We had coffee together."

She said the last sentence with as much shame as if she'd confessed to murdering someone. Billie closed the refrigerator door and faced her.

"This is good, Beth. Very good."

Beth shook her head, and Billie saw her eyes redden. She stepped closer and put her hand on Beth's shoulder.

"I'm just not sure what to do. If it's been long enough…If this would hurt Ryan and Callie…If I'm even ready." Beth gave Billie's hand a squeeze and then she sighed audibly. "I shouldn't have brought it up. Forget I said anything."

Billie shook her head. Beth had never mentioned anyone before, but Billie had no doubt other men had shown interest in her during the past few years. "Has he asked you out before this?"

Beth shrugged. "Once or twice. He knows about Mike and he doesn't push, but he's let me know he's interested."

"You've never mentioned this before."

Beth looked away. "I don't know why. I guess I didn't want to bother you with it."

"Or maybe it's because now you want to go out with him."

Beth was silent for so long that Billie thought she might have misread her. When she finally spoke, her voice was almost a whisper.

"You were his best friend, Billie. Sometimes I thought the two of you were even closer than he and I were, because of everything you went through together, everything the two of you shared and that he wasn't allowed to talk to me about." She paused and visibly inhaled. "I need your honest advice, Billie. What do you think he'd say to me right now?"

Billie wanted to launch into a series of encouraging platitudes. Time heals all wounds; it's time to move on; Mike would want you to be happy. There was some truth to them, but Beth wanted honesty. And Billie wanted her friend to have hope for the future again. She chose her words carefully.

"Mike was one of the most matter-of-fact people I've ever met, about both life and death." She thought back to the days before each mission, when they had to write letters home in case they didn't survive. Billie had written to her dad and sisters, feeling the distance between them measured both in miles and in emotional connection. The letters had been a chore to her, a necessity before she was allowed to go into the field. Hers had all been alike and as impersonal as a form letter, unlike the ones Mike wrote for Beth. "He knew the odds of being hurt or killed were high. He accepted it, and I know how proud he was that you did, too.

"If I could talk to him right now about you and what you're going through, he'd say *Of course she's moving on. Why wouldn't she?* He wouldn't be at all surprised that someone is interested in you because he always talked about how gorgeous and smart and wonderful you are." Billie paused and took a breath, making an effort not to look like she was gasping for breath. The nightmare and the resurfacing memories over the weekend had weakened her. Now, thinking of Mike and imagining what he would say to Beth, she felt her insides clench. But she kept her tension inside. Not on her face and not in her voice. It was what she was expected to do, what Beth needed from her. She exhaled and continued.

"More important, though, he wouldn't be surprised in the least to hear that you might want to let someone new into your life. He'd expect it. He'd see it as a natural and human thing to do because he understood more than most people that life would go on whether we survived a mission or not. He'd never judge you for moving on, or condemn you to the life of a martyr. He'd want you and the kids to live a full and happy life."

Beth wiped away the tears on her cheek and hugged Billie. "Thank you," she said when she pulled away. "You're pretty wise for someone who avoids romantic relationships of any kind."

Billie laughed. "I don't avoid them. I just move around too much to find someone and settle down. It's a family trait, I suppose."

"Hmm." Beth glanced around the apartment with an unreadable expression. She didn't say anything else, and Billie was about to ask what was on her mind but she had a feeling she knew what Beth was thinking. Billie had pictures crowded on the walls, and every surface was covered with something personal—mementos from her travels, more photos of the friends she'd made in the service and in the department, and pieces of tack she'd brought home from the police barn to either clean or repair. She looked like a settler here, not a temporary occupant. What Beth didn't know was Billie had always lived this way. She'd been shuffled from house to house because of her dad's job. He was on the boat for long periods, and she and her sisters had stayed with someone different almost every time he left. Spreading the wealth, he called it. Desperately trying to find someone willing to take in three kids was more like it, in Billie's opinion. Still, she and her sisters hadn't had much choice, and they'd gotten in the habit of unpacking and making each new room their own as soon as they arrived. Billie had never shaken the habit, no matter if she'd been at an army base for two weeks of training or here in Tacoma for almost a decade. She might give the appearance of being settled, but her heart was always prepared to move again.

Callie and Ryan came back into the room lugging their suitcases. Billie would miss the kids' company, but she was relieved to have the conversation end in the chaos of good-byes. She was willing to listen to Beth's issues but much less comfortable when the topic of her own love life—or lack of one—arose.

As soon as her guests were gone, Billie showered and got her police uniform out of the closet. She pulled on the tight navy pants and straightened the seams so the extra material designed to protect her inner thighs from the stirrup leathers was placed just right. She buttoned her freshly ironed shirt and tucked it in before buckling her duty belt around her waist. The belt was modified from the one she'd worn as a patrol officer to make it easier for her to move on horseback, but it still held everything she might need while at work, from gun to handcuffs to notepad.

Even the act of putting on the outfit of a mounted patrol officer soothed her. She loved Beth and the kids, but being around people who'd been through trauma always made her relive her own. She was as exhausted by their presence as she was uplifted by the children and her friendship with Beth. Soon she'd be with her horse, Ranger. Grooming him and riding the streets of Tacoma. He'd put her back in balance.

Her first mount, a gray mare named Corona, hadn't worked the same magic as Ranger. Billie had joined the unit with little riding experience, trusting her sergeant and fellow officers to help her transition from a beginner with only a handful of therapy lessons to a capable rider. Instead, she had found herself in the middle of an unanticipated battle to destroy the unit and take over the land where the police barn now stood. Billie had managed to seem confident even though she was never certain whether Corona would do her job or decide to bolt or buck, but she'd spent more of their training sessions on her butt on the ground rather than in the saddle.

Then Rachel Bryce had stepped in as sergeant and put her on Ranger. Billie had finally found the healing and strengthening kind of partnership she had been hoping for when she had joined the team, not just with Ranger, but also with Rachel and Cal—Rachel's girlfriend and the team's trainer—and her teammates Clark and Don. Don especially was an odd choice for someone she now considered to be one of her closest friends. They were far apart in age and interests and lifestyle, but they'd bonded over the horses and their friendship had carried over into everyday life beyond the barn. The mounted team had come to mean everything to her.

She checked her reflection in the bathroom mirror and straightened the small TPD pins on her lapels. She combed her hair and was clipping back her too-long bangs to keep them out of her eyes when her cell buzzed. A photo of her lieutenant, Abigail Hargrove, popped up on her screen.

"Hey, Hargrove. What's up?"

"Murder and mayhem." Abby was speaking in her work voice, crisp and no-nonsense. When they'd first met, Billie had doubted there were any other sides to Hard-Ass Hargrove, but lately she'd discovered the funny and playful woman beneath the controlled officer persona. Love had been good for her. Abby was all business today, though.

"Another homicide last night. Drive-by. I need you to canvass the area with the witness, so report to the one sector substation instead of the barn."

Billie sighed. No time with Ranger today. Instead she'd be subjected to the fresh trauma of a murder witness. "Fine. What are we looking for? Did they see the shooter?"

"No. She doesn't seem to have any useful information since she was looking for something on the floor when it happened, or getting carsick, or whatever. But driving around the area might jog her memory. Plus, she's pretty upset, obviously, and I want you to spend time with her. You're one of the best in cases like these, and I'm sure you'll be able to calm her down and get a clear story from her."

Great. An afternoon playing grief counselor. Billie was flattered by Abby's praise because she knew Hargrove never gave it lightly. The only reason Billie was so good at working with frightened or traumatized people, though, was because she had all her own grief sitting right under the surface of her skin. Maybe other people sensed it was there and knew she understood them, or maybe the currents of PTSD just made her more sensitive to the resonating vibrations coming from victims of trauma. Whatever the reason, these interactions eroded her strength a little more each time, and she was left fighting harder than ever to conceal and control her own feelings and memories. But she had to put aside her personal issues and do her job. "I'll be there," she said.

CHAPTER THREE

Merissa sat slumped over in the hard plastic chair. She'd been ferried around the city in cop cars since the police had arrived at the crime scene the night before. Everywhere she went, though, the picture of Dennis staring out the window of the BMW with unseeing eyes and a trickle of blood dripping off his chin superseded everything else. Brief flashes of other images came and went, but they shifted through her mind out of context and a little fuzzy. She couldn't describe the inside of the main police station, even though she'd seen the exterior hundreds of times. All she remembered of her time there was resting her clenched hands on a metal table in the stark room where she was interviewed by a string of detectives. The hospital morgue was reduced to a flash of Karen's horrified and confused expression after she identified her husband and before she rushed into Merissa's arms. And when Merissa closed her eyes, all she could recall from the tiny Hilltop precinct room where she was now and had been waiting for the past two hours was the curved, orange chair on which she sat. It must have been there since the seventies, but was the rest of the furniture in the room just as old, or was it more modern? She had no idea. Even when she opened her eyes and looked around, she couldn't make her mind register the rest of the décor. It slipped in and out of her head, unable to dislodge the image of Dennis.

She shifted in the uncomfortable chair. She was apparently waiting for yet another officer or detective to come see her. She knew the drill by now. Each time someone new was about to approach her, they'd first talk quietly with the detective who'd been in charge of her most of the night, both of them glancing her way as if she was a specimen in a lab. Then each new arrival would walk over to her wearing what they must have hoped was a consoling and reassuring smile. They'd gently ask her the same questions about what she'd seen and heard, she'd give the same brief and unhelpful answer—*nothing*—and they'd sigh and leave her alone again. She tried to make them understand that she wasn't trying to disappoint them or herself or Dennis. More than anything, she wanted to be the one to identify the shooter and have the horrible person locked away forever. Why had she been focused on finding her index card and not paying attention to what was going on around her?

The next awaited officer finally arrived. Instead of the grizzled older male cop Merissa had come to expect, this one was a woman about Merissa's age. A *gorgeous* woman. Her dark thick hair was blunt cut and held off her face with a plain clip. Her uniform was different from the ones the others wore, made of a clingy fabric and snug enough to show off her slender legs and small waist. She was beautiful with her combination of gentle curves and muscular strength, but Merissa's attention was drawn past her looks and to the expression on her face. Intense and shielded, as if she had powerful thoughts and memories and emotions below the surface, but would only show faint ripples on her controlled face.

Damn. Merissa had been feeling vulnerable and raw since she had first stumbled out of the BMW and called for help. She hadn't showered yet, and she was so tired she'd probably get lost if she stepped outside the precinct and tried to get back in. She hated feeling weak and at a disadvantage in any situation, but she had been managing her irritation just fine with the string of unappealing cops that had been interviewing her. Just because she found this one attractive and confident didn't explain why she was suddenly angry, but her emotions had been running the gamut from extreme to nonexistent all night.

The woman walked toward her, and Merissa realized with a start that this officer was the first person or thing to really register in her mind since she'd realized Dennis was dead. She felt an odd mix of guilt, like she was betraying him somehow, and gratitude that she wouldn't be stuck in the memory of the immediate moments after his death forever.

"Shitty day, isn't it?" The woman stopped next to Merissa's chair, no trace of the placating smiles others had worn. She carried with her a faintly spicy and sweet scent. Merissa couldn't quite define what it was, but she inhaled deeply and exhaled with a sigh, glad to have the momentary break from stale police precinct air.

"Yes," Merissa said. A simple answer, but she was as relieved by the honest words as by the respite from the sweaty, ferrous aromas of death and fear that she'd been living in for the past hours. No *Are you doing okay?* and *Yes, I'm fine* lies to suffer through.

"I'm Billie. I'm going to drive you around the neighborhood. I know it will be hard to be back where the shooting happened, but maybe something will jog your memory."

Merissa shook her head. Why go through all this when it was hopeless? "I didn't see anything until...after. I'm sorry, but I'd rather not—"

Billie put her hand on Merissa's shoulder and stopped her words with gentle pressure. "Don't apologize. Our minds can play tricks on us, making us forget what we actually remember. You might have seen or heard something that you don't realize will be important to us. Any clues we can discover will help us find who did this to your friend."

"Okay," Merissa said. She was distracted by the feel of Billie's touch. She felt a shiver pulse through her at the contact, and Billie must have interpreted it as discomfort because she pulled her hand back. Merissa could only call it awareness, as if her cells were turning toward Billie's palm and fingers, and drawing her mental focus there as well. Traitorous body and exhausted mind. Merissa shouldn't be feeling attraction after what had happened. Or was it a stress response and nothing more? Unlikely. Billie would have caught Merissa's attention in any circumstance. She wanted to explain away her body's response the same way she'd been rationalizing her unexpected reactions to everything happening to and around her since the shooting, but she couldn't convince herself. She needed distance and privacy before she could process what happened and understand her reactions, and she wasn't likely to get either one soon.

She stood up and only noticed she was a couple of inches taller than Billie when they were standing side by side. Billie's bearing made her seem larger than her physical size. They went outside and got in the patrol car waiting by the curb. Merissa buckled the seat belt. She'd managed to avoid being in police cars for all thirty-four years of her life. In less than twenty-four hours she'd been inside more of them than most felons probably had.

Billie got in the car and hesitated before she started the engine. "I'm sure you've gone over this a hundred times today, but will you tell me your version of what happened?"

Merissa sighed. The car seat was much more comfortable than the chair had been, and all Merissa wanted to do was wrap Billie's scent around her like a blanket and take a nap. No such luck. It was bad enough that she'd had to experience Dennis's death one time, and now it was time to relive it yet again. She'd sympathized with victims of violent crimes on news reports, but she had never realized that what happened to them wasn't a single event, a single moment in time. Instead, it was a repetitive series of internal reruns and external conversations. Over and over—how many more times? Her stomach clenched and growled, and she put her hand on her belly. "I had dropped some notes I'd taken earlier in the day and when I picked them up I missed one card. I leaned over to find it, and when I sat up again, I noticed something was wrong with Dennis."

Merissa shuddered at the understatement. *Something wrong* sounded as innocuous as the flu or a headache. Billie was frowning while Merissa talked, and Merissa interpreted her expression as one of judgment. She had felt judged throughout this entire process, by the detectives and even by Karen, although they all tried to deny it. She should have noticed more, done something different, saved her boss and dear friend. She heard the tone of her voice growing more defensive as she talked. "I heard a noise, but it sounded like a rock hitting the window, not a loud gunshot. And there was so little blood. It shouldn't have taken me so long to figure out what was going on, but I was sort of distracted because I was carsick, and it wasn't…it wasn't like you see on TV."

"Hey, I'm only trying to figure out what happened, not blame you for it." Billie's voice was soft and free of judgment. So very different from the harsh and berating one Merissa had been hearing in her own skull all night. The kindness in Billie's tone washed her free of recrimination for a moment, but Merissa fought with the freedom from guilt. She didn't believe she deserved it, and the realization made her want to weep. She was glad Billie didn't look her way as she started the car and pulled away from the curb. "This was a small caliber bullet and it would have been fairly quiet and with a small point of entry. I'm sure you, like most people, don't drive around expecting someone to shoot at you, so on the rare occasions when it does happen, it's perfectly natural for the brain to take a while to process what's happened. Start from the beginning and tell me about yesterday without beating yourself up in the process. Where were you when you took those notes?"

Billie managed to say the right words to ease Merissa's worries, but she struggled against the sense of being soothed. The other officers had been kind enough and had reassured her when she started to spiral out of control with guilt and sorrow, but Billie did more than comfort. She understood the heart of what was hurting Merissa and she reached inside and addressed it directly, closing the gaping wounds. Billie's strength only made Merissa's weakness even more obvious, though, and her ability to say the right thing threw Merissa's half-formed thoughts and sentences into stark relief. Merissa felt an irrational anger because Billie's help made her seem even more vulnerable than she'd been feeling. She wasn't sure how to handle her confusing reactions, and she focused instead on reliving the last moments she'd ever spend with Dennis.

"We'd gone to Seattle to scout some neighborhoods," Merissa said, focusing on the facts of yesterday and wishing she could change the day's end by changing her words. She thought even further back, to their discussion when she had wanted to take her car, but Dennis had offered to drive instead because she liked to sketch plans while they were on these trips. *If only I'd been the one driving* sounded like it might qualify as beating herself up.

"What exactly were you looking at in Seattle?"

Merissa, jarred back into the present, noticed they were driving downhill, toward the Tideflats and away from the street where Dennis had been shot, but she answered Billie's question instead of asking why. "Ideas for a renovation project we have in the works. *Had* in the works. During the planning phase, we'll look for inspiration in all sorts of places. Or we used to look for inspiration."

Billie reached over and patted Merissa's leg. The touch was brief, but somehow it pulled all of Merissa's focus to the spot on her thigh where Billie's hand rested. Her rioting thoughts and emotions centered, and then spun out of control again. She gave a deep sigh.

"Don't worry about getting the tenses right," Billie said. "Just talk. How long were you in Seattle?"

"About three hours. We got back here just after six."

Merissa kept her answers short and let Billie's calm questions lead her through the recounting of the night's events. Piece by piece, Merissa gave more details about their route from the freeway, her carsickness, and their conversation than she'd realized she could recall. Billie was like a puppeteer, making Merissa talk and seek out her memories. Merissa wanted to cut the strings and be left alone again, but at the same time, she was relieved to be remembering so much more than she'd expected. Her tale ended where she began, with the dropped card and the gunshot.

"Good," Billie said. "You have an excellent memory. We'll retrace your steps and maybe something new will come to you. First, though, let's get some food."

She pulled into the drive-thru lane of a McDonald's, and Merissa grimaced. She rarely ate fast food and she wasn't about to start today. She doubted she could keep anything down, let alone a greasy hamburger. "Nothing for me, thanks."

Billie ordered a meal and a Coke and then she inched the car forward in line. "When's the last time you had something to eat?"

"We had a late lunch in Seattle," Merissa said. Pad Thai at their favorite restaurant. She'd never eat there with Dennis again. The realization should have made her cry, but instead she felt curiously numb.

Billie paid for the sack of food and dropped it on Merissa's lap. "Eat."

Merissa was about to protest some more, but the scent of french fries made her stomach growl again. She reached into the bag. Maybe just one. Or maybe a handful. She finished the fries in a matter of seconds, barely pausing to wipe oil and salt off her fingers before she unwrapped the burger and took a huge bite. She'd been hungry before, of course, but this was nothing like a normal appetite, just like the fatigue from jet lag was more profound than normal weariness. The unaccustomed neediness accompanying her meal brought tears to her eyes. Great. *Now* she wanted to cry. Because of a stupid Quarter Pounder, not because her mentor had died right in front of her.

Billie drove down Pacific Avenue toward the freeway, glancing at her occasionally with an inscrutable expression in her intense eyes, but she didn't speak until Merissa had wolfed down the entire meal. "It's normal," Billie said. She accelerated onto the freeway heading north toward Seattle, but she didn't stay on I-5 long and took the Portland Avenue exit instead.

Merissa braced her hand on the dashboard as Billie made a sweeping turn and crossed under I-5. "What's normal?"

"Whatever it is you're feeling right now. You look upset, but don't be. After what you've been through, everything will seem upside down. You'll have extreme emotions at one moment, but when you think you should feel sad or scared or whatever, you'll be completely numb. You're not a monster if you don't feel grief at what you believe are appropriate times, and you're not overreacting if odd things make you cry. These are normal responses to stress, even though they seem weird and unpredictable."

Merissa nodded and wiped the tears off her cheek. She took her attention off the horizon long enough to look at Billie. Her words and expression seemed to show a calm compassion and understanding, but Merissa wondered if Billie knew the right words to say because she had been around other victims in her line of work or if she had been through trauma herself. Merissa was annoyed because Billie seemed to read her so well, but Billie even understood her confusing annoyance. A vicious cycle, with Merissa spinning out of control. Wondering about Billie's life and past distracted her from her own emotions. Still, she now felt a little less worried about her unexpected reactions to both the night's events and to Billie's calm presence. She wasn't used to being pissed at someone just because they were helpful to her, and she decided to chalk her responses—even her physical attraction to Billie—up to stress and nothing more. "Thank you," she said.

"You're welcome," Billie said. "Now keep your eyes on the road so you don't get sick."

Merissa gave a brief laugh, surprising herself with the sound. "Don't worry. I won't throw up in your car."

Billie shrugged. "Go ahead, it's a pool car. But if you're planning on it, I'll have to put you in the backseat because it's easier to hose down."

Merissa glanced back at the hard plastic shell in place of a normal, padded seat. With the surrounding plexiglass shield, it looked like a clear coffin. "No thanks," she said. "I'll stay up here."

They merged onto the freeway again, going south. "Okay," Billie said. "You took the I-705 exit. What was happening in the car?"

"We were discussing the neighborhood we want to renovate. I was telling Dennis I'd like to have an open pathway through the center, like the staircase over there, and he was trying to convince me to make it a more isolated community. Our usual argument. We turned here."

Billie retraced their route through downtown Tacoma. Billie rolled down the windows, and the bracing breeze helped Merissa focus. Billie didn't say much while Merissa talked about their plans to refurbish the city block, and Merissa thought the atmosphere in the car changed in some indefinable way but she had trouble reading the unflappable officer next to her. Billie seemed level on the surface— her voice, her reasonable words, the spare but graceful way she gestured with her hands while she talked—but Merissa sensed passion and movement beneath the calm. She was too consumed by controlling and understanding her own fretful insides to be able to truly see or understand what Billie might be thinking about her, and she gave up trying. Maybe Billie was just giving her a chance to remember the trip without distracting her with questions. As they were about to turn off Pacific Avenue, Merissa felt her thoughts swing back to the night before with a jolt.

"He saw someone. He was looking in the rearview mirror and made a kind of grunt. When I asked what was wrong, he said he thought he saw someone he knew."

"Good, Merissa," Billie said. Merissa felt a swell of pride because she'd finally remembered something potentially useful, but Billie's next words brought her down again. "Did you look back when he said that? Did you notice what kind of car he was looking at, or ask who he saw?"

"No," Merissa said. She felt her shoulders droop. "We turned off Pacific right after he mentioned it. Do you think it was related to what happened? And I completely missed it!"

Billie nudged her with an elbow. "It might have been connected, and it might be completely separate from what happened after. He lived in Tacoma, so the chances are good he'd see familiar faces while driving anywhere in the city. Just keep focusing on remembering details like that, not on what you should have done."

Merissa would try for now, but she doubted she'd ever get past the guilt she felt. How many opportunities to see the shooter or to prevent the murder completely had she missed? She wanted Billie to be angry with her, to blame her for what happened and validate her own guilt, but Billie remained as stoic as she'd been since the first moment she walked into the precinct. Merissa was sure Billie had strong emotions just like she did, but Merissa's were plainly visible to everyone around her. Billie's were tucked inside.

When they got close to the neighborhood, Billie slowed the car. She stopped at a red light next to a convenience store where a group of young men were lounging under a bus stop shelter.

"Hey, Mitchell," one of them called. "Where's your horse? You get bucked off?"

The group laughed and Billie grinned in response. "He's off today," she said. "He gets more vacation days than I do."

"He deserves them, having to haul your ass all over the city." The guys laughed harder, and Billie waved when the light changed and she drove forward again. Merissa was surprised by the easy banter between a cop and what looked to her like potential troublemakers. "Your horse?" she asked. "Is that street slang for something?"

Billie chuckled. "Yes. It's slang for a large animal with four hooves. I'm with the mounted unit, and I'm usually riding on my patrol beat, not driving."

Merissa suddenly realized why Billie was wearing a different uniform than the other officers, and she also remembered where she'd seen her before. The Daffodil Parade through the streets of Tacoma and nearby Puyallup in the fall. Of course, she hadn't recognized Billie's face because then she'd worn sunglasses and a helmet.

"You ride a chestnut Thoroughbred, with a small white sock on his left hind."

"Yes," Billie said, looking at her with raised eyebrows. "Ranger. How'd you know?"

"I'm on the Daffodil Festival committee and I saw you riding in the parade. I couldn't see your face, but I remember your figure." Merissa waved vaguely at Billie's body, feeling her face heat with embarrassment. She'd thought Billie was sexy even before she got a good look at her edgy face and gorgeous eyes. "I mean the way you rode. Your team, that is. You're all good riders, and I…"

Her voice trailed to a halt. She pointed with a suddenly shaky finger. "I saw that car."

Billie braked swiftly. "You saw it last night? Are you sure?"

Merissa stared at the old brown Chrysler. Snatches of memory came back to her when she was distracted by either anger toward or attraction to Billie and not focused on remembering, like seeing flashes of the past in her peripheral vision. "Yes. At least, I think so. Or one just like it." She shook her head, hating the uncertainty in her voice. "It passed us right before I could scream for help, right after Dennis was shot."

Billie frowned and took out her notepad and pen. "Good job, Merissa," she said, but her praise sounded flat. Merissa wasn't sure why, since she'd finally uncovered a shred of useful information from her confused mind.

"There wasn't a lot of traffic," she said. "Maybe the shooter was in that car."

"Maybe," Billie said, her frown deepening. "Let's get back to the precinct."

Chapter Four

Billie parked in front of the precinct again. She wished she had a few minutes to herself, to compose her thoughts and formulate a plan, but her charge was looking at her expectantly. Merissa had been pushed and pulled in all directions since the shooting, and she was waiting to be told what to do next. She was Billie's first responsibility right now, and everything else would have to wait.

Billie was proud of being the department's go-to person for witnesses and victims like Merissa, even though the experience of constantly reliving pain through someone else wore her out. She should be elated because her probing questions and calm method had helped Merissa uncover a new clue that might help them catch the killer, even if the potential evidence she'd brought to light left Billie reeling.

But Merissa wasn't helping Billie's attempts to remain calm and in charge. The time with her had been exactly what Billie had expected in some ways—Merissa was traumatized by the homicide and by the whirlwind of interviews and questions following it. Talking to her and helping her through it had, as always, scratched the scabs off Billie's personal wounds and left her feeling raw and exhausted as she fought to maintain the illusion that she was feeling detached sympathy and not a unifying empathy.

Oddly, though, she hadn't been as depleted as usual while driving Merissa around town. Instead, she'd felt her own emotions churning—not just resonating with Merissa's, as Billie had come to expect, but diving and soaring on their own. Merissa needed Billie to explain how to process the alien emotions she was feeling, but she'd remained strong. The ordeal had left her vulnerable, but not fragile, and Billie felt respect for her. Beyond that, Billie's response to Merissa wasn't comfortable to acknowledge. She'd been sensitive to Merissa's closeness and the heat of her skin the few times they touched. The scent of almonds and lavender lingered in the car, teasing Billie's senses with its subtlety. Most of all, though, the sound of Merissa's rich and melodious voice gave her goose bumps. She had the hint of an accent, but Billie couldn't define it further than to say she sounded urbane. Cultured. With a trace of French thrown in. Merissa had been at times sad and silently raging and coldly numb, like most other victims Billie dealt with. Had she felt any attraction to Billie? The question was pointless, and Billie was angry with herself for even asking it.

Billie had to stay focused on the words Merissa had used and not her delivery. Merissa's voice made her want to tear Merissa's clothes off right there in the patrol car. But what Merissa said about her plans to tear down the decrepit old city and transform it into something artificial and new left Billie cold. And the identification of the car had been a bucket of ice water.

"Come on," she said. "You'll need to give a statement about the car, but then you should be able to go home. I'm sure you're ready for a rest after all this."

Merissa got out of the car and followed Billie to the door. She hesitated before going through. "How do I get home? Dennis picked me up this morning, and I don't have my car here."

Billie paused, holding the precinct door open. "We'll arrange a ride for you. Or call you a cab if you'd rather. Or I can take you." Billie wanted to pinch herself hard for offering, but she had an obligation to fulfill.

"Are you sure?" Merissa's voice was tinged with despair, but she seemed surprised again by her reaction and tried to downplay the relief Billie had seen on her face when she made the offer. "I guess I can go with you, if it's not too much trouble?"

It was way too much trouble. "Of course it's not," Billie said. Hargrove and the detectives on the case would be happy to have Billie spend more time with Merissa, hopefully prying more information from her. Billie, however, didn't feel the same enthusiasm. "I just need to rearrange my schedule a little, and then I'll be right back here to take you home."

Apparently reassured by her words, Merissa finally went into the precinct. Billie had already called in the information about the car, so she left Merissa with the detective in charge and made up an excuse about needing to stop by the police barn before she took Merissa back to her house. She felt Merissa watching her as she left, but she didn't look back.

Instead of going to Point Defiance Park, where the police horses were stabled, Billie drove back the way she and Merissa had come. She saw two squad cars with flashing lights boxing in the brown Chrysler, and she turned into a back alley before the officers noticed her. She parked under an empty carport and jogged down the alley, keeping as close to the privacy and chain-link fences lining it as garbage cans and overgrown shrubs allowed. She wasn't used to hiding while at work unless she was chasing a perp, and the action triggered old memories of sneaking through empty, shell-torn streets in dusty desert villages. Here in Tacoma, she would face only a reprimand or confused questioning if another officer saw her, but the feeling that a misstep might mean her life—illogical as it was in this setting—was difficult to ignore. Especially after a day of dealing with both Beth's and Merissa's traumatic memories. She had to stop once to lean against the faded wooden slats of a fence and brace her hands against her knees, taking slow, deep breaths until her heart rate and respiration were under control again.

Merissa was pushing her out of her comfort zone, and out of her usual obedience to the authority figures and laws that governed her job. Normally when she talked with victims, Billie felt pulled even deeper into herself. She became aware of every fragile spot where her control was beginning to slip and her memories and pain were seeping through. She was more herself—raw and wounded. But it was different with Merissa. Merissa made her feel strong, made her expand outward, made her feel too many conflicting emotions. Annoyance at the cavalier way she was going to raze Tacoma and rebuilt it, fear that Merissa's memories might hurt one of Billie's friends, compassion for someone so clearly out of her element in the world of police and crime. Most of all, Billie had felt a tenderness so sharp it hurt. It reached out from her to everyone around her—Merissa, the owner of the brown car, and even herself. She was unrecognizable to herself after one short car ride with Merissa. Billie never would have come up with the plan to sneak down a back alley to avoid the cops before she met Merissa. But here she was, and she had to hurry.

Billie finally reached a dilapidated three-story apartment building with a tarpaper covered roof. The landlord had been promising to shingle it properly for six months, and Billie doubted it would get done until the leaks got too bad to ignore. She climbed the stairs two at a time, bypassing her own floor and going directly to the third.

When Merissa had been rhapsodizing about the beautiful new high-rise condos she wanted to build as an urban renewal project, Billie hadn't bothered to mention that she herself would be homeless if it happened. Merissa hadn't seemed to realize how many tenants would be evicted if their affordable—meaning dirt-cheap—housing was demolished. Billie was certain Merissa never would have even considered whether Billie would be one of them.

Billie strode down the hall and banged on the door of apartment 3F. She heard shuffling inside, and shoved open the unlocked door before anyone on the other side could throw the bolt and bar her entrance. Four men and two women were scattered on the sofa and around the small dining room table. Two of them reached toward concealed guns, but once they recognized Billie their hands stopped and remained in plain sight.

"Yo, Mitchell, you scared the shit out of me," Carlyle said. He dropped onto the ugly suede recliner and grabbed his chest. "About gave me a heart attack."

The other five were about to settle into seats again, but Billie pointed at the door.

"Out," she ordered. Carlyle was about to join them as they filed out, but she stepped in front of him. "You stay. We need to talk."

"Uh-oh. You breaking up with me, Billie darling?" He tried to slip into their usual banter. Billie wasn't going there. She had a jump on the other cops—it would take them time to track the beat-up old car to Carlyle since she was sure it didn't have a legitimate registration or insurance card handily sitting in the glove compartment. But they'd find him soon enough. She might have a few hours, or they might get lucky and she'd only have minutes. Either way, she wanted to get out of here before anyone from the department showed up.

"Where were you last night?" she asked. "Between five and seven."

Her seriousness had seeped in at last and Carlyle sat down again with a thump. His suddenly pale face made his slicked-back hair and thin mustache stand out darkly. "I was with Lois, all night. I swear, Billie. Go ahead and ask her, just make sure you do it when her boyfriend isn't around or she'll have to cover her ass. We went to McGinty's for a drink and then back to her place. What's going on?"

Billie frowned. He looked like he was telling the truth, but she couldn't be sure. He was a practiced liar and had spent more than a few months behind bars during the five years she'd known him. They were friends in a way, joking when they passed in the hall and sharing a beer now and then, but she couldn't afford to trust him completely. A man's life had been taken. Even worse, until Billie knew exactly why Dennis Morgan had been shot there was a chance Merissa was in danger. Billie had just met her, wasn't even sure she liked her all that much, but she felt a fierce desire to protect her rise inside.

"Are you in trouble, Carlyle? You'd better tell me now, while I can still help you. If you don't, you're on your own."

"Help me with what? I didn't do anything, Billie, you gotta believe me." He stood up and shoved his phone toward her. "Call Lois right now. Hang up if a man answers, but call her now and she'll tell you where I was. I didn't do whatever it is you think I did."

Billie pushed the phone away. The detectives would eventually follow this same trail and contact Lois. Billie wasn't going to bother. His alibi was a known prostitute who would deny being with him to protect herself from her violent pimp. Billie had to either accept what he was saying on faith or not. She wasn't going to have proof until the metaphorical smoking gun was found either in his possession or someone else's.

"Where was your car last night?" she asked. She felt defeated as her adrenaline seeped away. No matter what Carlyle said or did, he was going to look guilty to every detective and every cop who'd dealt with him on the street. There wasn't anything she could do.

"A friend borrowed it. Said some other dude needed it for the night, and he owed this guy a favor. It wasn't back yet when I went out to look this morning. Is it there now?"

Yes. Being dusted for prints as we speak. Billie kept quiet about that part, though. "What's your friend's name?"

"Percy. We hang at the Fifty-Five sometimes."

Billie translated his sentence into *I often buy drugs from him at the convenience store at 2455 Sixth Avenue.* She didn't bothering asking *some other dude*'s name. The car had likely been through a longer chain of occupants than two last night. She tilted her head when she heard footsteps coming down the hall. A lot of them. Damn, they'd found Carlyle fast.

"Gotta go," she said. She yanked open the door to the small balcony and checked for officers before she went outside.

"Wait," Carlyle said. He followed her and tugged on her shirt. "Please, Billie. I didn't do anything," he said again. "Help me, please."

She watched his expression shift. He was scared now, but she thought she saw innocence on his face, too. Confusion. She didn't trust herself enough to read him well—didn't trust him altogether—but she believed him somewhere down deep. Otherwise she wouldn't have risked coming here at all. "I'll try," she promised. She had no idea how she'd do it, but she'd try.

"Find Percy. He'll be scarce once he gets wind of this, but he hangs out near the tracks on Ruston. He might hide around there."

Billie nodded before pulling away from him and swinging her legs over the balcony ledge. She jumped across the five-foot gap between balconies and repeated the process until she reached the one outside the end of the third floor hallway. If any tenants saw her, none raised an alarm. They were accustomed to minding their own business around here, even if someone was using their balcony as a thoroughfare. She pressed against the wall and out of sight in case anyone looked down the hall and out the sliding glass door, and then she carefully eased over the edge and swung forward to drop to the second floor balcony. She jimmied open the locked door and went to her apartment where she sat for fifteen minutes while she listened to the creaks and footfalls coming from upstairs. Then silence. She went over to the window and peered around the curtain as Carlyle was escorted to a waiting squad car.

She went into the bathroom and splashed cold water on her face. She stared at herself in the mirror, surprised she didn't see any residual emotion from the day. She looked as calm and unruffled as she had this morning, but she felt the turmoil inside. She'd do what she promised and check Carlyle's story. And if she found out he was behind the murder? That he was the one who'd put Merissa's life in danger and forced her to endure the horror of watching her friend die? She'd lock him away herself and toss the key into Puget Sound.

Chapter Five

B illie wanted nothing more than to climb on Ranger and go cantering through the park until she was worn-out and free of the emotions of the day, but she resolutely pushed open the precinct door and went inside. Abby had assigned her to Merissa, and Billie had to get her charge safely home and settled—away from police stations and interview rooms—before she'd feel she'd accomplished her mission. The memories of trauma, as well as Carlyle's obvious and warranted fear, clung to Billie like a film of sweat.

As soon as she saw Merissa, though, her own discomfort and tension were pushed aside by the desire to do whatever it took to make Merissa feel better. She was sitting in the same plastic chair Billie had found her in earlier. Billie had only been gone a little over an hour, but Merissa seemed to have imploded since then. Dark circles shadowed her eyes, and her beautiful dark blond hair was limp. She sat with her eyes closed. After a night of being questioned and told what to do and where to go, she had an air of passivity around her. Billie was fairly sure this wasn't Merissa's regular state of being. She'd only talked to Merissa for a short time today, but she had seen stubbornness and passion in her. Now, exhaustion had kicked in, and she was merely waiting for her next instructions.

Billie felt different, too, but she was confident no one would notice. Her heart still felt wobbly after sneaking down the alley and into Carlyle's apartment. The action itself was nothing new to her and was part of her routine work as a cop. Today had felt nothing like a routine, though. She was still operating under the effects of nightmares and beyond the scope of her legitimate job. And Merissa…Billie had expected to be shaken by spending a morning with a crime victim, but Merissa had spread tendrils more deeply into Billie than had been anticipated. Frightening, arousing, electrifying tendrils.

Billie looked away from Merissa with an effort, and checked with the detective to make sure Merissa was free to go home. She walked quietly over to her chair, determined to hold herself together for another hour.

"Do you want to get out of here?" she asked.

"More than anything." Merissa remained still for another moment before she opened her eyes and stood with a groan.

"Do you use these chairs to force confessions out of people?"

"Works every time," Billie said with a smile. "Are you ready to tell me your darkest secrets?"

Merissa looked directly at her, and Billie saw a flash of what must be her normal demeanor. She briefly imagined meeting her in a bar and exchanging similar banter. She'd be happy to leave with someone like Merissa for a night or two of passion. If they had met as strangers.

"I'll tell you anything you want to know," Merissa said, stepping a little closer and lowering her voice to a soft breath of a whisper. She seemed to remind herself of the situation she was in, because her eyes widened slightly and she leaned away from Billie.

"Then this should be an interesting car ride," Billie said, with a short laugh she hoped sounded casual and relaxed. She had just caught a quick glimpse of breezy confidence in Merissa, and then it was gone as quickly as it had arrived. She put her hand on Merissa's back as they walked outside. The touch was meant for support, but Billie felt the same well of conflicting emotions she had felt in the alley earlier. She felt sorry for Merissa and felt an obligation to take care of her because it was her duty today. She had negative emotions toward her as well. Merissa was pretty and distraught and obviously out of her element in the seedier side of downtown Tacoma, and

Billie knew Carlyle—guilty or not—wouldn't stand a chance if a jury watched Merissa's tears flow and saw one of her slender and expressive fingers point him out in a courtroom. Billie had even taken a risk by blurring the line between cop and friend—something she rarely did—because of Merissa.

Despite everything flooding through Billie, she wanted to keep her hand on Merissa's back. Rub away the tension she felt there and let her hand ruffle Merissa's hair back to life. Instead, she pulled her hand away and opened the car door for Merissa. She was good at helping trauma victims because she let herself get close to them and feel their pain. She had to remind herself where the boundaries were and keep a professional distance from Merissa.

She got in the car, her right arm only inches from Merissa's. The best way to create space between them was to bring up Merissa's urban renewal project again. The thought of being homeless ought to be the cold shower Billie needed right now.

"What exactly does Morgan Consulting do?" she asked. She started the car and realized she wasn't sure where Merissa lived. "And I'm taking you home, but I don't know where your home is."

Merissa shrugged. "Sometimes I'm not sure, either. But I live in Gig Harbor."

What did she mean by her first statement? Merissa was too vulnerable right now, and her inner thoughts—most likely kept private in normal situations—were showing every so often. Billie herself was struggling not to be anything more than a casual shoulder to lean on, so even though she was curious about the hint of resignation in Merissa's voice, she kept silent as she headed toward the harbor, giving Merissa time to answer her initial question.

"I guess the best definition of what we do is we design urban spaces. We'll find a run-down neighborhood, or a place where there are lots of foreclosures or vacant buildings, and we'll draw up a plan for what we'd like to see there. We get quotes from construction companies, and then we get financial backers to invest, buy the property, and pay for the renovations."

Billie whistled. "You must have some very wealthy clients. How do they make money from this investment?"

Merissa tucked her hair behind her ear. She kept staring forward while they talked, not looking in Billie's direction. Billie was glad not to have the full force of Merissa's blue eyes on her. They held more depth and pain than Billie was ready to see. They threatened to draw her in.

"It depends on the concept. Sometimes the area will support stores and restaurants, sometimes condos or homes. Usually a mix of both. The investors make dividends on the various types of leases or a percentage if the property is sold instead."

Billie noticed that Merissa winced every time she said *we*. Billie understood the way certain words and memories chafed against the open wound of loss. "What are your plans for the neighborhood you were circling last night?"

Merissa grew a little more animated as she explained her open courtyard design, and Billie secretly thought her vision was an impressive one. Too bad she wouldn't be able to afford to live there anymore once her apartment building was replaced by the fancy high-rise condo. She sped up and merged onto Highway 16. "Sounds amazing. And much too pricey for the residents who live downtown now. Where are they supposed to go?"

"We haven't addressed that so far, although I have some ideas," Merissa admitted. "Like I said, we often buy buildings that aren't inhabited, so we aren't always displacing people. And we're only able to renovate small chunks of the city at a time. There are still plenty of less expensive living options."

"I suppose." Billie wanted to drop the subject but she stubbornly kept picking at it. "Your eventual goal, though, is to remake Tacoma into what you consider to be an ideal city."

Merissa looked at her then, and her words were full of the passion Billie had sensed in her earlier. "Not just what I think is ideal. What a lot of people would consider to be so. A home where neighbors know each other and take care of each other. Not a series of anonymous, walled-off houses and apartments, but a community."

Billie thought of Carlyle, of the people she lived next to, protected, and sometimes arrested. They were her extended family, whether they were pillars of society or the opposite. "Just because you venture downtown and drive along the streets with your doors locked and your windows rolled up doesn't mean the existing community isn't close-knit and friendly."

"It didn't seem that way last night," Merissa said quietly. There was no censure or accusation in her voice, but Billie felt like she'd been slapped. Merissa had seen the worst of the city last night, and no matter what she planned to build there, she hadn't deserved to have her friend wrenched away right in front of her. And most likely, Dennis had simply been in the wrong place at the wrong time and hadn't deserved his death.

"I'm sorry," she said.

Merissa leaned her head against the back rest and closed her eyes as Billie drove over the westbound span of the Narrows Bridge. The twin suspension bridges crossed high over the strait, connecting Tacoma to the Kitsap Peninsula. Billie wasn't sure if Merissa was nervous of heights or just tired—or just tired of talking to her. She remained still, without talking, until they reached the end of the bridge. Billie didn't mind the height at all. She loved the views from the bridge, with the steep cliffs rising on either side and the lush greenness of the Point Defiance Park on one side and the less crowded peninsula on the other. Occasionally, when she crossed here, she would spot a seal bobbing in the water or, more rarely, an orca's fin cutting through the choppy waves. Her first experience as an informal department crisis counselor had occurred up here, when she'd been dispatched to check into a caller's report of someone about to jump off the bridge. She'd managed to talk him down before anyone else arrived on the scene. She felt her palms grow sweaty as she thought about what might have happened if she'd been a few minutes later, or if she'd been too afraid to walk onto the bridge.

"Take the next exit," Merissa said, breaking Billie out of her memories. "You're right, I guess."

"About what?" Billie asked with a frown as she tried to recapture the thread of their conversation. She was tired herself, more emotionally than physically, and getting caught in the cycle of what-ifs from past experiences was one of the signs she knew to watch for. If she wasn't careful, she'd spend the night immersed in nightmares. As soon as she dropped Merissa at her house, she'd get to the barn for some equine therapy. Even an hour spent grooming Ranger should be enough to ease her mind back to the present.

"You were right about me being an outsider in places like the Hilltop. I've driven on those streets lots of times, but it was different when I was with you. You knew people. You were joking with those guys, and several others waved at you or called out. Turn right at the light and follow this road around the harbor." Merissa guided them away from the more commercial and increasingly populated areas of Gig Harbor and down a steep hill toward the older part of town. "What you have in Tacoma because you work there is what I want everyone to be able to experience. It's what I envision, but for more people."

Or just the richer ones. Billie didn't say it out loud because she wasn't quite sure she believed Merissa thought that way. She wanted to lump Merissa in the pile of evil developers who booted out undesirable tenants in favor of wealthier ones, but there was something that sounded like longing in Merissa's voice when she spoke of her dreams for Tacoma. As if she lacked something in her own life and wanted to provide the missing feeling or connection for the city. Billie didn't know how to reconcile the two images in her mind, especially since she'd only known Merissa for the day, so she decided to stop trying. Her responsibility toward Merissa ended as soon as their car ride did.

Billie slowly navigated through Gig Harbor. Tiny one-of-a-kind shops and restaurants lined the main road that curved along the edge of the harbor. Pedestrians crossed the street at random places, and mannequins dressed for an afternoon at the yacht club watched their progress through clothing store windows. Hundreds of boats were moored here, their stick-like masts bobbing as the water from the Sound rocked them. Billie looked to her right as she drove. The view of Mount Rainier would be stunning when there wasn't a heavy layer of gray clouds in the Washington winter sky.

She followed Merissa's directions up another hill and out of the historic district. Without much segue, they were in farm country. Businesses disappeared, and the lots became more spacious as they drove. After a few miles, Merissa told her to turn onto a gravel road and gave her the code for the large iron gate that blocked their path.

Billie drove slowly as the road meandered between thick stands of fir trees. She thought they were entering a housing development, but she rounded a bend and a large property opened up in the valley below her. She bit her lip to keep from gasping out loud. She was familiar enough with some of the beautiful equestrian stables around the area. Callan Lanford was dating Billie's sergeant and trained the mounted team, and Billie had spent many hours at Cal's family's fancy polo farm over the past six months. She'd visited other large barns to watch horse shows and polo matches with Rachel and Cal, but Merissa's place dwarfed them all. The house was a grand brick mansion, complete with a pool and columns and what seemed to be several separate wings. Large grazing paddocks lined the driveway, and an enormous field was dotted with horses and an entire cross-country course of jumps. A large barn stood close to the house, and three smaller barns were stepped up the hill behind it. A polo field, an oval training track, and an outdoor arena were scattered around the barn. Billie sighed. She'd just found heaven.

She cleared her throat. "Nice little place you have here." Seeing Merissa in the context of this farm made perfect sense to Billie. The richness in her voice and the feather-light scent of her hair. Her casual, lived-in but obviously designer clothes. Beauty and elegance, but somehow down-to-earth.

Merissa laughed. "It's a bit much, isn't it? It belonged to my grandfather, and he left it to me when he died."

A tall bay gelding stood near a white board fence and watched them drive past. Billie wanted to stop and visit him, but she kept going until she reached the circular drive in front of the house's main entrance. "I take it he was a horse person?"

"Actually, no," Merissa said as she unbuckled her seat belt. "I am. I was living with my parents in Europe, and the three of them were usually in a sort of battle for my affection. He found out that I was taking riding lessons, and he built this."

Merissa's gesture encompassed acres of beauty. Billie shook her head. She'd spent most of her childhood living with her dad's friends and distant relatives. She'd have been happy if he'd built a tiny shack for them to live in together, and she'd never even have dreamed of a place like this.

"Did it work?"

"Yes," Merissa said. "I came to live with him when I was thirteen, but not because he gave me a fairy-tale farm."

Merissa got out of the car without explaining why she *had* chosen to come here. Billie followed her up the arched staircase and waited while Merissa unlocked the large wooden door with its ornate metalwork design.

They went inside, and Merissa tossed her keys on what looked like an antique table. Everything was as regal inside as Billie had expected after seeing the exterior. Marble flooring, elegant furniture, vaulted ceilings. Huge picture windows looked over the pool and the woods beyond. When she stepped into the main room, she could see a showroom-ready kitchen to her right and a glimpse of a formal dining room. Everything was picture-perfect, but nothing looked like home. There weren't any photographs or knickknacks to be seen. The kitchen counters were bare, without even a coffeemaker to prove someone lived here. It was one of the most beautiful houses Billie had ever seen, but she suddenly hated to leave Merissa alone in it.

"Will you be okay?" she asked, watching as Merissa gave a huge yawn. "I can take you somewhere else, if you'd rather not be alone. To a friend's house, maybe?"

"I'll be fine," Merissa assured her. In a gesture Billie had come to recognize over the past few hours, Merissa tucked her hair back with fingers that trembled. Their movement was out of place here. Her shaky weariness would be safe with the horses or in the welcoming barn, but not inside the house. Here, everything was rigid and cold, and Merissa would be made even more numb, not comforted. "I want a hot shower and a bed, that's all."

Billie took one last look around before she nodded in acceptance. This was Merissa's home, and she had no reason to stay longer or try to convince her to leave. The enticing image of Merissa luxuriating in a steamy, fragrant shower and then sliding between cool, freshly laundered sheets made the former option Billie's favorite by far. She had to get out of here. She handed Merissa a card with her number on it, not hesitating to give her one of the rarely used cards with her personal and not her work number. "This is my cell. Call me if you need anything."

"I will." Merissa followed Billie to the door and put her hand on Billie's arm. "Thank you. You made an unbearable day a fraction more bearable."

"It's my job," Billie said, although her response to Merissa's touch was anything but professional. "Good night."

Billie drove back toward Tacoma, where Ranger and her tiny but homey apartment waited for her.

Chapter Six

Merissa watched through one of the leaded glass windows next to the door until the police car was out of sight, then she turned away and walked across the shiny marble floor of the living room. Billie's presence was confusing—she stirred up emotions Merissa couldn't process right now. For most of the night, Merissa had felt chunks of feelings and half-formed notions roiling around inside of her. Pain, sadness, fear. And, once Billie had arrived, attraction and defensiveness. Too many sensations and thoughts to sort through and understand. Instead of coming to mind in an orderly way, they had bumped through her like objects in a pan of boiling water, their sharp edges cutting into her wherever they collided with her raw mind and heart. Eventually, the sharpness had worn away, and she'd gotten numb. The collisions were less acutely painful now, but still uncomfortable and jarring.

Merissa left the main wing of the house behind and walked through a breezeway to the little suite where she actually lived day to day. No one got much farther into her real home than Billie had tonight. The few people she invited into her house saw the main section her grandfather had designed. He had entertained there quite often, using the opulent surroundings to impress business clients and to give himself an aura of power. Merissa wouldn't be the same. When she started meeting for business, she would prefer a place like the Morgan firm or her potential investors' own offices. She wanted them to feel in control and powerful enough to invest the kind of money she needed from them, not for them to feel intimidated by her or that their contributions would be unnecessary.

Merissa had brought the occasional friends, including Dennis and Karen once, over to the house for a meal in the grand dining room or drinks on the terrace. She'd had several girlfriends who made it as far as the beautiful guest room decorated in shades of blue and the shiny kitchen for romantic midnight snacks, but no one came into her private sanctuary, the suite of rooms that had once belonged to a string of nannies hired to care for her when she was young.

Merissa shut the door behind her and breathed a huge sigh as some of her tension released. Tomorrow she'd probably feel fear from her ordeal, needing to check under beds and behind curtains for imagined gun-toting intruders, but right now all she felt was relief to be home and alone, although she'd very nearly invited Billie back here with her. A definite sign that she was overtired and overwrought.

She pulled off her clothes as soon as she got into her bedroom and dropped them on the floor next to the hamper. Later, she'd decide whether to wash them or to just toss them and the memories they'd always contain into the trash. She caught a glimpse of herself in the mirror above her dresser and quickly looked away from the sight of her haggard expression. She wasn't able to define all the emotions inside her, and her face revealed the confusion and weariness she felt inside. She went into the small bathroom and took as hot a shower as she could stand, washing away the grime of murder and police stations.

She got out when she didn't feel she could stand upright much longer and lay down on her bed, naked and flushed red from the heat of the water. Billie had been too present in her thoughts, and Merissa's exhausted mind couldn't summon enough common sense to keep her from imagining Billie in the shower with her. She had washed her hair and scrubbed the nasty precinct smells off her body, but it had been Billie's fingers she felt skimming across her slick, sudsy skin and massaging the tension out of her scalp and neck. Merissa stared at the posters on her wall without really seeing them, taking some comfort in familiar surroundings and childhood memories even though she felt a gaping loneliness that she hadn't experienced since she was a child. Since no one saw her rooms back here, she'd decorated more like a teenager than an adult. Instead of framed prints, she had posters thumbtacked onto the wall. Horse figurines she'd collected over the years pranced across dressers and every flat surface. Her books were stacked on shelves instead of sitting upright because she found it easier to locate the title she wanted when the books were horizontal. Her drafting table stood in one corner of the room, covered with experimental plans for the Hilltop neighborhood project. Billie had seen her at her weakest today, and bringing her to this room would only have made Merissa feel even less capable and controlled than she did.

Her phone rang, and she rolled onto her stomach and reached for it. In an unguarded moment, reason be damned, she hoped it was Billie on the other end of the line—although she couldn't recall giving her this number—but a man's voice spoke instead.

"This is Jeff Kensington. I just heard about Dennis, and Merissa, I'm so sorry. Is there anything I can do?"

She accepted his condolences and gave vague answers about the night before, hoping she was saying the correct things. She'd been in charge of her grandfather's estate when he died and she'd fielded calls from distant relatives and business associates pretending to be sorry while they were in reality trying to determine who would be in control of his wealth and how they could get some. This seemed different. Dennis had been more of a friend to her than her grandfather had been. She'd loved him, of course, and he had been exceedingly generous with her, but their relationship had never been characterized by warmth or affection. She'd mourned from a distance.

She made small talk with Kensington for as long as she could bear, and when she started to wrap up the call, he changed the subject back to business.

"I understand you were going to be with Dennis when the firm pitched this new development proposal to me," he said. Merissa felt herself grow cold and she shivered, pulling the comforter over her naked body. She had only learned the news last night, but Kensington seemed more aware of her role at work than she was. "I know your firm will be in turmoil for a while, but give me a call when you're ready to get back to the project. I'm very interested in working with you."

"I'll let you know," Merissa said vaguely before she ended the call. She'd been a fool to think Jeff was merely calling to say he was sorry about Dennis. And what had he meant by the phrase *your firm*? He wanted something from her, something she couldn't yet identify and that wasn't hers to give. Just like the scores of people who called as soon as they heard about her grandfather's heart attack. Merissa had only a few minutes with her cynical thoughts before her phone rang again. Another number she didn't recognize. "Hello?"

"Merissa?" A voice much louder than Jeff's boomed over her phone. She held it a few inches from her ear. "It's Ed Lemaine. I was shocked to hear about Dennis today. How are you holding up, my dear?"

They went through the same routine of sorrow, and then small talk, and then a leap back to business. At least Merissa was ready for it this time.

"Dennis mentioned you have a project in the works. I'd be glad to hear your proposal once you've recovered enough to get back to work. I know it will be challenging for you to fill his shoes, but I'll be there to walk you through every step of the way. Dennis and I had a great business relationship, and I foresee the same for me and you."

Merissa frowned at her phone. Dennis must not have mentioned his intention to use Jeff for this neighborhood's renewal, but he had apparently brought her name into a conversation at some point. In less than twenty-four hours she had gone from elation over being asked to be present at a pitch meeting to hearing Lemaine practically name her as successor. She wasn't sure what to say and was going to give him as noncommittal an answer as she'd given Jeff. Edwin spoke again before she had a chance.

"You're new to business on this scale, sweetheart, so I'm going to give you some helpful advice. You're going to need someone with power on your side. You'll need a lot of money backing this project and any others you plan in what could be an extremely successful future for you. I have influence over most of the investors in this area. They'll listen to me whether I tell them to invest or not." He paused before delivering his final words. "I'd prefer to tell them to back you, but it depends on how you handle yourself once you're in charge. Let me know what you decide."

Merissa barely managed to say good-bye. Her hands were shaking as she ended the call and dropped her cell on the bed as if it was burning hot. Was she really the one everyone expected to take over now that Dennis was gone? These men seemed to think so. She felt a surge of undeniable pleasure because they were looking to her as the new Morgan Group leader. Dennis had always ruled the firm on his own, employing a creative staff but never developing partners to have equal say in the business. Merissa had been an employee, not a peer, although she knew she had the potential to be more and had always dreamed of working in a more collaborative environment with Dennis and other planners. People beyond the private walls of the Morgan offices had apparently taken notice of her, and the knowledge fanned the sense of pride she had felt when Dennis told her about the pitch last night.

Along with her pride came a wave of reservations. She wasn't ready to lead the firm. Dennis hadn't even come close to training her as a replacement boss, and until last night she hadn't realized he had the intention of bringing her more deeply into the business. She'd consider taking the promotion if Karen chose to offer it to her—maybe even buy the firm herself if Karen wanted out but she had her doubts. Not about her ultimate career goals and her belief that she could make beneficial changes in the city if she had a chance and a strong team to lead, but concerns about following so closely in Dennis's footprints. She had felt uncomfortable talking to the contractors, but she wasn't sure whether it was due to their personalities and their past relationships with Dennis or just to the traumatic events of the night before. She hadn't been able to read either Jeff or Edwin until they laid their cards out for her. She'd naively thought they were sad about a fellow businessman's death, but instead one was pushing for a contract that would put his fledgling business on the map, and the other was threatening to use his already strong reputation against her. She'd sat next to a good man as life drained out of him drop by drop, and instead of really caring how she was handling the horror of it, they were pushing their selfish agendas.

Merissa had hoped her hot shower would relax her enough for sleep to come, but now she was as wide-awake as she'd been exhausted only minutes earlier. She put on a sweater and jeans and sat on her bed fiddling with the card Billie had given her. Billie had been the one honest part of this mess, and she was tempted to call her and let Billie's calm presence ground her. Billie had been assigned to her, Merissa knew. She was only doing her job hauling Merissa around Tacoma and back home again, but she'd been more than an escort around the crime scene. Merissa suddenly felt lost, without anyone to trust completely. She let two more calls with unrecognized numbers go to voice mail before she saw a familiar name. She tucked Billie's card in her pocket and answered the call.

"Hey, Callan," she said. Her voice was surprisingly steady, buoyed by the realization that she had a friend out there. Cal had no reason to want anything from her.

"How are you, Merissa?" Cal's voice came across the phone with honeyed depth. "I heard about the homicide when I went to work with the mounted unit today. I knew Billie was assigned to help out with the investigation, but I didn't realize you were the witness until she got back to the barn a few minutes ago."

"You work for the police? I had no idea." Merissa knew Cal from friendly conversations at polo matches and awards banquets. They'd never gotten together off the field, but Merissa had admired Cal's riding and had been impressed by her down-to-earth humility, even when she beat Merissa's team. Which she always did. "Any chance they'll keep you too busy to school your ponies so someone else can have a chance at the regional championships?"

Cal laughed. "I'll tell you a secret. The three words that will win you that trophy."

"If you say *practice, practice, practice* I'm hanging up on you."

"Nope. I was going to say *join my team*."

Merissa grinned. She felt some of the effects of last night uncoil inside her.

"Seriously, Merissa, are you surviving?" Cal asked. "Billie didn't give any details—she's the epitome of discretion—but she seemed worried about you. I didn't want to call and bother you, but she said you might want to talk."

"I do," Merissa said. She settled back against her headboard. From the first moment they met, Billie had seemed to sense what Merissa was feeling and how best to help her. Of course she was the reason Merissa was getting a phone call she desperately needed. If Merissa wasn't so relieved to have Cal on the line, she'd be infuriated that she'd been so transparent to Billie. Consistent with her oddly inconsistent and unfamiliar emotional swings, she even found her angry response to Billie arousing. She usually was proud of her even-tempered approach to life, especially after the depth of pain and emptiness she had sometimes felt as a child. Dennis's murder had set off a chain of cascading moods in her, and Billie seemed to swing between calming them and making them fiery and pronounced.

Right now, Cal and polo and horses might be able to distract Merissa enough to shut off her mind and rest. "Nothing about last night or about the future of my career, please, but just talk. If you have a few minutes to spare, of course."

"I have as much time as you need," Cal assured her. "Especially if you'd care to discuss certain rumors about a certain someone who recently imported a fancy new polo pony from Argentina."

"Are you digging for insider information to help your team beat mine?" Merissa asked. "Because I won't say a single word about the gorgeous black mare currently trotting around my pasture."

"Good. Then I won't mention the fact that I desperately need a new horse for my string."

Merissa heard a voice tinged with laughter in the background, telling Cal that she absolutely did not need another horse.

"That was Rachel," Cal said to Merissa. "Love of my life and voice of reason. I listen to everything she says." She dropped her voice to an exaggerated whisper. "I'll pay you double what you paid for the mare."

"I guess I'll be staying on Rachel's good side, then, because there's no way she's for sale."

"Rats. Okay, wait. What?" Cal carried on a murmured conversation in the background. "That's a great idea, Rach. I'm back, Merissa. Rachel says that since you are kindly refusing to support my horse buying addiction, she'd like you to come ride with the team tomorrow. It's a training day, so we'll be at the barn in Point Defiance. We can help take your mind off everything, for a couple hours at least."

Merissa sighed. The thought of a fun day spent with horses and some nice people unrelated to Dennis and the firm was exactly what she needed. She wasn't sure how she felt about seeing Billie again, but she was interested in seeing her ride. She would bet that Billie's intuitive way of handling distraught murder victims was part of her nature, which meant she'd connect easily with horses. Prey animals and traumatized people required similar approaches, and Merissa felt a curious tingle in her stomach at the thought of watching the confident and caring Billie in her normal work mode.

"I'd love to come," she said. The invitation settled her more than the shower had, and she was only able to talk to Cal for a few more minutes before her near-constant yawns ended their conversation. She turned off the ringer on her phone and slid out of her clothes again before falling into a deep sleep.

Chapter Seven

Billie got to the barn early, after missing her ride the day before because of Merissa, and she hooked Ranger to the crossties in the barn aisle. She took her time grooming the patient chestnut gelding, currying him gently to loosen the mud from his thick winter hair. He had the thin, sensitive skin of a Thoroughbred, but as long as she was careful with the grooming tools, he seemed to enjoy her attention as much as she loved lavishing it on him. She used a stiff-bristled brush to flick the mud off him, and then finished the job with a softer brush to bring a shine to his red-gold coat.

By the time the others began to arrive, she was cleaning his hooves with a metal pick, and she'd worked out most of the remaining tension from yesterday. She had worried about leaving Merissa alone, but once she'd discovered that Cal knew her and would call and check up on her, Billie had relaxed. Better to have Cal contact Merissa than Billie. She was attracted to Merissa on the surface, and she appreciated the intelligence and strength she'd noticed in her, but their relationship was a work-related one and didn't need to seep into Billie's personal life. Merissa was an idealist—and who could blame her, given the mansion in which she'd grown up? Billie was a realist. She'd lived in hellholes and through hell during her years in the army. Most of her childhood had been spent as an unwanted guest in other people's homes. Opposites might attract, but they probably wouldn't have much to talk about after the initial fireworks were over.

Billie went into the tack room and got her saddle. She seemed to be spending a lot of time and energy convincing herself that she was better off without Merissa. Last night, she had nearly handcuffed her wrist to the bed and thrown the key across the room to keep from driving back to Gig Harbor and knocking on Merissa's door. The handcuffs might have come in handy then, too…

Billie forced her attention back to the task at hand. The police unit needed her to be fully present these days, since the new horses and riders joining the team meant every training session was mission critical. Everyone was here today except for Clark, who was away for an afternoon of departmental training. He'd been riding Legs lately since his horse Sitka had been injured the month before, pulling a suspensory ligament when he slipped while he was turned loose in the arena. All of them realized they or their horses could be injured in the line of duty, but the freak accident in the relatively safe confines of their stables had come as a surprise to the entire team. Clark would be rotating out of the mounted division at the end of their season anyway, when he would be promoted to sergeant, and he had bought the injured gelding from the woman who had leased him to the police department. After a few months of rest and rehab, Sitka would be sound enough for trails and light riding. Clark hadn't been the most horse-oriented of the riders when the unit was formed, but each of them formed an undeniable bond with their equine partners.

The gray Thoroughbred Legs had been in the police string for two months now. Abby had ridden her at the Puyallup Fair, where she'd been well-behaved except for the minor issue of putting their lieutenant in the hospital with a fractured wrist. The team would bring on one rider for her, to replace Clark next spring, as well as expanding to include a fifth member. And after Sitka's accident, Rachel and Abby had gotten permission to have a sixth horse trained and on standby in case another was injured.

Billie came out of the room with her bridle over one shoulder and her saddle balanced on her other arm. She saw Abby, Rachel, and Cal huddled in the parking lot, discussing something with large gestures and animated faces. Every once in a while, one of them would glance at Billie with a suspiciously conniving expression. Billie sighed as she smoothed the navy saddle blanket on Ranger's back. She recognized plotters when she saw them. She had no clue what they were talking about, but whatever they had in mind, she wouldn't go along without a fight. If they were up to something good, they'd come right out and talk to her without the obvious subterfuge.

Don led his pinto mare, Fancy, to the crossties near Ranger and started to groom the homely but impeccably behaved little horse. Billie had ridden her a few times since the mounted unit was formed almost a year ago, and she was sure she still had bruises on her ass from Fancy's rough gaits. Don loved her, though, and the two of them had surprised everyone with their talent both in mounted police work and search and rescue.

"I heard about your neighbor, Carlyle," Don said. "They're calling him a flight risk and holding him for twenty-four while they try to find some solid evidence against him. D'you know anything about that?"

Billie shook her head, checking to make sure the other riders were still in the parking lot. "I talked to him yesterday, after Merissa ID'd his car. He claimed he didn't do anything, and I didn't get the sense he was lying. His alibi won't back him up even if he was telling me the truth about where he was the night before, though."

Don stopped brushing Fancy and looked at her. Billie avoided his gaze because the more time they spent together, the more adept he was becoming at reading her.

"What aren't you saying? What else did he tell you?"

Billie sighed. She'd been a private person since she was very young, and had grown more so after Mike's death and her return from the Middle East. Being part of this mounted team had initially been appealing to her because of the horses, but she'd grown closer to the people in her unit as well. The connection to them, the way they really seemed to look at her and see her, was still foreign to her. She was uncomfortable with the sudden visibility, but part of her liked it.

"There's this guy, Percy. Druggie. He borrowed the car for the night and said a buddy of his needed it. Carlyle told me Percy would probably stay away from his usual spots in case Carlyle sent the detectives after him, but he told me where he might be found on Ruston Way."

"And you're going to try to find him?"

"I promised Carlyle," she said. Plus, she wanted to understand the reason behind this shooting. If Dennis had just driven into the middle of a messed-up drug deal, she would be sad about his fate but relieved to know Merissa was safe. If Dennis had somehow been targeted, Merissa might be in danger, too. The imperative to follow orders and respect the chain of command was strong in her—drilled into her by the army—but she was ready to launch a brief investigation into Percy's whereabouts if it meant she'd have a chance to reassure herself about Merissa's safety and to protect Carlyle if he was innocent.

"Fine. And I'm going with you."

"No way, Don. I just want to talk to the guy, see if Carlyle's story checks out and find out who Percy's buddy is, if there even is one. In and out." What she planned to do wasn't technically against any rules since she had as much right as anyone to talk to someone on the streets of Tacoma. However, if the detectives found out she had withheld information by not giving them Carlyle's name, and then had used that information to interrogate a possible murder suspect...well, she wasn't dragging Don into this. She put her hands on her hips and stared him down, putting as much forceful determination as she could into her look. During her army days, she'd scared the secrets right out of tougher men than Don with the intimidating expression she'd perfected.

"Oh, Lieutenant Hargrove," he called loudly, not breaking eye contact with Billie. "Can I talk to you for a minute?"

He raised his eyebrows as their boss walked toward them. "Fine," Billie whispered in a hiss. He was probably bluffing, but too much was on the line for her to take a chance. "You can come with me."

"What's up, Don?" Abby stopped next to him. Even in Billie's slightly miffed state, she couldn't help but recognize the changes Abby had gone through in the past two months since she'd met and fallen in love with Kira. Her thick auburn hair, usually bound in a tight chignon, was instead caught in a ponytail with a few loose strands waving along her cheekbones. Her face had softened, losing some of the taut determination she used to show, as if she was fighting a battle against the whole world and doing it alone. Now she smiled more easily and she often rode with her team when they trained, instead of bossing them around from the ground. Still, as different as Abby was from the woman they'd called Hard-Ass Hargrove, Billie didn't want to be on her shit list and she was relieved when Don came up with a reason for calling her over that had nothing to do with Billie.

"Fancy needs a new bridle. The one she has is rubbing her cheekbones. Do we have money in the budget?"

"Sure, Don," Abby said, with the same indulgent tone they all used when talking to Don about his beloved mare and something he'd decided she needed, like another piece of equipment or change in diet. "Just have Rachel put in a req form."

"Will do," he said with a wink in Billie's direction. She gave him her best scowl, but he just laughed.

Billie led Ranger away from Don's laughter and out to the practice arena. Cal had made an obstacle course for today's session. Billie looked it over as she mounted Ranger and adjusted her stirrups. There was a tarp that had been cut into strips and hung so the horses had to walk through it, and a bridge that rested on a round pole so it would teeter back and forth as the horses walked over it. None of the obstacles would pose a problem for her and her experienced gelding.

Cal and Rachel came over and stopped her before she could walk into the arena. They were a striking couple, with Rachel's dark and wild good looks and Cal's golden hair and elegant bearing. "Change in plans," Rachel said. "We want to work the new horses through the course, and each one will be paired with one of our seasoned mounts. Cal thought you'd do well with Juniper."

"Oh, okay," Billie said, sliding to the ground again. She was pleased to be put on the challenging young mare, but she had to force down her possessive desire to be the one to ride her own horse. "Who'll ride Ranger?"

"Merissa. She sounded like she could use a distraction after what she's been through, and she'll have fun with this course. She's a great rider, so don't worry about how she'll handle him."

Merissa was coming today? Billie—usually calm and single-minded during training sessions—felt tension rise from her twisting stomach to her tight throat, and Ranger fidgeted in response. She didn't want Merissa here, riding Ranger, but she wasn't sure why. Was she jealous? Worried Merissa would be a better rider and outperform her on Ranger? No. Billie had no doubt Merissa was a high-class equestrian. She'd assumed as much after seeing her barn and before Cal had told her what an excellent polo player she was. And of course expensive trainers and lessons had been part of the massive equestrian complex her grandfather had built for her, while Billie's own training was limited to therapy lessons for a year and the schooling she'd gotten from Cal and Rachel. But she didn't mind having her riding compared side by side with Merissa's. She had no illusions about her level of expertise and was always happy to learn from riders with more experience.

She knew the real reason behind the clenched fists holding Ranger's reins. She wasn't prepared to spend more time in Merissa's company. The barn was her place of refuge. Merissa's presence had brought a turmoil of conflicting emotions into Billie's life yesterday, and Billie wasn't sure she wanted those feelings to invade this healthy space. Merissa sparked passion in her—unexpected and overwhelming—both the passion of attraction to her and a passionate desire to argue against her and her plans to destroy Billie's neighborhood.

"Well, I'll get Juniper ready," Billie said. She'd have to keep control of herself not only for her own well-being, but also for the young mare and for Merissa, who would be dealing with the fallout of her traumatic night with Dennis for a long time. They both needed Billie to be the calm one. "Can one of you hold Ranger until she gets here?"

Rachel reached for the reins, and Billie managed to loosen her grip and let Rachel take them. "Wait a sec, Billie. There's more." She exchanged a glance with Cal. "You know we were going to send the horses to Cal's farm for a month of rest and then a month of training before we start patrolling again in the spring."

Billie nodded. She loved riding on the trails and lovely polo fields at the farm. She'd been looking forward to the change of scenery for her benefit, as well as Ranger's.

"We've decided to ask Merissa if she'll take them instead. Her barn is closer for most of the riders, and she's got plenty of space for them."

Billie snorted at the understatement. Merissa had plenty of space for the entire Royal Canadian Mounted Drill Team to perform on her front lawn alone. "Whatever you think is best for the horses," she said. The commute would be easy for her and she wouldn't mind a chance to get an up close and personal look at Merissa's horses. She started to turn away when Cal put a hand on her arm.

"There's more," Cal repeated Rachel's words. Billie rolled her eyes. The two of them communicated with looks alone, finished each other's sentences, and now were echoing each other. The whole lovebird thing was cute to an extent. Right now, Billie was finding it annoying as hell since she seemed to be on the outside while they shared some secret that had something to do with her. "Spit it out in unison, you two. What's going on?"

"We don't talk in unison," both Cal and Rachel said at the same time. Rachel blushed and gestured toward Cal, letting her share their news with Billie.

"We'd like you to be in charge of the horses while they're at her farm," Cal said. "They'll need grooming and some light riding for the first month, and the newbies will need desensitizing work. Merissa and her grooms have their hands full with her polo string, but at the same time, we don't want to have a bunch of riders descending on her property every day. You seem like the ideal choice."

Rachel nodded. "You're great with the nervous horses. And, well, with people, too. Merissa needs a friend right now, and someone who will be there while she processes what's happened."

"And she's beautiful," Cal added. "And single."

"You weren't supposed to say that part out loud," Rachel said, playfully shoving at Cal.

Billie watched their impromptu wrestling match for a few seconds before she had to stop them. "Save it for tonight, when you're alone," she said. "Look, I'm flattered that you think I'd be good enough to be responsible for the horses, but I don't think I'm the right one to help Merissa beyond what I did yesterday." She struggled to find the right way to express what she was trying to say. Merissa wanted to tear down Billie's home, her neighborhood. They didn't seem to understand each other on a fundamental level. Too much contact on a daily basis with a trauma victim might be damaging to Billie's soul. Too much Merissa might overwhelm her heart. "You've seen my apartment, and you've heard about her estate—"

"I wasn't suggesting your houses date," Cal interrupted. "Although they seem to have a sexy wrong-side-of-the-tracks thing going for them."

Rachel pulled Cal behind her and her voice changed to what Billie and the others called her Sergeant Voice. "Look, Billie, we were going to ask you to be in charge of the horses at Cal's, too. Just the venue has changed, and we didn't make this job up for you just to push you and Merissa together. You'd be doing this for the team first, and if you happen to help Merissa at the same time, that's just a bonus."

"I'll think about it, Sarge," she said. She walked back to the barn and took Juniper's halter off a hook on the wall. She wasn't sure whether she completely believed Rachel or not, but the thought of being the sole person in charge of the horses excited her. She'd eventually like to step into Rachel's boots, once Rachel was promoted to lieutenant, and this experience would be a step toward her goal. And if Merissa was part of the deal? Billie felt an involuntary smile forming on her face, but she bit her lip and pushed it away. As long as she and Merissa avoided any talk of Billie's home or Merissa's plan to turn Tacoma into a wealthy utopia, they might be just fine together. Talking was overrated, anyway.

CHAPTER EIGHT

Merissa drove through the high chain-link gate and parked her red Dodge pickup next to an ancient Camry. She sat inside for a moment before joining the group of riders who were standing outside the arena. She immediately recognized Billie from the back. She sat with one hand on the reins and the other resting on her hip, looking relaxed and confident on the pretty buckskin mare. She was talking to two of the other riders Merissa had seen in the Daffodil Parade. Judging by Cal's glowing descriptions from the night before, the tall, dark-haired woman was Cal's girlfriend, Sergeant Rachel Bryce, and her liver chestnut quarter horse named Bandit. The other was an older officer who was riding a pinto mare that seemed asleep, with one hind leg cocked and her eyes nearly closed. Cal was standing a few yards away, holding the reins of two horses, the one Billie had ridden in the parade and an enormous black-and-white paint. An auburn-haired woman on a stunning gray completed the colorful tableau. Merissa thought she might have seen her at the police station yesterday, but she couldn't remember clearly.

Merissa seemed to have lost control of her eyes, and her gaze moved back to Billie of its own volition even though she tried to pay attention to the horses, the arena, the trees in the park across the street—anything but Billie's seat in the saddle. Her riding outfit had looked sexy yesterday, but now that she was on a horse it was even more appealing. Billie shifted her weight as the buckskin started walking toward the arena, and the navy fabric stretched across her toned ass as she moved in the saddle. Merissa's own response was less subtle and graceful, probably as obvious to everyone as if a cartoon tongue had rolled out of her mouth and across the parking lot.

She was about to make as dignified an exit as possible—or at least a fast one—when Cal waved her over to the arena with a welcoming grin. Merissa smiled in return as she approached them, but inside she struggled to find some composure. The group seemed friendly and comfortable together, and Merissa would be on the outside today. She was accustomed to the role since she wasn't as quick to form relationships as other people seemed to be, but she felt a wave of jealousy at the sight of the tightly bonded unit. Merissa would have bet that Cal had played a big part in creating the cohesion, especially since her polo team showed the same connection with each other. While Merissa liked the members of her own team, they never socialized off the polo field, and probably as a result, their play was uninspired on it.

Billie turned in her saddle as Merissa approached and gave her a quick wave before getting back to work. Her expression was friendly but distant, and Merissa wished her own reaction to seeing Billie was as calm. She was a professional chore to Billie, but Merissa's reaction to her was far more personal. Inside, she felt the churning of desire and residual irritation and grief from the day before.

Cal welcomed her with a hug, awkward with two horses attached to her, and then she introduced Merissa to everyone. "You'll be riding Ranger," she said, handing the Thoroughbred's reins to Merissa. "We're going to have a more experienced horse lead the rookie over the obstacles, so you and Billie will be paired together. Don and Fancy will be with Abby and Legs, and I'll ride Merlin with Rachel and Bandit. Why don't we start by warming up along the rail."

Abby hung back with Merissa and Cal while the rest of the riders filed into the arena and trotted around the edge of the ring.

Merissa patted Ranger and talked quietly to him while she tightened the saddle's girth and adjusted her stirrups.

"Billie was raving about how beautiful your farm is, Merissa," Abby said.

Merissa couldn't imagine Billie *raving* about anything since she seemed so composed. She wondered what the result would be if Billie's control slipped away and the intensity under the surface was released. "Thank you," she said. "It's a nice place to live."

"Close to the city, but private," Abby said with a nod. "Which leads me to my proposition."

Merissa listened while Abby and Cal told her about the mounted team's two-month rest period, but after they mentioned having Billie be the one to come out to her home and care for the horses, she let their voices fade into the background. She glanced over at Billie, who was trotting around the arena and who seemed to be carefully not looking their way. She must know about this plan for her and the animals that would be her responsibility, so why wasn't she the one asking Merissa to board them? She had a feeling both the raving about her farm and the decision to make it their home base for the next months had come from Abby, Cal, and Rachel. Billie was as much a pawn here as Merissa was.

She held up her hand to stop Abby's long and detailed discussion about commute times for the team. "I get it," she said. "Everyone would save time coming to Gig Harbor for training instead of driving to Cal's. But we're talking fifteen minutes' difference, maybe less if there's traffic on the bridge. And I've played in matches at your farm, Cal. You can't tell me you don't have space for six extra horses. You could fit sixty more out there with no problem. I don't need extra income from boarding, and you certainly don't need to pay me when you could keep them at cost. So what's the deal?"

Abby looked at Cal, and then back at Merissa. There was a frankness in her expression, and Merissa suddenly realized her team would follow her anywhere, without question, if she led with the integrity Merissa sensed in her. "You're a friend of Cal's, Merissa, and anyone connected to her and this unit is family to us. You've been through something very traumatic, and the effects will last longer than you realize right now. Billie is, by far, the best person to have around when you need to talk or simply want someone there to understand what you're going through."

"And she can kick ass if anyone tries to hurt you," Cal added.

Merissa felt her eyes widen in surprise. The thought of Billie going to battle for her was enticing, but the image was overshadowed—barely—by fear. As far as she'd been able to tell, the detectives agreed Dennis's murder had been a fluke. He'd gotten in the way of the shooter's real target, or he'd been the victim of a gang initiation. "Why would I be in danger? I didn't see anything worth witnessing and no one seemed to believe the killer was aiming for Dennis in particular. There's no reason anyone would. He is... was a great guy, and everyone loved him. Why would anyone want to...?"

Merissa stopped herself when she heard the note of hysteria creeping into her voice. Abby was right. She might have gotten past the acute pain of losing Dennis the way she had, but the underlying emotions were still jumbled and hard to control. She turned away from them and mounted Ranger while she blinked away tears. He sensed her agitation and danced sideways, but she took a deep breath and made her body, at least, relax. When he was standing still, Abby spoke again.

"Chances are, you're correct about the motivation behind his shooting. We're just being cautious and we want to take care of you. We'll feel better if we know Billie is hanging around for a few weeks, while the investigation wraps up, and you'll have someone close by in case you need to talk." Abby raised her hands in a beseeching gesture. "Merely precautions."

"I'll think about it," Merissa said. "For now, let's ride."

She nudged Ranger forward with her calves, but she squeezed harder than she had intended, and he jogged into the arena instead of walking like she had planned. She kept trotting, determined to look as if she had meant to ask him for the faster gait. Everyone was a winner in their plan except Billie. What did she get out of the deal? A chance to babysit Merissa and the horses? Since they'd be riding partners today, Merissa would talk to Billie about the situation before she accepted Abby's proposal.

She moved Ranger onto the rail behind Billie and tried to keep her eyes to herself as she let the horse draw out her personal pain. Ranger was soft to her aids and seemed to know the warm-up routine better than Merissa did. She watched the rest of the team occasionally as they maneuvered around the edges of the obstacles, but her focus kept returning to Billie. All the riders were technically very good—a testament to Cal's teaching methods—but Billie had a different spark. She blended with the buckskin mare, even when the horse shied away from a flare Cal set on the ground near the gate. Merissa pulled Ranger to a halt and watched as Billie used her legs and seat to get the mare back on track. Soon, without any fuss, they were trotting along as if nothing had happened. The mare's ears flicked back toward her rider more often than they were pointed at the scary tarps and contraptions in the arena, indicating that her focus was now on Billie.

Merissa had been around plenty of talented riders and lots who had excellent formal training but little natural ability. Billie had a sense of feel that couldn't be taught. Merissa had experienced her intuitive abilities the day before, and she'd had the same response as Billie's mount. All her attention had centered on Billie since the first moment they'd met. The mare didn't seem interested in fighting against Billie's magnetism like Merissa did.

Once they had trotted and cantered their horses around the arena, Cal assigned each pair to an obstacle. She and Billie were standing next to a wooden platform balanced precariously on a round log when they finally had a chance to speak.

"Thank you again for yesterday," Merissa said as soon as Billie rode up next to her. "I don't know how I would have gotten through the day without your help."

Billie shrugged, but her smile looked pleased. "I didn't do much except get you a burger."

"That's what I meant," Merissa said with a quick wink. "No one else thought of feeding me. Even though I'd been there for hours." Hours, after witnessing a homicide. She pictured Dennis's face again and shuddered, all teasing disappearing. She suddenly wanted Billie—anyone—to understand what she had gone through yesterday. "Seriously, you were what I needed at a time when I really hated needing anything or anyone."

"I'm glad," Billie said quietly.

Merissa felt tears threaten again, and she changed the subject. "So, how do we do this? I've never trained a police horse before."

"Ranger has seen obstacles like this plenty of times, so why don't you take him over the bridge a few times to get accustomed to it. Then I'll follow with Juniper."

Merissa walked Ranger in a circle and aimed at the arched wooden surface. She gathered him into a balanced position and carefully kept him steady as he stepped onto the bridge with his front hooves. He hesitated a moment, but she nudged him forward, and as soon as his front end passed the halfway point, the bridge tipped forward. She felt her balance shift back in the saddle, and Ranger hopped off the moving platform. Not bad. She gave him a pat on the neck. Most of her own horses would have freaked when the bridge rolled underneath them.

"Try again," Billie said with a less enthused expression than Merissa guessed was on her own face. "Remember, he's a police horse and not a polo pony. He's supposed to think for himself." She hesitated for a second. "I can't explain the difference. I guess I mean that you shouldn't think of it as riding him over the bridge but more of going with him while he walks over it."

Billie was obviously floundering to describe what to her was a reflexive way to ride. Merissa sighed. She'd been riding since she was seven years old, starting with excellent teachers in France and continuing with the trainers her grandfather hired to instruct her. She just hadn't been expecting the jolt of the moving bridge.

She gave him a tap with her heels and walked toward the bridge with more impulsion, but she was getting tense and trying too hard. He balked and sidled around the bridge instead of walking over it. She gritted her teeth and turned him in a circle before trying again with more determination. Ranger walked over the bridge this time, but not even as smoothly as the first attempt. Merissa felt her short nails dig into her palms as she tightened her grip in frustration and she rotated her wrists to relax them. She was on a horse, the one place where everything usually made sense and felt right, but she couldn't find herself amidst the turmoil surrounding her.

"Why don't you let me show you once," Billie said. She slid off Juniper and reached for Ranger's reins.

"Because you're the perfect horse trainer?" Merissa asked. She was out of sorts and embarrassed. She had expected to feel comfortable with any riding she had to do, not to feel like a green beginner. Billie had yet again managed to make her feel weak. "Just like you're the perfect victim's advocate?"

"I'm nowhere near perfect, but I've been working with him for months now. I think I have a better feel for what he needs than you do. I just want to show you how he prefers to be ridden."

"Okay, Horse Whisperer. Wow me." Merissa climbed off Ranger and handed him to Billie. She stood with her arms crossed over her chest and Juniper's reins draped over her wrist while she watched Billie settle in the chestnut's saddle. Was she imagining it, or did Billie look less at ease than she had during the warm-up?

She wasn't imagining it. Billie's first walk over the bridge wasn't much different from Merissa's. Billie stopped for a moment and closed her eyes, apparently trying to pull herself together, but on the second try Ranger stopped and raised his head, refusing to go forward.

"What's up?" Cal asked in a deceptively casual voice. Merissa hadn't realized she had walked over on her large paint until the pair was looming over her.

"There's something wrong with Ranger," Billie said. "He doesn't seem to be feeling well."

Merissa fumed. "So if I can't get over the bridge right, it's my riding. But if you can't, the horse is sick?"

Before Billie could answer, Cal walked in between them. "Whatever is going on, get it fixed right now. We're here to train the horses, not snipe at each other."

Cal was scowling, but she glanced over at Rachel and gave her a quick wink. Merissa was certain Billie noticed it, too, because she rolled her eyes with an expression of annoyance.

"They seem to think there's something going on between us," Merissa said to Billie, her gesture including Cal and Rachel. "They don't realize I'm still tense after yesterday, and I know the day was a strain on you, too. I'm sorry I was snotty about my riding."

"I'm sorry, too," Billie said. She seemed uncomfortable with the entire unit staring at the pair of them. "You're an excellent rider. I didn't mean to imply otherwise."

"And you *are* more experienced with these sorts of obstacles. I should have listened better." She looked at Cal. "Satisfied?"

"Maybe," Cal said with a shrug, but she was grinning widely. "Let's see if either of you can manage to walk Ranger over the bridge before it gets dark outside."

Billie's face was a mask of tranquility again, and she took Ranger over the obstacle flawlessly. Merissa took notice of how she handled him, and when it was her turn again, she managed to imitate their performance. Once she let go of her frustration with Billie and turned it on Cal instead, she enjoyed the new experience.

"Abby talked to me about boarding the horses for the next couple months," she said as they walked to the next obstacle. "I'd be happy to have you use my place for their vacation and training. And if you ever need to stay the night and ride early, there's an apartment over the barn." She saw Billie's expression shift, but she couldn't read her at all. She'd been prepared to say no to Abby— she didn't need the caretaker they were obviously trying to supply in the form of Billie—but she wanted to prove to Cal that Billie's presence meant nothing to her. And hopefully prove it to herself in the process. What was wrong with her? Were her swings really a result of stress from watching Dennis die? She heard the nearly indiscernible tremor when she spoke again.

"Not that I'd be keeping you in the barn like a groom. It's a nice apartment, but I'm sure nothing like your own home. You could stay in the house if you'd rather, since there's plenty of room. Or just commute. Whatever."

Her last word, meant to convey a casual air, was squeakier than she'd have liked. Billie was still watching her without any readable emotions on her face, but Merissa was certain she'd felt a wall go up when she'd talked about the apartment.

"I'm sure the horses will love staying at your farm." Billie didn't mention herself, and Merissa sensed that Billie didn't believe she'd enjoy the months as much as the animals would. Would she enjoy having Billie there? She wasn't sure, and she fought to take her mind off the question and focus it instead on walking Ranger across a crinkling sheet of plastic.

CHAPTER NINE

Billie pulled the clip out of her hair and let the short waves cover the sides of her face. She wore a tight black sweater and jeans that were faded and worn from hours rubbing against a saddle. She studied herself in the mirror, rounding her upper back and slumping her shoulders as she tried to look less like a cop and more like someone who belonged on the dark street at night. She used to be able to blend more easily, fitting in by silhouette alone while on a mission, but she'd gotten out of practice. Even her poor posture looked stiff and rehearsed. She sighed and stood straight again. She'd always thought of herself as a chameleon. When had she gotten complacent and rigid? She wiggled her shoulders and tried once more, this time better approximating the shape of an urchin who didn't have Cal hounding her about a tall riding position or Lieutenant Hargrove calling her to attention whenever she was angry.

She turned away from the mirror and sat at the kitchen counter while she waited for Don to arrive. She tapped her fingers on the faux granite laminate and thought about the day's riding lesson. Merissa's effect on her was confusing. She was such an open book, probably because her defenses were still weakened by the murder. Somehow, she'd managed to transmit her turmoil to Billie, who had gone on to make a fool of herself at the training session. They had finally begun to work as a team and help the younger mare through some tough obstacles, but not before they'd caught the attention of the entire team. And now—because of Merissa, again—Billie was about to do something crazy and go against department policies. She usually followed rules and kept to herself, not wanting the negative attention of standing out. Something about Merissa brought out Billie's extremes, both high and low, that she rarely showed. Merissa was anything but average, and Billie couldn't be, either, when they were around each other.

She frowned and clicked her short nails in a repetitive rhythm on the counter. She didn't even know what had made her mad when Merissa offered the apartment over the barn. Far from thinking she was being offered servant's quarters, Billie had been quite sure the apartment would be better appointed and nicer than her own. She would ignore the hastily added offer to stay in the cold mansion. She needed more distance from Merissa than one house, no matter how large, would provide, and the atmosphere inside the marble living room was more mausoleum than home.

Still, Billie had been tempted to accept for a brief moment. Given the way Merissa had been nervously rambling, she might have offered a place in her own bed if Billie hadn't spoken up and declined. She would take the safe option and commute back and forth, sleeping in her own place and working the horses at Merissa's.

So why had she been rubbed the wrong way? Merissa had her inherited money, but she seemed to treat it as a fact of life and not a status symbol. She dressed nicely—looking freaking gorgeous in the skintight tan riding pants she'd worn today—but not ostentatiously. Billie really didn't see the same chasm between haves and have-nots that other people believed was there. She'd grown up with a father who left her and her sisters behind to fish the rough seas off the Alaskan coast. Yes, he'd made a lot more than he would have elsewhere, but the sacrifice, in her opinion, had been high. She wasn't naive enough to believe that having buckets of money necessarily made a person happier than others. On the contrary, she figured the more money one made, the greater the sacrifices as well. She wasn't going to be anyone's sacrifice ever again.

Billie sighed. She heard Don's footsteps approaching through the thin walls of her shoddy apartment and she got to her feet.

Merissa just made her feel too much. She was used to keeping most of her emotions under wraps, but Merissa wore hers in plain sight. She was innocent and worldly at the same time. She seemed to desire community and neighborhoods, but she was willing to tear down existing areas with those qualities just to build her personal vision on the rubble of broken homes and evicted tenants. The conflicts she raised were too much for Billie, who had wanted nothing more than a steady and predictable life when she was a child. She'd grown up with conflicting messages—I love you, but I have to leave you—and she'd had enough of them for a lifetime. She had become a nomad like her father, but she still appreciated what home meant to other people. Not everyone in this building had the option to move on or find a new place like she would if evicted.

She opened the door just as Don was about to knock. "Ready?" he asked.

She patted her lower back, where her gun was tucked out of sight. "Yep. Let's do this."

She locked her apartment, although a determined poodle could break down her door if she had doggy treats on the other side, and followed Don down the narrow hallway. "We're just asking some questions," she reminded him.

He looked over his shoulder at her and laughed. "What do you think I'm going to do? Water board the guy?"

"I'm just saying, all I want to do is corroborate Carlyle's story. Get Percy to make a statement if we can. If he really did borrow the car for someone else, he'll have nothing to lose by telling the truth."

Don slowed before going down the wider staircase and they walked side by side. "It must be nice living in the rose-colored world in your head. I wish I could visit sometime."

"It's worth a shot," Billie said. She didn't believe she was the optimist he seemed to think she was, but even her years in the military and on the force hadn't been able to squash the persistent hope she felt at times like these. She'd believe Percy was at heart a good guy who wouldn't want Carlyle to suffer for someone else's mistake. If he proved her wrong? Then she'd still be likely to get what she wanted. She'd had confrontations like this a million times, and the routine was always the same. He would deny everything, and then rat out someone else to take the fall. He'd protect himself, and she would get the information she needed to protect her friend. Whatever his motives, he'd talk.

"I owe it to Carlyle to try."

"Yeah, Carlyle," Don said with a snort as he got in his car.

Billie slid in beside him. "What's that supposed to mean?"

Don pulled away from the curb and cut across town toward Commencement Bay. "It means you're really doing this for the long-legged blonde you were staring at all afternoon."

"I was not staring at Cal," Billie said, pretending to misunderstand him and making an attempt at humor. "Don't you dare insinuate I was to Rachel. She'd kill me and drop me in the Sound wearing cement-filled riding boots."

Don laughed. "Yes, she would. And good job deflecting by the way. Your joke completely threw me off the fact that you're really doing this tonight because you want to make sure Merissa is safe."

Billie rolled her eyes. "I'm sure she's sleeping safe and sound in her grand mansion. She doesn't need me for anything." Merissa might have needs—someone to keep her warm in that cold house, and someone to help her understand Dennis's death—but Billie wasn't the one to supply either one. If her investigation proved Carlyle innocent and also gave Merissa a sense of peace, then she would be happy, but she was doing this for her friend Carlyle first, because Merissa had the power to destroy him. Or did he want to destroy Merissa? Billie wouldn't be able to relax until she knew for sure.

She kept quiet while they slowly drove up Ruston Way. The road wound along the waterfront, and the seafood restaurants and bars alongside had drawn crowds of people to the area. Once they moved beyond the bright lights and muffled music, they saw fewer people on the sidewalks and piers. During the day, especially in the warmer months, the paved path would be full of joggers, strollers, and families. The mounted unit had made their debut ride with Rachel as their leader down here, weaving among the people and pets while fireworks exploded over the bay on the Fourth of July. It had been one of the most exhilarating nights of Billie's life, and she'd been proud of both herself and Ranger as they had overcome the internal demand—innate for the horse and learned for her—to flee from the booming rockets and had instead calmly and coolly patrolled the citywide party.

Billie watched the shadows, noticing the people lurking among them and deciphering their actions based on the few clues she could see. A hooker over there, leaning against a tree trunk as she watched cars go by. A couple sneaking out to a rundown wooden dock, its pylons rising in dark relief against the moonlit and city lit sky. A drug deal—but not their target dealer—going down in what was supposed to be a closed construction site, where fancy new condos would soon be built. The darker side of Tacoma had emerged. Two nights ago, Merissa had been caught in the midst of this world that was so unfamiliar to her. Billie fought down a wave of nausea at the thought.

When she spoke, she continued her train of thought. "Merissa and Dennis didn't belong in that part of the city, so they weren't the targets. They were bystanders who got in the way of a drug deal or gang fight. I don't need to talk to Percy to know Merissa is safe from whoever shot Dennis. I'm doing this to help out a neighbor. I don't even like her all that much."

Don laughed, and Billie couldn't blame him this time. She'd sounded almost petulant, as if she'd been caught with Merissa's pigtail in one hand and an inkwell in the other. She changed tactics.

"Did you know that she and her boss were planning to demolish my apartment building? Build some sort of community square, with shops and cafés and a little park. In the middle of the Hilltop."

"Oh, no," Don exclaimed, clutching at his chest with his left hand. "I'm getting choked up thinking about all those homeless cockroaches and rats! Wherever will they go?"

Billie punched him in the arm. "There'll be homeless people, too. Including yours truly."

"I've been trying to get you to move for a year now," Don said. "I've worked in the bowels of this city long enough to be thrilled when I see any sign of improvement that benefits the taxpaying, law-abiding citizens. Like the Sixth Avenue and Stadium districts."

Billie frowned as Don drove around a traffic circle and back the way they'd come. "I want to see the city grow and become a safer place, but Merissa needs to care about the people she'd be displacing. They matter, too. She needs to see past the appearance of these buildings to the heart inside."

"Please. You care just as much about appearances. The only reason you stay in that fleabag apartment of yours is because you like the impression it gives."

Billie stared at him in disbelief. Did he know her so little, after all the time they'd spent together? "What impression? That I'm poor and possibly covered with bedbug bites? You really think I want people to see me that way?"

"No. You want them to see you as someone compassionate and connected to the community you serve. You're making as much of a statement by choosing to live in squalor as someone who wears designer jeans and polo shirts with fancy logos. Hey. Over there."

Billie had been looking out the window blankly, struggling to decide if there was any truth to Don's statement, and she'd almost missed their quarry.

"Go to the next street and park up the hill," she said. "We don't want to spook him."

Don did as she said, and they quickly moved along the sidewalk, staying in the cover of some tall shrubs. They stopped and looked across the street, toward the bay, where Don had spotted Percy in a small green space next to a kiosk that sold ice cream bars and soda during the summer months. They'd have to cross the open road to get to him.

"I'll go," Billie and Don said at the same time. Billie shook her head and dropped into her druggie posture. "Me first. I'll distract him, and you come up from behind." She pointed to an information board with a map of the city and a ship's wheel on it. "We can take him back there and talk, so we won't be disturbed."

Don nodded and she noticed his gun was in his hand. She left hers tucked in her jeans—Percy would understandably bolt if she ran toward him with a drawn weapon—and jaywalked across the street. She made no attempt to move furtively and stayed within

Percy's line of sight, wanting to seem like a customer hoping to score.

"Hey," she called softly as soon as she was nearing the other side of the road. "You selling?"

"Do I know you?" Percy asked. He stood his ground as she got closer, and she angled her approach to make it seem like she was aiming for the glowing circle under a weak streetlight. In reality, she wanted to buy Don some time and get Percy's attention off the road, but she couldn't see Don anywhere.

"Whoa," Percy said putting his hands up as soon as her face was lit enough for him to see her. He either recognized her from some past dealing or her movement and bearing had given her away. "Ain't no law against walking in the park."

Billie was about to answer, but suddenly Don was behind Percy. For an old, overweight guy, he moved like a cat. Percy's hands stretched higher and his expression shifted from belligerence to fear. Billie assumed the barrel of Don's gun was pressing into his back.

"Over here," she said, nodding toward the sign. She drew her own pistol and her eyes scanned the area for any indication that they had unwanted company.

"I didn't do nothing," Percy said, as expected. Billie heard the same phrase every day she worked, even in response to a simple *excuse me*. It was most often uttered by someone who had actually just done something bad.

"We just want to ask you a few questions," Billie said. She looked around again, suddenly nervous. She wasn't the type of cop to go outside of department regulations this way, unless the fate of someone she cared about was on the line. She'd do the same for any one of her team members, and she was putting herself at risk now for Carlyle. An image of Merissa, her face moving from the happiness Billie had seen during today's training ride to terror as she stared at Dennis's unmoving form, flicked through Billie's mind. She pushed it away quickly. She needed to concentrate on what was happening right in front of her. In and out.

"Two nights ago you borrowed Carlyle's car," she started, but Percy interrupted her.

"No, I swear I—"

"That wasn't one of the questions," Billie said with a snarl in her voice. She stepped closer to him. He was taller than she was, but seemed intimidated and tried to back up. Don's gun held him in place.

"He said you needed it for a buddy. Just give me his name, and you can go."

Percy's face had a look of terror on it that Billie didn't understand. This was a game, and they all knew the rules. How many times had he ratted out other people to save his own skin? Dozens. Billie would bet money on it. Why would he hesitate to shift a murder investigation onto someone else?

"Give her the name," Don said, pushing from behind. His face had the same look of confusion Billie was sure was on her own.

"No. You can shoot me if you want. Take me to the station and book me. But I'm done talkin'."

Billie and Don exchanged a look, and he backed away. He came to her side with his gun still drawn.

"You'll want to change your mind," he said in a low voice. "Whoever you're so afraid of will find out we were here. Maybe he'll think you talked to us more than you should've. Give it some thought and make a smart decision for once. Come and turn yourself in, and we'll protect you. Come on," Don continued, pulling on Billie's sleeve. She backed around the sign, and then they turned and jogged toward the street.

"That was odd," Don said. He sounded as spooked as Billie felt. They'd both questioned suspects countless times, and Percy'd been on the other end of those questions often enough. There was a routine to the interrogations, a cat-and-mouse posturing. Percy was the kind of guy who scared most people he came into contact with. A long-time dealer who wouldn't be afraid of two cops asking a few questions. Who had terrified *him*?

They were halfway across the street when an unmuffled gunshot cracked the silence of the night. They ran back to the sign and saw Percy lying face down in a pool of blood. A .22 was several yards away, in plain sight. Don knelt by the still form and felt for a pulse. He tossed Billie the car keys. "He's dead. Get my phone and call for backup."

Billie nodded and ran as fast as she could. She wasn't worried about leaving Don alone because this had been a message. If someone just wanted Percy dead, they'd have shot him after Billie and Don were long gone. If they had wanted to kill either of them, they'd be in the middle of a gunfight right now. Billie felt her heart grow cold, and the ice spread to her fingertips, making it hard for her to use the phone. Someone wanted to keep Percy from talking permanently, and specifically to her. This was a message, clear as could be. She couldn't hide from the final assumptions along this trail of clues. Dennis's death hadn't been an accident. Whoever had him shot was covering tracks and blocking even her off-the-record investigation. Merissa—who had recognized the car and witnessed the murder—wasn't as safe as Billie had originally thought.

Chapter Ten

One day—and three very long sessions with the detectives on the Morgan case—later, Billie stood in the apartment over Merissa's barn and dropped her suitcase next to the couch. The furniture was upholstered in a heavy brocade embroidered with scarlet-coated riders and hound dogs giving chase to wily foxes. The coffee table and end tables were carved out of gleaming mahogany, and the walls were painted a deep burgundy. The room opened into the small kitchen with its matching cabinets and green-tinged quartz countertop. Bookshelves filled with paperbacks and horse books lined one wall, and a window curtained in heavy tan fabric had a view of a huge horse pasture and a pond. Damn. Billie hadn't been wrong when she'd guessed that this apartment would be better than hers.

Although, to be honest, the stalls in the barn below her would be an improvement over her home. She loved her little space, with its photographs and Impressionist prints on the walls and her police manuals and mystery novels stacked by her bed, but this room would be a pleasant interlude while she was here. Even with a stable full of horses underneath, the room smelled fresh and piney. Don said her place smelled like a dead moose had been smoking cigarettes under the stairs. A slight exaggeration, of course.

"The bedroom is through that door, and the bathroom is here on the left," Merissa said. She stood next to Billie, and her subtle scent of almonds drifted below the overt and artificial lemon and pine cleaning products. "There's a washer and dryer in the tack room, but we use it for horse blankets and saddle pads, so you probably won't want your clothes in there." Merissa fumbled in her pocket. "I put a key to the main house on the ring with the one to the apartment. If you go through the side entrance, the laundry room is the first one you come to. You can use it anytime you'd like. I didn't expect you so soon, and I haven't had a chance to stock the fridge with food."

Billie held up her hands to stop Merissa's speedily delivered words. She sounded nervous, and with good reason. She'd originally been told the horses would arrive in two weeks and that Billie would come by a few times a week to ride and groom them. Suddenly, Billie was moving in and Cal would deliver the horses tomorrow morning. Billie had gone from being someone who would be around if Merissa needed to talk, to a guard posted outside her house. They had barely reached a truce at their last meeting, during the training session, and Merissa was probably as thrilled to have her here as Billie was.

"This is beautiful, Merissa," Billie said. "I stopped by the grocery store on my way here, so I have all I need for now. I'll try not to be an intrusion while I'm here."

Merissa sank down on the couch. She was wearing jeans and a pink sweatshirt, with her hair tied back. She looked young and worried. "You won't be. I meant it when I offered to let you stay, and I'm looking forward to having some new horses and training methods around here. But something changed. I could hear it in Abby's voice when she called, and Cal's when she called immediately after. Why won't anyone tell me what's going on?"

Billie sat next to her and almost groaned as the soft cushions enveloped her. Definitely an improvement over her hard, green seventies-style sofa. She didn't want to frighten Merissa, especially when they still had no idea who had killed Dennis and if it really had been premeditated—even though Billie didn't have a doubt in her mind after seeing the fear on Percy's face and finding out how warranted it was. But even worse in her mind than scaring Merissa for no reason was not giving her the information she needed to keep safe and protect herself.

"The car you recognized when we drove around the city together belonged to my neighbor," she said.

"Your neighbor? You live on the Hilltop?" Merissa asked the first questions with a casual curiosity, but then she seemed to put several pieces in place at once. "Near the block we were planning to develop?"

Billie raised her eyebrows and didn't answer.

"Oh. On the block we were planning to develop?"

"The very same."

"So…" Merissa drew out the word for several seconds. "When I called it a—"

"Disgusting eyesore, I think is the phrase you used," Billie supplied the words for her with an exaggerated look of despair. "I won't lie. It hurt. You were right, but still. Ouch."

Merissa winced, but she was holding back a smile. "I'm sorry. Very tactless of me."

"I agree. You really should see the inside of the place before you pass judgment on it." She poked Merissa's upper arm with her index finger. "You'll need a round of shots first, of course, but then you should be safe to visit."

Merissa laughed and pushed playfully at Billie's hand, but her smile was fleeting. "Now back to your story. Was your neighbor involved in the shooting somehow?"

Billie wanted to say no, but she shrugged instead. She gave Merissa an abbreviated version of the events following the sighting of the car—Carlyle's arrest and Percy's shooting—downplaying her more behind-the-scenes activities.

"You think someone was trying to kill Dennis?" Merissa's eyes widened as she came to the same conclusion Billie had. "Or me? I was planning to drive us to Seattle. If someone was hired to shoot the driver of the car, maybe Dennis was a mistake and the bullet was meant for me."

"Don't go there," Billie warned, although the same worry had flooded her nightmares the few hours she had managed to sleep the night before. "We still don't know if it was intentional or who the target really was. I'm here just in case, but you should take some precautions as well."

Merissa nodded, her face resolute. Maybe she would completely break down when she was alone, but in front of Billie she seemed to be holding together well. Billie was relieved. She'd gone through hell after she called in Percy's shooting. Abby had yelled at her in the middle of the station for thirty-seven minutes—Don timed the tirade—even though she didn't have any right to berate Billie for the same actions she had been committing for years. It still wasn't widely known on the force, but every member of the mounted team knew about Hargrove's illicit investigations into her family's misdeeds in the department. She had even sought to rectify a lot of them on her own, finally calling on her team members for help when Kira's life was at stake. Billie wasn't trying to save the love of her life like Abby had been doing. She'd just wanted to absolve her neighbor and ensure Merissa's safety, although until now she had never fully understood the gut-clenching need to protect that Abby must have felt when Kira was in danger.

After all the screaming, Abby had fought like a fiend to keep Billie from getting into serious trouble, resulting in Billie's forced vacation at the Casa Merissa. She rarely used leave and had enough stored up for the next two months. She just had to stay here and keep both her nose clean and an eye on Merissa. She could do it, no problem. The pain of not doing her part as a cop was tempered by the idea of having weeks to ride and play with all six horses. She'd never had such luxury. As long as no one shot at them and she and Merissa stayed away from any controversial urban renewal topics, of course.

"What should I do?" Merissa asked. Her hands were clenched between her knees and she wore a worried frown. Billie stood up and held out her hand.

"Can you give me a tour of the barn while we talk?" she asked. Merissa took her hand and let Billie pull her to her feet. Billie had made the suggestion because she thought Merissa might be more at ease if they interjected horse talk in between Billie's suggestions, but one touch of Merissa's hand and she decided it had been a good idea to get off the comfy sofa where they had sat so close to each other. Another concerned expression on Merissa's face, and Billie might have been tempted to reach over and cup her cheek. Slide her hand along Merissa's jaw and let her fingertips graze those pink, luscious lips.

Billie dropped Merissa's hand and they each took a step back at the same time. Merissa cleared her throat and gestured toward the stairs. "After you," she said.

Billie led the way to the barn aisle. To her right and left, large box stalls lined the aisle. A feed room and tack room were directly opposite her staircase, and the causeway leading to the second row of stalls was a few feet up the aisle and to her left. The barn was a huge H, and the short but wide causeway was lined with grooming stalls and a wash rack.

"Your horses will be in these stalls," Merissa said. The six stalls were airy and bright, with Dutch doors in the back of each one, leading into a private paddock. Merissa had put them in prime spots, close to the causeway and everything Billie would need to groom and care for them. She figured these stalls were usually full, and the normal occupants had been moved to give her and her horses the most convenient spots.

"Your turn," Merissa said. Apparently the tour and Billie's safety lecture were going to alternate.

"Don't go anywhere alone if you can help it. Take me with you, or ask a friend. At the very least, let me or someone else know where you'll be."

Merissa gave the suggestion some thought. Billie understood her hesitation because she liked her own independence and would chafe under the restriction of checking in with someone or having a chaperone at all times, but she was beginning to realize how difficult it would be to guard Merissa. Just one suggestion from Billie, and Merissa already looked ready to stage a formal protest.

"I can do that for a short time, I guess, but I don't like it," Merissa said. She walked down the aisle, introducing Billie to the few horses that were inside. The day was brisk, but partly sunny, and most of the animals were in the pastures. Merissa walked across a loop of the same gravel drive that wound around the property and pulled open a large sliding door. Billie gasped at the size of the indoor arena. She'd ridden at the fairgrounds, in the metal and cement lined Paulhamus Arena, but Merissa's had it beat both in size and atmosphere. Arching wooden beams crisscrossed the ceiling, and a low tongue-and-groove cedar fence separated the riding area from a series of bleachers. On the far side was a space for storage, and Merissa opened the locker doors to show her where the polo mallets and balls were kept. There were also piles of brightly colored poles and standards for building jumps, a few stacks of cones, and some plastic barrels.

"You can use whatever you need for training your horses. There are more jumps in the outdoor arenas, and you saw the cross-country course when you drove in."

Billie looked over the equipment, mentally designing obstacle courses for her rookie horses, but Merissa was watching her expectantly so she continued with her mini-lecture.

"I always should know where you are, but don't let anyone else anticipate your movements. Don't travel the same route twice in a row, don't ride the same trail every afternoon, and don't leave the house or office at predictable times."

Merissa sighed. "I'm not accustomed to having so many rules," she said.

Billie gave a snort of laughter. She was right—Merissa wasn't going to be compliant at all. "So many rules?" she repeated. "I've only given you two so far."

"*So far?*" Merissa imitated Billie's bemused tone. "You mean there are more?"

Merissa changed the subject again, apparently not ready to hear more of Billie's demands on her privacy and autonomy. She pointed at a small cottage situated between the arena and the smaller barns on the hillside. "Jean-Yves Lucier lives there. I met him at a horse show when I was at university in Montreal. When I came back here, I asked him to come with me and take over as manager and head groom. He takes care of the upper barns, and there are three others who help him in the main one. You'll meet all of them in the next day or two, I'm sure."

They went around the far side of the arena. "We have trails cleared on the wooded section of the farm. You can access them through that gate and up the hill. Do you see the big tree stump? It's at the entrance to the trail system. There are different forks along the way, but they all loop back to the same place, so you can't get lost on them."

"How long have you been riding?" Merissa asked as they walked to one of the big, grassy paddocks. She stopped and leaned her forearms on the top rail of the fence. A coal-black mare was grazing along in the far corner, and what little sun there was made her coat glow like polished onyx.

"About three years," Billie said. She didn't want to elaborate. She'd started riding at a therapeutic center when she could no longer handle her PTSD on her own. She had dropped out of life, barely getting to work on time, barely making it through the day. She'd never been much of a drinker, but the temptation to lose herself in a bottle was overwhelming. At first, she'd simply sat on top of the horse while volunteers led her around and around the ring. Eventually, she'd started noticing the animal moving underneath her, and one day she picked up the loose reins and started to take control again. The healing was slow and ongoing. The difference between her riding experiences and Merissa's—with her fancy barn and French Canadian stable manager—was almost laughable. But when she watched Merissa's expression soften while she looked at the black beauty in front of them, she wondered if they weren't more similar than she thought.

"I'd have guessed a lot longer after watching you ride," Merissa said. "You must have had good teachers."

Billie felt her face heat at the compliment. "I did. Cal's taught me about classical equitation and being a balanced rider. And Rachel has more of a natural horsemanship approach, and I've learned a lot about horse psychology from her." Billie didn't mention the instructors at the therapy program, although she sent them a silent and heartfelt thank you in her mind. She had learned the basics from them—not just in riding, but in living through pain.

Merissa looked at her for a moment, as if about to ask more questions, but Billie's face must have said the topic was closed. Merissa turned and gave a piercing whistle instead.

"Wow," Billie said as the mare floated over to them in a breathtaking trot. She seemed barely to skim the surface of the grass as she moved. Billie tried to come up with a more intelligent observation about the horse's movement or conformation, but she couldn't come up with a thing. "Wow," she repeated.

"I know," Merissa said as she stroked the horse's neck. "Billie, I'd like you to meet Mariposa. I imported her from Argentina. And if Cal asks about her, she has a swayback and only three legs."

"I take it she's going to be your secret weapon on the polo field next season." Billie rubbed the mare's forehead, and she lowered her head over the fence and pressed it against Billie's chest.

Merissa watched them in silence for a moment. "Any more advice?" she asked.

Billie twisted the mare's forelock around her fingers. "Listen to your intuition. If you feel uncomfortable with a situation or person, don't second-guess yourself. Trust yourself and no one else."

"Not even you?"

Billie thought about that. Had she made the right choices for Merissa so far? "No," she said. "Not even me."

Chapter Eleven

Merissa was cleaning a stall the next morning when her phone vibrated in the pocket of her jeans. She propped the manure fork against the wall and read the name on the display. Karen. Merissa had only spoken to her twice since the shooting, and each time Karen had been too distraught to talk long. She and Dennis had been married for over forty years. Merissa knew they'd had trouble on and off in their marriage, but Dennis had said they were growing closer over the past few years. His last words were meant for her, and when Merissa told Karen about them, she had filled in the blank and told her Dennis said, *Tell Karen I love her.* Even if that wasn't what he'd really meant to say, Merissa had no qualms about her little tiny lie.

"Hi, Karen," she said when she answered the call. "How are you?"

She automatically adopted the same annoying tone most people took with her these days, as if she were a child who needed a pat on the head. *How are you holding up, Merissa, dear?* Merissa usually wanted to smack them, but here she was using the exact same baby-talk voice with Karen.

"Not well. Not well at all. Oh, Merissa, I miss him so much." Karen sobbed on the other end of the line, and Merissa stood there, unsure what to say beyond some soothing words and sounds. She waited patiently until Karen was in control again.

"My lawyers are going to the office today," she said with a sniff. "They'll go over the books and Dennis's files to find out if we need to pay any bills or collect money. I was hoping you could be there to make sure they have what they need. You know I'm not good at that sort of thing."

Merissa frowned. Karen did just fine with the financial side of the business, always showing up when a client's account was in arrears, but she liked to play the helpless game sometimes. Dennis had loved it, and always rushed to her aid. Merissa wasn't as fond of the act, but if lawyers were rifling through files at the office, she wanted to be involved.

"Are you planning to sell the business, or keep running it?" Merissa asked. Karen seemed to recover once she was talking about money, and Merissa decided to ask the question she had been dwelling on for a while now.

"Oh, dear, I couldn't possibly keep it going as well as Dennis did. I'll have to sell. You were his favorite employee, and I'm sure he'd want you to have the first option to buy. Once my lawyers have gone through the accounts, we'll decide on a fair price and let you decide."

Merissa believed Dennis had been closer to her personally than to any of his other employees, but she also knew she was the only one who could possibly afford to buy the firm. Of course Karen would come to her first. Merissa had been hoping decisions about the fate of the Morgan Group would be tabled for a few months, until she could make her own decision about her future and not be forced to follow the path everyone seemed to assume Dennis had had in mind for her. Besides, her grandfather would return and haunt her if she didn't make sure the business's affairs were in order before she made the choice whether or not to take over.

Dennis had kept sole control over the financial side of his firm, and Merissa wanted a chance to examine everything before she made an offer. *If* she made an offer. The extra time would have given her a chance to decide what she really wanted to do, but Karen was pushing too fast. Merissa had loved working for Dennis, and the work was satisfying and thrilling, but a big part of her joy was tied up in her friendship with Dennis and his role as her mentor. There was a big difference between working for someone she respected and who taught her so much, and making a long-term commitment to buy the company.

She had too much going on in her head to make such a huge and life-altering decision right now. She had hoped for more time. Time to grieve, to think, to plot a new course for her future. Everything was happening too fast.

"I appreciate having the option," she said. "But we don't have to rush. I can run the business for a while, until everything is settled and we're ready to make more rational and less emotional choices."

"Oh no, dear. I couldn't possibly drag this on any longer than necessary," Karen said, the weepy note creeping back into her voice. "Dennis would have wanted me to move on and you to take the reins of the company. I'm sure of it. On the subject, I know you needed to take some time off before coming back to work, but is there any chance you can be at the office to help them find the files and ledgers they need?"

"Yes," Merissa said without hesitation. She wanted to see what they took. This would give her a chance to look through Dennis's files and learn more about the stability and solvency of the firm. Would Billie want her to go? Probably not. Good thing she was at the feed store. "What time?"

"Two o'clock. And the lawyers will expect you and the others to turn in your files for the time being. Protocol, you know, until we make a decision about the future of the firm. Anything deemed unrelated to the business will be returned promptly, of course."

Promptly. Right. "I'll be there," Merissa said. She'd be early.

When she ended the call, she rested her palm against the wall and replayed the conversation in her mind. She was about to lose all her contacts, all the sketches and designs she'd created while working with Dennis and during graduate school as well. If she bought the firm, the lawyers would return her files. But what if she didn't and they didn't know how to determine which designs were her own? She had too much to lose and if she got to the office before two, she could clear out everything that wasn't directly related to one of Dennis's projects. Those personal visions should be hers to keep.

She checked her watch—five after one—and pulled the wheelbarrow full of used shavings out of the stall, leaving it in one of the grooming areas. She'd finish the work as soon as she got home, hopefully before Billie arrived and found her missing. To ease her guilt, she left a note telling where she was going tucked under the brow band of Ranger's bridle in the tack room. It wasn't hidden, and it was in a place where Billie would see it. Eventually. Like, tomorrow. Merissa would have to pretend she hadn't already seen Billie riding the chestnut toward the trails this morning.

Merissa rushed through her shower and threw on a pair of khakis and a blue shirt. She felt uncomfortable deceiving Billie, even though she was probably perfectly safe going to the office when a posse of lawyers was scheduled to be there, too. Besides, it had been a few days since Dennis was killed, and no one had shown even the slightest interest in harming her. Her brilliant move as a witness—saying she might have seen a car that looked similar to the one Billie's neighbor drove—had literally hit a dead end. Maybe the first reason the detectives had told her had been the real one. She and Dennis had unknowingly driven into the line of fire, and the bullet hadn't been meant for either one of them.

She got in her car and sped along the gravel road, wanting to be on her way before Billie rounded a turn and they came face to face. Then again, maybe Billie wouldn't be angry at all. She'd probably understand Merissa's need to collect her personal belongings before they were confiscated. She seemed very protective of her own privacy and obviously wouldn't want someone pawing through her belongings.

Merissa gripped the steering wheel as she took a corner too quickly. She didn't know Billie well at all yet, even though she had been living at the farm, and they exchanged small talk several times a day when they passed in the barn. Billie was friendly with all the grooms, present in the barn but not obtrusive in Merissa's life, and she always seemed to intuit what other people needed. But she had a wall built around herself, behind a warm, seemingly open exterior. Merissa wanted to call it an illusion of friendliness, but she honestly believed that Billie was the genuinely kind persona she showed everyone she met. That was the reason she was so good at helping people through traumas and tough times. She was like a still pond, reflecting others' emotions back to them with empathy, and never revealing her own depth.

She was driving Merissa crazy.

She had only been on the farm for two days, and already Merissa felt like she'd become a fixture of the place. Merissa could smell a hint of sandalwood soap whenever she entered a room or section of the barn where Billie had recently been. Almost every time she looked out a window in the house, she saw Billie in one of her fitted long-sleeved T-shirts, hand grazing a horse or riding one around the polo field. Her section of the barn had become police central, with matching halters, blankets, and nameplates hanging tidily next to her six stalls. She seemed as unconcerned by her close proximity to the bed where Merissa slept as Merissa was hyperaware of it. Merissa wanted to connect to Billie somehow, reach past her barriers and discover who she was, but Billie had defenses calmly and solidly in place.

Merissa frowned as she wove through the traffic heading off the bridge. Was she purposefully trying to get a rise out of Billie by ignoring her suggestion and going off alone? No. Instead, she was following Billie's final instruction, to listen to her own intuition. She didn't have a bad feeling about this short trip. On the contrary, she was anxious to get there before anyone else.

Merissa took an exit leading to the Old Town of Tacoma and she drove a couple blocks before turning up a side street. She parked in a residential neighborhood where she was less than a quarter of a mile from the firm's office, but still out of sight of anyone approaching from a more conventional route. She hurried along the sidewalk and down a back alley before letting herself in the back door with her key. The offices were in an old brick building settled on the slope leading down to Commencement Bay, which also housed a tearoom, a photography studio, and an antique book and map store on the ground floor. The outside was worn and surrounded by rosebushes and rhododendrons, but Dennis had decorated the inside with a modern flair. Clean lines, neutrals and gleaming metals, and an open-concept main room with desks and groupings of white sofas scattered throughout. Large windows looked out over Commencement Bay, the Tideflats, and Mount Rainier.

Merissa gently shut the door and cringed when it made a loud clicking sound. She'd been so convinced she was doing the right thing while in the car, but here in the office, all alone, she started to second-guess herself. Should she have come here on her own? No one knew she was coming today except for Karen, and she could certainly trust Dennis's widow. Couldn't she?

Merissa stayed close to the wall and skirted the large open area on her way to her own enclosed office. She thought back to Karen's phone call. She'd done her grieving wife crying bit, although Merissa now thought it might have sounded forced. Then she'd completely changed her tone when she started talking about selling the business and collecting all the files. Had she made up the story about lawyers just to lure Merissa here?

She opened her office door and went inside, closing and locking it behind her. She was overreacting to being near downtown again, and to being in the empty offices where everything was silent except for Billie's warnings echoing through her mind. She leaned against the door and surveyed her file cabinets and messy desk. She had only a little time to make decisions and grab what was hers. She'd leave everything connected to Dennis's projects behind.

She hadn't thought to bring boxes, of course, so she dumped a case of paper reams onto the floor and started to fill the box with her drawings. She skimmed through the file cabinets and pulled anything personal. Some books on architecture, her address book, and piles of newspaper clippings. She left photographs and the few knickknacks she had on her desk behind—if she took them it would be obvious she'd been in here, and she assumed the lawyers wouldn't care about photos of her horses. She'd come get them later, when the rest of the employees were here to do the same.

Merissa was carrying the heavy box through the main room when she passed by Dennis's office. She set her things down and laid her hand against the door as if she could sense what was inside. Was there some clue in there? Something to tell her who had wanted him dead and why? Or was it empty of such evidence because there was none to be had and the murder was a random event?

She checked the time on her phone. She still had fifteen minutes. She fumbled on the key ring for the one belonging to Dennis's office, but her hands were shaking and she dropped them on the floor. When she bent to retrieve the keys, she flashed back to the car and the dropped index cards, the ping of the gunshot, the expression on Dennis's face as he pulled to the side of the road.

A loud click came from her right, and Merissa gasped and spun around. Her mind took a while to connect the sound with the heat pump kicking on. She frantically jammed the key in the lock, opened Dennis's door, and kicked her box into the office before following it inside. Her heart was beating so hard her ribs felt bruised. She had to try three times before she was able to slide the latch and lock the door. She wasn't cut out for a life of cat burglary. She laughed to herself, a little hysterically, imagining what damage she'd do if she were after a priceless work of art.

The laughter helped, insane as it sounded in the empty room. She walked to Dennis's desk and looked at the piles of papers. She didn't have time to sort through all of them, so she took what was on top of the stacks, hoping she was getting the most recent notes. She opened the desk drawers and pulled out two manila folders and a date book. Somehow, she felt as if he was with her, guiding her as she yanked open file cabinets and took folders out at random. She had to find out who had killed him. If there was evidence here, it would soon be swallowed by Karen's lawyers, and who knew when the truth would come to light.

Her phone chimed loudly and she had to smother her shriek of surprise. She answered without checking the ID.

"Where the hell are you?"

Billie. Apparently Merissa had been wrong to think she wouldn't be angry.

"I'm at my office picking up some files." Merissa spoke just above a whisper even though she was alone in the building.

"Yes, I know. I saw your note and came to find you, but I had to search for your car. Do you mind explaining why you parked on a deserted street instead of the more populated and safe parking lot right in front of your building?"

Merissa was about to explain herself when she heard a creak and the murmur of voices. She lowered hers even more, partly so no one would hear her and mostly because she suddenly couldn't get enough breath in her lungs to talk normally. "Where are you?"

"That was my question."

Merissa double-checked the door to make sure it was locked, and then she hurried across the plush carpet and looked out the window. Billie was just coming around the corner and heading downhill toward the front of the building. Even from a distance she looked furious. Merissa tugged open the window as quietly as she could and leaned out. "Look up," she whispered as Billie passed below her.

Billie looked up and saw her. With a shake of her head, she stopped and tucked her phone into her pocket.

"Shh," Merissa said before Billie could say anything loudly enough for whoever was in the building to hear. "Wait there."

Merissa grabbed the box she'd packed in her own office and crammed the papers she'd taken from Dennis's desk and cabinet in it as well. She lugged the heavy box to the window. "Catch," she said to Billie as she let it drop. Billie stood and watched it land in a rhododendron with a rush of cracking branches.

"What are you…Merissa, don't you dare jump."

Merissa straddled the windowsill and swung her other leg out until she had one foot precariously balanced on the wide ledge. She held on to the wooden frame, gripping it tightly even though the rough wood cut her hand. She used the other one to shut the window. She couldn't lock it again from the outside, but hopefully no one would notice.

Because of the slope of the ground, the drop would be less than a full two stories, but it still looked like a long way down. She closed her eyes and let go of the window frame, hoping the bushes below her would break her fall enough to keep any body parts from snapping in two. She felt a moment of nothingness as she fell, and then Billie's strong arms grabbed her and they both crashed to the ground in a heap.

Chapter Twelve

B illie got the first-aid kit from the tack room and stacked it on top of the box of files. She carried everything up the stairs to the apartment while Merissa called Karen and made up an excuse for not being at the office. She had wanted to go around to the front door and pretend she'd just arrived, but Billie had managed to talk her out of it. Merissa would have had a hard time explaining why she showed up at the office with a cut on her temple and a bleeding hand. Not to mention the leaves in her hair and the dirt stains smeared on the left leg of her khakis. If anyone noticed the destroyed shrubbery under the window, they'd have connected the dots pretty quickly.

Billie's most important reason for taking Merissa home instead of agreeing to have her meet the lawyers was one Billie wouldn't admit to her. When she had come back to the farm and found Merissa gone, Billie's stomach had clenched in a too familiar way. And when she couldn't find Merissa's car near the office? Billie's tension had turned to outright dread. She couldn't even justify the response to herself—it was as overpowering as the ones she'd experienced during the moments when she realized one of her teammates was missing during a mission or when her gut instincts had kicked in and warned her of danger before there were any real signs to be seen. Like in the brief seconds before Mike was killed.

An overreaction, nothing more. She was keyed up because of her responsibility to the horses and to Merissa. Otherwise, she wouldn't be having these reactions simply because her charge was out of her sight. Unreleased tension was giving her more flashbacks and nightmares than normal, and they—not Merissa herself—were the explanation behind the panic Billie had felt today.

She pushed open the door to the barn apartment and saw Merissa sitting on the couch. Her normally tidy hair was still a little leafy, and her pale skin was marked with bright red scratches and one deeper gash. She held her phone in one hand and cradled her cut left one in her lap. Billie sighed and leaned against the doorjamb.

Her reaction had *everything* to do with Merissa.

Billie set the box on the coffee table and sat next to Merissa on the couch. She inhaled and noticed an earthiness from Merissa's roll in the rhododendron garden layered over her usual scent. She smelled like a lavender field on a warm summer day, with rich soil and blossoming plants. Billie shook her head to dislodge the heady fragrance, and she distracted her wandering thoughts by listening to one half of a conversation about rescheduling a time to meet with the lawyers and about Dennis's funeral arrangements.

She put some antiseptic on a gauze pad and dabbed at Merissa's head wound. It was superficial but dirty. Billie cleaned it thoroughly, ignoring Merissa's wincing, and covered the cut with a Band-Aid. She took her time with the job, letting her fingers brush against Merissa's unblemished skin and removing leaves from her silky hair, feeling a sense of wonder at the way her own body responded to the gentle touches. She always cared about the wounded people she helped while on the job, whether their pain was emotional or physical. She had to let herself become them, in a way, and feel what they were going through from the inside out. Those experiences were never easy to dismiss, and they necessarily drew her closer than was comfortable to aching hearts and bodies. Even with the closeness, though, she always managed to keep a barrier deep inside, not letting anyone cross it. She'd learned the hard way, with her father and friends like Mike, what happened when someone broke past her defenses.

In a few short days, Merissa had managed to do just that. Billie had tried to think of her as just another victim to help, just another rich woman who wanted to clean up the city. But she'd seen more sides to her than those generalities. She'd watched her around the barn, joking with and working alongside her grooms, and she'd seen her riding and caring for her horses with a compassion and gentleness that she had been too tense to show at the police barn. Billie's initial attraction was developing into something stronger as she watched Merissa change from a static victim to a real person moving through life.

When she'd finished with Merissa's head, she held her wounded left hand in her own and wiped off the blood, probing for splinters. She rubbed her thumb across Merissa's palm, where her skin was soft and pliant, and over the ridge of calluses from long hours spent holding reins and pitchforks. The sensations flooded through her as each nuance of texture created an exponential response inside her. She finally realized Merissa had put her phone aside and was watching her in silence.

"Why did you stand under me when I jumped?"

"Why do you think? I was there to catch you." Billie eased her leg into a straight position and rubbed her knee. Tomorrow, she'd be bruised on one side from hitting the ground, and on the other from having Merissa land on top of her. "Okay, maybe I didn't exactly catch you. But I did break your fall."

Merissa smiled. "You were cushier than the ground. So thank you."

"You're welcome. And thank you for nearly knocking me out when you threw this box out the window and at my head."

"I thought you'd catch it."

Billie shook her head. As if she'd risk her life by jumping under the box, but just let Merissa tumble to the ground. What could possibly be so important? She didn't have an excuse to keep holding Merissa's hand, so she placed it back in Merissa's lap. "I don't want to know, but I have to ask. What's in it? And please, please don't say anything illegal."

"It's my work," Merissa said. "My personal drawings and plans. No one has any right to take them from me."

"Who was going to try?"

"Karen said the lawyers were going to confiscate all our files. They'd go through them and give us back anything that didn't belong to the firm." Merissa examined her hand without meeting Billie's eyes. "I was trying to be helpful and save them the trouble of sifting through all the paperwork."

"Very kind of you," Billie said. She didn't need years of police experience to tell her Merissa was holding something back. She leaned forward and poked through the contents of the box, as wary as if there might be a ticking bomb inside. "I understand why you might want to clear out some things from your office, especially if the office will be closed for the time being and if the lawyers might not be sure what items are yours and what rightfully belong to the firm. But..." She drew the word out for several moments. "If there's anything illegally obtained, whether you took it by accident or not, we need to return it right away. And I'm just adding the *by accident* phrase to protect you when you're inevitably sued for stealing documents from the company."

Merissa gave a derisive snort. "Stealing documents. Really. *Pfft.*" She made a beseeching gesture with her hands. "Although, I might have—by accident—gotten some of Dennis's files mixed in with mine when I passed through his office to exit out the window."

Billie covered her face with her hands while she tried to come up with some way to get Merissa out of this mess. Nothing came to mind. Hargrove was going to have her drawn and quartered for letting Merissa do this while she was supposed to be on guard duty.

She dropped her hands and sat straight again. "Be sure to use that wide-eyed innocent expression when you attempt to explain this to the jury. Even so, though, they might ask if the route through his office window was your usual one."

"It's a shortcut to the coffee shop," Merissa said, batting her eyelashes.

Billie fought for a moment, and then gave in to her laughter. "Okay, tell me the truth. Why did you steal his files?"

"I thought they might have some clue in them. Some way to tell if Dennis was in trouble, or why anyone would want to hurt him."

Billie's heart wrenched when she saw the dejected expression on Merissa's face. The eyelash batting had been an obvious joke, and just as clearly she was now being honest. She had lost someone very close to her and wanted to understand why. Billie could relate to the need for answers more than Merissa knew.

"Here's what's going to happen," she said after giving the problem some thought. She wanted to extricate Merissa from the trouble she'd be in while at the same time help her find some closure. What harm would it do to look at papers Dennis had in his office? "You're going to call Karen and tell her you went through some files you had at your house and you found some that belonged to Dennis. Maybe you had them here to review and forgot about them until now. And then you will return all of them."

Merissa opened her mouth, likely to protest, and Billie held up a hand to stop her. "Before you give them back, though, I think it would be wise to go over them quickly. To make sure none of your own papers are mixed in."

"I think that's a brilliant idea," Merissa said with a happier smile than Billie had seen yet. "Will you go through them with me? I might miss something a cop would notice."

"Yeah, you've seen where I live," Billie said with an answering grin. "I'm clearly an expert when it comes to urban renewal."

"You've got the before part down cold," Merissa said, fishing through the box and dumping a pile of folders on the table in front of Billie. "These sketches will show you the afters."

While Billie opened the first file, Merissa sorted the rest of the box's contents. Two manila folders, lots of files, and some scrap papers. Merissa pulled out a date book and set the box on the floor beside her. Apparently the rest was hers.

Dennis had been fairly organized, and Billie quickly figured out the files. He had sketches and preliminary plans, a list of notes from staff meetings, and the final plans and a contract from the builder, all carefully kept in order. Some projects never got out of the development phase, and others were in progress. A handwritten memo in black ink on the outside of each folder gave the dates for each meeting and draft deadline. She had a mishmash of dates in front of her. Some of the files Merissa had pulled during her foray into the world of crime were from three or more years ago, and others were more recent.

"I don't know for sure what I'm seeing here," Billie said. She handed Merissa one of the older files. "Walk me through this."

"I had just started at the firm when Dennis was negotiating this project," Merissa said, looking at the sketches and not the date. She set two drawings side by side. "This is what he proposed for the site, and this is what he drew up after getting input from the contractor and investors. You can see some of the design elements are the same, but the floor plan was changed to make larger office suites."

"Is this common?"

"Compromise?" Merissa asked. Billie nodded. "Yes. It's part of the process. Not my favorite part, but a necessary one if we want to get the financial backing we need."

"Okay, then look at this folder from two months ago. Here are some sketches from your meetings."

"Oh," Merissa said with a soft exhale. She picked up the piece of paper and ran her fingers softly over the lines of the drawing. "He put most of my ideas in here. The way the bungalows are grouped around a central courtyard and you can access any of them by these paths here and here. This site is near the hospital, and we wanted to create a complex for medical offices."

"It's beautiful," Billie said. "Very open and inviting."

"I guess I wanted to make it pretty and comforting," Merissa said, putting the paper aside. "I imagined nervous people going there, maybe getting bad news or going through scary tests. I wanted the setting to help them through the process, make them feel just a little calmer and more hopeful."

Billie was quiet, watching Merissa talk. She was passionate about her work and had the people who would be using the small parts of the world she created in the front of her mind. She just didn't always think about the people who were being ousted to make way for her visions.

"Do you know who used to live on this property before it was flattened?"

Merissa rubbed her hand over her face. "Don't tell me, let me guess. Your best friend and the hundred homeless cats she rescued?"

Billie laughed. "No. Actually this one was a vacant lot. But you should know what you're destroying every time you create something new."

Merissa rolled her eyes at the mini-lecture. "Did you have a point to showing me this project?"

"Yes," Billie said as she pulled another sketch out of the file and unfolded it. "This is what Dennis actually proposed at his meeting with this Edwin Lemaine guy."

Merissa took the paper from Billie. "He's the contractor Dennis uses most often, but he...Wait, this sketch is from a project he did several years ago, for some business offices. The scale of the rooms is changed a little, but it's basically the same plan. It must have been put in the wrong folder."

"Look at the date."

Merissa frowned and started pulling files from Billie's stack. "These are the same, as well. Everything from the past six months or so is just a recycled version of other projects. Our recommendations and ideas are in his original drawings, but only a few little elements are added to the final ones. I can see some of my touch in these"—Merissa put three sketches on the table and pointed to cornices and windows—"but otherwise, they're nothing like the vision we had as a group."

"Is that normal? Wouldn't you have noticed this before?"

"Dennis did all negotiations on his own. This current project was the first time he was going to let me take part. I knew when he signed contracts, but I never saw these final plans. I just assumed he'd gone with the proposal we'd come up with, except for the minor compromises he had to make."

"Wouldn't you notice when the buildings started going up?"

"Of course, but the lag time between concept and actual building is huge, so none of these have even broken ground yet."

Merissa silently shuffled through the sketches. Billie opened the manila folders to give Merissa time to process what she was seeing. She pulled out several blank legal forms and a few handwritten notes.

"He was slipping," Merissa said, barely loud enough to be heard. "For at least a year, maybe more. I can't tell without seeing more files, though. His designs are poor, and there are mistakes a contractor would need to fix. He's just copying old plans with minor changes for size and to add some of my ideas, but even those are just tacked on and not in a practical or visually effective way. It's like watching someone's mind go…"

Billie put her hand on Merissa's shoulder, hearing the anguish in her voice. "Had you noticed anything different in person? Did he seem more confused or tired lately?"

"No. Well, he took a few personal days scattered over the past few months. Nothing unusual for your average person, but before that I'd never seen him take a sick day. He claimed he was spending more time with Karen because they were working on their marriage, but maybe something else was going on."

Billie put the forms she had found on the table, covering the sketches. "He was planning to sell the firm, Merissa. He's got the paperwork here, but nothing is filled in."

"So we have no idea who was going to buy it?" Merissa picked up one of the documents with a shaking hand.

"No, but he has a list of clauses he wanted to add, and he uses *she* and *her* in them. If he was starting to involve you in the business more, he might have been preparing to hand over the company to you."

"Karen said it was what he wanted," Merissa murmured. "What were the clauses?"

Billie squinted at the paper in her hand. "I can't decipher his writing well, but something about monthly financial audits by an independent party and a requirement to use a minimum of three contractors every year. Do they sound like normal expectations?"

"I don't recall the firm ever having an audit. We had an accountant who would come during tax time and twice a month for payroll, but nothing more elaborate. And he usually used Lemaine, except for our current project."

"What was different about this one?"

"He said Jeff Kensington might be more suitable for my style of planning. And something about it being time to try someone new."

Billie looked through the pages again, trying to make sense of what they'd discovered. Was Dennis's decision to change contractors due to his decision to sell, or were all his choices related to the decline Merissa was noticing now, as she looked through his drawings?

"Was any of this worth killing for?" Merissa asked, saying aloud what Billie was wondering in her own mind.

"I don't know," she said. And until she knew for sure, she couldn't guarantee Merissa's safety. If someone would kill Dennis because of the changes he was going through, what would they do when they learned Merissa had seen the files? She put everything back in order and stacked the folders in a neat pile. "We need to get these back to Karen. The information in here isn't a secret since the contracts are signed and the plans are already on file with the city."

She took the forms and handwritten list of clauses out of Merissa's hand and shoved them back into the manila folders. The information on them, scant as it was, might be dangerous to Merissa because she had likely been part of Dennis's plan for the firm. But was he trying to protect her, somehow, with these clauses, or trying to protect a secret of his own? "These are blank forms and a few scrawled notes. Nothing to do with the business. For the time being, let's consider them missing."

She tucked the folders under the sofa's cushion. She wouldn't hide them forever, just long enough to figure out what exactly had been going on with the Morgan Group, and how it affected Merissa. She was taking yet one more step away from her old life by hiding this information. How far would Merissa lead her? How far was she willing to go?

Chapter Thirteen

Merissa walked into the barn the next morning wearing a blazer and gray slacks, with her portfolio tucked under one arm. Billie was in the central aisle, grooming Legs after their trail ride, and Jean-Yves was next to her putting a saddle on Juniper. Billie took one look at her in her business attire and gave a long-suffering, eye-rolling sigh.

Merissa held up one hand. "Spare me the dramatics," she said, hiding a grin at Billie's exaggerated annoyance. Well, maybe it wasn't exaggerated, but it was still amusing. "I was going to sneak out while you were riding, but I didn't this time."

She had considered doing just that, and until this morning she hadn't been sure whether she would tell Billie she was leaving or run off like she'd done the day before. Last night, after they'd gone through Dennis's files, she'd spent hours lying on her quilted bedspread and staring at the ceiling while she thought about Dennis, their past, and her uncertain future. She wasn't sure what to do with the information she'd gotten yesterday, but she needed to know more before she could make a decision. When she'd called Karen about the missing files, she'd asked a few vague questions about Dennis and the company, but Karen hadn't given her any more information. She'd sounded unfazed about the files, and asked Merissa to drop them at the front desk of the office whenever she was in Tacoma.

Merissa had immediately called both Kensington and Lemaine and told them she was thinking of buying the business. She asked for meetings this morning and both eagerly accepted, despite the short notice. Of course they would. The amount of money they'd make from an alliance with the Morgan Group, whether she or Dennis was leading it, was worth an impromptu meeting or two.

Since she'd already gotten Billie involved in the file theft, something Billie clearly wasn't happy about, she had originally planned to leave her behind again. But the guilt of dragging Billie along with another scheme was outweighed by the betrayed expression she'd likely see on Billie's face when she finally came home. She'd be up-front about her meetings, and Billie could decide whether to come with her or to stay behind. Either way, Merissa was going.

"I have appointments with Kensington and Lemaine today," she said, trying to look anywhere but at the pulsing beat near Billie's jawbone. She must be grinding her teeth with frustration. "Both are in public places, and I'm just getting a feel of what our relationship will be if I buy the firm. This is a completely reasonable and expected course of action given the amount of money I'll be expected to pay for Dennis's company. It would almost look more suspicious if I didn't meet with them."

Her logic had sounded infallible last night, when she was alone, but Billie didn't look swayed by it. "What's your end goal here, Merissa? Are you going to accuse them of killing Dennis and hope they confess?"

"No." Merissa was telling the truth. She didn't have any sort of plan, just a desire to get a feel for the two men in person and to learn more about what had been going on in Dennis's life. If she happened to stumble across a clue or two, all the better. "I'm going to show them my sketch for the new project and get their input. And then I'll come right back out to the car where you'll be crouching in the backseat."

Billie tossed her brush into the wooden tack trunk and unsnapped the crossties from Legs's halter. "I'll sit in plain sight in the front seat. And I'm only going along with this for two reasons. One, I believe you when you say you'll go even if I try to stop you, and two, you're right that this would be a reasonable step for anyone about to buy a business."

"How much did it pain you to say I'm right?" Merissa asked with a laugh as Billie led Legs into her stall. She felt a sagging sense of relief that Billie would be going with her. She hadn't realized how tense she was about the meetings until just now. She'd met Edwin in passing, when he'd come to the firm's offices, but she only knew Jeff by hearsay. Maybe she'd be more confident now if she'd been involved with Dennis's negotiations from the beginning, but she had a feeling Dennis hadn't wanted her or anyone else to see him losing his edge. She had thought he was finally letting her be more involved because he was willing to give up a little control to her, but now she wondered if his condition—whatever it was—was getting worse and he felt he had to move some responsibility to her shoulders.

"Do you mind taking Juniper on a short trail ride, Jean-Yves?" Billie asked.

"Not at all," he answered. He was already swapping Billie's saddle for his own. The mare danced as he buckled her girth loosely. "I'll let her have a short gallop along the track first, to work off some of this energy."

"Good idea. Remember she's still a little nervous walking through water. If you go on the trail that crosses the stream, be sure to—"

Merissa grabbed Billie's arm and pulled her down the aisle. "Have a good ride, Jean-Yves," she called.

"But—"

"We're going to be late if we don't hurry. Besides, he has more horse knowledge than the two of us put together. He'll probably have Juniper happily doing laps in the pool by the time we get back."

"Fine," Billie said, allowing Merissa to pull her along toward the car. "Where are these meetings of yours?"

"Kensington's office is in Gig Harbor," Merissa said, starting the car and heading out. "Lemaine is in Tacoma, just on the other side of the bridge."

"Okay. Let's go over exactly what you're going to say."

Merissa gave the speech she'd spent most of last night preparing. "I'm interested in taking over the firm, but I don't have

Dennis's experience with the business end of submitting proposals and working with investors to solidify plans. Would you please take me through the process and give me some input on these sketches?"

"Be careful not to sound too naive," Billie warned. "No one would believe you're anything other than smart and capable, and you don't want them to think you're there for any reason other than the business one." She reached around and pulled Merissa's portfolio off the backseat. "Are these the firm's plans for my neighborhood? If they are, we need to turn around right now."

"I'm smart and capable, remember?" Merissa asked with a laugh. She was pleased with the compliment, but now had to rethink her approach. She had been planning to sound a bit dim so the contractors might let down their guard a little, but if she had been, then Dennis never would have put her in the position of his possible successor. "Those are some drawings I made last night, based on ones I did during grad school. They're my vision."

"Good. What else are you planning to say?"

Merissa gave the rest of her speech, and Billie tweaked the words until they came up with a short presentation both could agree on. Billie still didn't seem completely happy with the day's plan, but she was resigned to it. Merissa knew she'd have to ad-lib a little since their prepared speech wouldn't cover all possible turns of conversation, but she kept that from Billie. Her main objective was to find out what had happened to Dennis, and she'd do whatever it took to do so.

She parked next to the restored Victorian where Jeff Kensington had his office space and left the car running so Billie had heat. She tried to get her portfolio out of Billie's hands, but she had a tight grip on it.

"Should we go over what you're planning to say again?"

"No," Merissa said. Her portfolio finally came free when she gave it a determined tug. "If we do, I'll sound like I'm reading cue cards. This has to sound natural to be convincing."

"You're not convincing anyone of anything. You're honestly checking into these contacts before you agree to commit to buying the firm."

Merissa shut the car door without answering and gave Billie a wave as she walked up to the front door. She stepped into the foyer, filled with antique furniture and nautical maps of Puget Sound, and went around the corner. She was expecting a receptionist, but she emerged from the hall directly into Jeff's office. He stood up from his desk as soon as she came in. He was in his early thirties, with already thinning blond hair. He wore a blue plaid shirt with a brown tie and blazer. His clothes looked as worn as the furnishings in his office, and Merissa figured he wanted to create the image of someone unpretentious and in touch with the past.

"Merissa, it's nice to finally meet you in person," he said, coming around the desk after she introduced herself and walking toward her so briskly that she thought he might be about to hug her. She almost took a step back, but stayed still with effort. He held out his hand instead, and she shook it with relief. He gestured toward a wood chair upholstered in a heavy maroon damask and went behind his desk again. "What can I do for you?"

She went through her rehearsed spiel and opened her portfolio. She had come up with a new design for a downtown city block, this one including the affordable rentals as well as the fancy-view condos. She described the details to him, and then sat back in the stiff chair and tried to look comfortable while he scanned the drawings.

"I like your style," he said. "You blend contemporary and traditional elements in a very pleasing way. I'm excited about the idea of creating some housing options that are more cost effective and more accessible to the residents of the Hilltop. I have some investors who have strong philanthropic interests and I'm sure they'd be interested in working on a project like this."

"Wonderful," Merissa said with a smile as she stood and gathered her papers. She was caught in the vision of her plans coming to life, and she almost forgot why she had come in the first place.

"I'm glad you stopped by today," he said. "I've been interested in working with the Morgan Group, but Dennis and I could never seem to get beyond the initial meeting phase. Even when we agreed on the design elements, he'd go back to Lemaine."

"You've met with him before?" Merissa had thought Dennis wanted to switch to Jeff because of her style. He'd never mentioned going to other contractors before signing with Lemaine.

"Several times. He kept talking about being ready to make a change, but I guess he really wasn't. It's not easy breaking into the upper levels of this business, and when I heard I'd have the chance to deal with you I was excited. Two newcomers helping each other out, you know? Still, it's a damned shame he's gone. Last I heard, the police think he happened to drive through the line of fire during a gang shooting. Is there any more news on what happened?"

"I'm not allowed to talk about what I witnessed that night," Merissa said vaguely. It was true. She wasn't supposed to even mention the murder to him or anyone else, but she watched his expression to see if he seemed nervous when she mentioned the word *witness*. He merely looked curious, and she didn't bother to add that she hadn't seen anything worth noticing, except for a generic brown car. She shook his hand again and walked out of the building. Had Jeff worried Dennis might change his mind again? Had he thought his chances were better with Merissa at the helm? How far would he go to break in to the business he so desperately wanted to be part of?

She sighed. She had come looking for answers and now she had more questions than ever. She dropped her portfolio in the backseat and told Billie about their conversation, carefully glossing over the last part of it, as they drove the short distance to Lemaine's office.

Merissa, feeling as if she was in the touring company of a play, went through her same speech in Edwin Lemaine's gleaming modern office. Everything here was as black and white and geometric as Kensington's place had been faded and old-elegant. She'd prefer a mix of the two. Jeff's business had a rustic charm that seemed forced and overly casual. Edwin's, on the other hand, was too overtly formal, from the pencil-skirted receptionist to the boss himself. He was slightly overweight and had reddish-blond hair cut in a style more suited to someone about a decade younger, as were his thin hipster tie and the colorful sneakers he wore with his carefully tailored and pressed suit. She knew he was in his early fifties, but the attempt to dress and appear younger had the opposite effect.

He listened to her presentation and scanned her drawings quickly. "The low-income housing will be a tough sell, Merissa," he said, tapping her sketches into a neat pile and handing them back to her. "Most of our investors—the ones who have money to burn—are expecting to make a strong profit with every square inch of building space. They're not all as caring and generous as you are."

She nodded, impressed with the way he said a lot in few words. He'd just complimented her, told her he wouldn't accept her proposal as it was drawn, and let her know he was aware of her financial situation.

"We could possibly market plans for a less exclusive neighborhood, with lower rent and more basic amenities, in the future. For now, I'd suggest staying within the standards the Morgan Group has already set. Dennis and I worked long and hard to develop a good base of investors, and to create a set of plans suitable for a variety of uses."

Merissa nodded, her mind whirling. Dennis had given her the same advice. Stick to what's been working. Had his lack of imagination and skill been less a sign of a weakening mind and more a result of his longtime work with Lemaine? She had assumed that he was losing his edge for some reason and was unable to come up with more innovative ideas, but now she wasn't sure. Had Dennis been producing low-quality, derivative work on purpose?

Lemaine stood and held out his hand. She rose as well, feeling as if she'd been dismissed from the presence of the king. "Let me know when you make a decision about the firm. I believe we'd make as great a team as Dennis and I did. He will be sorely missed, but his legacy can continue."

What legacy? One of static and uninspired designs? "I'd like nothing more than to keep his best qualities alive," she said. "He had a great sense of style and innovation, especially earlier in his career. I plan to build on that if I buy the firm."

"Innovation is good," Lemaine said as he escorted her to the door. "But the ability to please the people who matter is a more predictable sign of success. It's a game, Merissa, and you need to learn how to play it. I believe we'd make a great team, you and I."

Merissa walked out of the low-slung building and got in the car with Billie. She had been ready to give Edwin the same hint that she'd witnessed something, but except for mentioning Dennis's legacy, he hadn't asked about the investigation. Kensington had seemed enthusiastic about her designs, but he might just be telling her what she wanted to hear. Maybe Dennis had never signed with him because he lacked follow-through and didn't deliver the investors he promised. On the other hand, Lemaine expected more than just the compromise she disliked. He seemed to want a sort of obedience she wasn't prepared to give. It seemed Dennis had been willing to do what he wanted, though, and Merissa didn't know why. Both talks had left her confused, and she was glad to drive out of the city and back to the peace and quiet of the farm.

CHAPTER FOURTEEN

B illie left Merissa at the main house and went back to the barn to check on her horses. All six of them were contentedly munching hay. Juniper had, as Billie had expected, been cooled down and groomed to a shine after her trail ride with Jean-Yves. She went into Ranger's stall and spent a few minutes leaning against his shoulder while he ate, feeling the rhythm of his breathing and chewing seep into her.

The day hadn't been a bad one. She had been upset by Merissa's insistence on going out and meeting with people who might have played a part in Dennis's murder, but at least Merissa had told her this time. Merissa needed to feel in control again, and planning these interviews had helped her achieve that. Besides, if Dennis had died of natural causes and Merissa had been looking into buying his firm or going out on her own, she would likely have met with these contractors like she'd done today. Even though she saw the logic behind the meetings, Billie had sat in the car and turned pages in a book without really seeing any of the words. In reality, she had been watching the doors, waiting for Merissa to scream for help.

And nothing bad had happened. After they left Lemaine's office, she and Merissa had gotten lunch in tiny downtown Gig Harbor, eating fish and chips next to a huge picture window. The afternoon had been sunny, but cold, and the restaurant had logs sizzling and crackling in the fireplace. They had gone grocery shopping at the small and overpriced general store before coming back to the farm.

Somehow, the casual afternoon had set Billie's nerves on fire like the logs in the restaurant. They had talked mainly about horses, avoiding any talk of Dennis's shooting or Merissa's impromptu investigations. They had shopped for everyday items like bread and milk. Nothing extraordinary, but all made more invigorating because they were together. Billie didn't understand her reaction, and she wasn't sure she liked it at all. Merissa upset her balance.

She was relieved to be here, alone with Ranger, for some time to decompress. She walked out of his stall more centered and relaxed, but the soft feeling disappeared when she saw Merissa standing in the middle of the barn aisle, her face unnaturally drained of color and her blue eyes wide with shock.

"Merissa? Merissa, what's wrong?" Billie shut the stall door and ran over to her.

"My house," Merissa said in a hoarse voice. She cleared her throat and tried again. "Someone was in my house."

"Are you sure? Did they take anything?" Billie had an image of the elegant kitchen and living room in disarray, curtains and cushions slashed and littering the clean marble floor. Had someone been looking for the files Merissa had taken?

Merissa merely shook her head and turned toward the house, beckoning for Billie to follow her. She didn't speak as they walked across the gravel drive and into the house. Billie looked around. Everything was as pristine as it had been the last time she was here. "Are you sure?" she asked again. "It looks fine to me."

"Not here. In my rooms." Merissa led her down a long hallway, with several closed doors on either side, and through a breezeway into a suite of rooms. The sudden shock of change from harsh whiteness to the rooms full of color made Billie's breath catch in her throat. This was where Merissa lived. She belonged here. Drawings and paintings covered the walls, most of them prints and posters thumbtacked in place. A bright orange and pink patterned blanket was tossed over the arm of a beige suede sofa, and the bookshelves were full of mismatched volumes. The kitchen counter was cluttered with a waffle maker, an electric coffeepot, and some of the groceries they had bought today. The rooms looked a little messy and lived-in, but not tossed like Billie had been expecting.

"Through here," Merissa said, still eerily terse.

Merissa's bedroom. Billie had pictured her in a grand room, with a four-poster bed and lots of fluffy pillows. This was a normal bed, covered in a pastel quilt that coordinated nicely with the soft sage walls. Horse pictures hung on the walls, and figurines were everywhere. Nothing looked harmed. Several framed photographs sat on top of a pale blue dresser. Billie walked toward them, unable to resist this glimpse into Merissa's world.

"Everything looks okay, Merissa. What makes you think…" Billie stopped when her sentence did. "Did you touch any of these?"

"No. I ran out to the barn as soon as I saw them."

Billie groped for her cell, unable to tear her gaze away from the pictures. The frames were mostly made out of wood, with decorative horseshoes and championship trophies painted on them. Most of the photos were of Merissa at various ages on horses, except for two of them. In one, Merissa was leaning out a second-story window, holding a box while Billie watched from the ground. In the other, they were sprawled in the rhododendron, next to the box full of files.

"Nothing else was touched? Was there any sign of forced entry?" Merissa shook her head, and Billie quickly gave the desk sergeant directions to the house. She called Hargrove next, and then turned back to Merissa.

"Let's wait outside," she said. "Someone will be here soon to dust for prints." She doubted they'd find anything. This wasn't the bumbling job of an amateur. This was a cold expert, sending a message. Billie was tired of getting them.

Merissa sat on the steps while Billie jogged to the barn to find Jean-Yves. He hadn't seen anything since he'd been trail riding on Juniper for over an hour, and then in the upper barns. The only other groom on duty during the day had been cleaning stalls and hadn't noticed any strange people or cars on the property. Both seemed genuinely shocked when Billie told them what had happened, but she wasn't sure she could read either well enough to tell if they were lying or not.

Billie slowly walked back to where she'd left Merissa. Who knew they'd be away for the morning? Jean-Yves. Karen, because Merissa had returned the files while they were in town. Lemaine and Kensington.

Like she'd told Merissa, she didn't trust anyone. Everyone was a suspect.

Merissa seemed deflated, and Billie sat next to her on the steps until a detective arrived and she took him to the room. When she came back outside, Abby was with Merissa. She said something and touched Merissa briefly on the arm before walking up the steps to meet Billie.

She held up her phone. A snapshot of one of the photos was displayed on it. "Carl sent me this. Looks like a picture of you helping someone B and E, but there's no way one of my officers would do such a stupid thing. Would she?"

"I wasn't helping. I just caught her when she fell."

"Are you making a joke?"

Billie bit her lip. Apparently not a good one. All the softness she'd been seeing lately in Abby was gone, replaced by the full force of Hard-Ass Hargrove. Billie wasn't the type to get in trouble. She followed the rules and did her job. Merissa came into her life, and suddenly she was breaking rules on a daily basis.

"No, ma'am."

Hargrove sighed. "Don't call me that. Just tell me exactly what's been going on here, from the beginning. Well, not the beginning. What's been going on since you and Don pulled that stunt on Ruston."

Billie did her best to make light of Merissa's trip to the Morgan offices, but there was no way to easily explain the picture of them rolling through the bushes. "We returned all the files today," she said, remembering too late that she had those blank forms tucked inside her sofa. "Well, most of them."

She got the forms from her apartment while Abby talked to Merissa about the inferences she'd made from Dennis's files. When Billie got back to the house, she joined them on the stairs and handed Abby the manila folders.

She glanced at the contents, and then slid them inside the folders again. "So, we have a dead guy who borrowed a car for an unknown second person, who may or may not exist. The car may or may not have been involved in the shooting. And we have some conjecture about the mental state of the original shooting victim based on stolen files. All in all, some excellent detective work, you two."

Merissa and Billie looked at each other. Merissa had a little more color in her face and actually seemed ready to laugh at Abby's statement. Either she was near hysteria because someone had been in her home, or she was slowly coming out of shock and returning to her normal self. Billie gave her a quick wink, impressed by her resiliency. Billie didn't feel she had nearly as much.

"I messed up, Lieutenant. I'll turn in my badge and gun tomorrow," she said, only partly joking.

"Oh for God's sake. Just try to keep our only witness from committing any more crimes. Karen Morgan hasn't filed charges, and you returned the files, so I'm going to try to ignore this event. You and Don had every right as officers to confront a known drug dealer while he was dealing, even if you were off duty. I'm running out of technicalities, though. One more questionable action, and I'll happily accept your resignation, Mitchell."

"Yes, Lieutenant."

"Now I'm going inside to find out whether Carl found any evidence. Please wipe those grins off your faces, and if I hear any laughter before I shut the front door behind me, I'm having you both arrested. I'll come up with a reason later." She paused. "Not that I'd need to look far."

"You are such a bad influence on me," Billie said once Hargrove was out of earshot. Merissa gave a sad sort of laugh and leaned her head against Billie's shoulder. Billie put her arm around her. Aside from occasional touches, this was the closest Billie had been to Merissa. She felt strong and solid in Billie's arms, but pliable at the same time. Her body molded along the length of Billie's. She fit. Billie let the tingling warmth she felt everywhere Merissa was in contact with her ease into her mind and dislodge the helplessly spinning question of who had been taking photographs of them.

"I'm sorry," Merissa said, her voice muffled against Billie's shirt. "I need to understand what happened—why it happened—and there doesn't seem to be any good way to get answers."

Billie knew she should tell Merissa that maybe she'd never find the answers she sought. And maybe the best she could hope for was to have whoever killed Dennis disappear from her life—no questions asked or answers given. Instead, she changed the subject.

"I never could picture you living in this house, until I saw your rooms. Are you sleeping in what was meant to be the servant's quarters?"

Merissa laughed and sat up. She stayed close enough for Billie's arm to remain over her shoulders, though. Close enough for her scent to seep into the deepest corners of Billie's mind.

"The nanny's. I had a string of them even though I was thirteen when I came here to live. Most of them were nice, and I spent more of my time back with them than in the front rooms. They never stayed long, though, since Grandfather liked to pick fights. He said letting any help stay too long was inviting trouble because they'd get too close and learn family secrets."

"What were the secrets he was trying to hide?"

Merissa shrugged, pressing against Billie's side when she moved her shoulder. The feeling bruised Billie's nerve endings, increasing the intensity of Merissa's closeness. "I don't think there were any. He was just a cantankerous old man who didn't trust anyone."

"You're not like him at all," Billie said. Merissa might be questioning the motives of people in her life right now, given what had happened to her and Dennis, but she seemed to be caught by surprise by the doubts, not to be expecting them. She had a sincerity about her, an openness Billie envied. Lately, Merissa's negative emotions of fear and frustration were readily seen on her face, but Billie suspected this wasn't the case when her life was normal. She'd bet Merissa usually was an open book, but with optimism and kindness as the most prevalent and visible traits. "Do you take after your parents more than him?"

"Yikes, I hope not."

Billie felt Merissa's tension, but she didn't pull away. "Tell me about them."

"Dad grew up with money and a lot of resentment. He never felt he lived up to my grandfather's expectations, so he stopped trying—if he ever really tried in the first place—and turned into sort of a playboy. He traveled around the world with an entourage of hangers-on, and eventually fell in love with one of them. Or, according to my grandfather, he got one of them pregnant with me and then married her so he wouldn't lose his inheritance. That's my parents' romantic love story."

Billie felt Merissa's sigh roll through her. Merissa's grandfather didn't sound very kind, and her dad sounded like an entitled spoiled brat. She didn't like to make judgments about people she didn't know, but Merissa's memories held tangible pain when she talked about them. No child, especially one as bright and loving as Merissa must have been, deserved to be told they were unwanted. She tried to look for a bright side to the story. "It sounds like you had a chance to travel more than most kids do. Where did you live when you were with your parents?"

"All over Europe, but mostly Costa de la Luz in Spain and Aix-en-Provence in the south of France. My parents loved the sun, and they were beautiful places, but I was on my own a lot because they were either partying at night or sleeping it off during the day. I'd wander the streets while they were in bed. It sounds scary here in the States, but over there it was different. I made friends with the shop owners and street sweepers. The city was more home and family to me than the cottage where we lived or my own parents were."

"And now you create similar communities for people right here." Billie had seen small indications of Merissa's remembered loneliness. Imagining her as a little girl, left on her own, gave Billie a whole new perspective. Merissa wanted to create beautiful spaces, yes, but what she was hoping to provide was much deeper than the outward appearance of fancy condos or classy cafés. "Why did you decide to come live with your grandfather?"

"I guess I had read too many books like *Heidi*. I pictured a loving family reunion when I came here, and I had a secret dream that my parents would miss me so much they'd come here, too. Grandfather and my dad would hug and forgive each other, and we'd all live happily ever after on this beautiful farm."

Billie felt cold inside at the way Merissa spoke. Her words were beautiful and painted a hopeful picture, but her delivery was flat and emotionless. "I take it they didn't come live here?"

"As far as I know, they're still living off Grandfather's money somewhere in Italy. But I made friends with the horses, and I was happy enough here."

Happy enough. Merissa deserved to be ecstatic. Joyful. Loved. Billie hoped she would find someone who could settle here and help her make it a real home instead of merely a big house with a handful of warm rooms.

"What about you?" Merissa asked, pulling away from Billie's arm and looking at her. "What was your childhood like?"

Billie shrugged. She had started the conversation as a way to get Merissa's mind off Dennis. She was flattered by Merissa's trust in her as she shared the painful—and most likely private—story of her past, but she wasn't sure how to respond. She rarely told anyone about her own life, choosing instead to listen to others more than she spoke. Most people were happier when they were talking about themselves, and Billie was comfortable letting them take center stage while she prompted from the sidelines.

"I don't know. My mom died when I was little, and my dad worked on a fishing boat. I lived in one town, but sort of moved around a lot."

Merissa watched her for a moment longer, obviously waiting for more of a revelation than Billie had given. She wasn't sure how to continue, though. Her childhood led to the army, which led to Mike and her PTSD and her old wounds. Who wanted to hear any of that?

Luckily, Abby and Carl came outside, and Billie jumped up to find out if they'd discovered anything in Merissa's room. They hadn't, as Billie had expected. Carl left, and Hargrove hauled Billie to one side by the collar of her shirt and delivered another stern lecture about keeping Merissa in line and obeying every law that had ever been written.

Once they were alone, Merissa looked at the house with a pained frown.

"Stay in the apartment with me tonight," Billie said. "I'll sleep on the sofa and you can have the bed. Don't stay here, knowing someone was inside your room." The violation was upsetting to her, and she could only imagine what Merissa must be feeling.

"I guess I will," Merissa said. "I can't bear to be in there alone. Thank you."

Her words were polite, and she was accepting Billie's offer of company and support, but something had changed. She had been sharing her story, opening herself up to Billie, and now there was a distinct and deep chasm between them. One full of ice water. And alligators. Billie felt her chest and neck grow hot when she pictured Merissa in the intimate little apartment with her, but Merissa's tone and expression were cold. Billie didn't know how to bridge the temperature gap between them.

"I'll get my things," Merissa said. She started to walk up the stairs, but then stopped and faced Billie. "I forgot to mention it, but Cal called right before I noticed the photos. She wants me to fill in for a team member at a polo match this weekend. I usually take Jean-Yves with me to help me with the horses..."

"I'll go instead," Billie said. Jean-Yves seemed like a good guy, but Billie didn't know him well enough to be sure. He claimed he hadn't seen anyone near the house today, but he was the one person who knew exactly when she and Merissa had left the property. Besides, she and Merissa needed to stick close together for the time being, until they found out who was responsible for switching the photos. "I'll be your groom."

"Fine," Merissa said, without a fight or a protest. She'd given up, and Billie wondered how much it had to do with her and her inability—or unwillingness?—to share much about her life.

It wasn't until later, when Merissa had gone to bed and Billie was lying alone on the couch, that she started to understand what had happened between them. Merissa had given her a gift. The present of her past and her pain. Billie always thought the gift she gave other people was understanding and the freedom to talk about themselves, but Merissa hadn't wanted that. She had wanted Billie to give something of herself as well, some part of her insides, her history, her scarred-over wounds.

Billie wasn't sure she'd ever be able to reciprocate that way. Just like she would never be the settled and stable woman to help create a home, she'd also never be the type to freely chat about her deepest parts. Sometimes she whispered stories to Ranger, but even he wasn't given everything she had. Today on the steps, she had seen the disappointed expression on Merissa's face before it was replaced with a more neutral one. She couldn't bring herself to make it better, though. Merissa might think she wanted to hear about Billie, but did she really need to be burdened with her stories? Billie rolled over and faced the back of the couch, shutting her eyes and letting the world behind her disappear.

CHAPTER FIFTEEN

By the time Billie woke up the next morning, Merissa had already gotten dressed and snuck out of the apartment. Billie found her in the feed room, measuring breakfast rations for the horses.

"Good morning," Billie said. She felt tentative around Merissa, both because of the scare Merissa had the day before and because Billie wasn't sure where they stood. She understood that Merissa had offered something of herself, and Billie hadn't reciprocated. She hoped they would be able to move past the awkward moment and go back to their normal relationship whatever that was. Billie hadn't known Merissa long enough to have established anything normal with her, but she had been getting more comfortable in Merissa's presence. This morning, she'd managed to convince herself that Merissa's revelations had been prompted by circumstances, the illusion of closeness, not by real feelings. Billie had done the right thing by stopping the increasing intimacy when she had. If she had opened herself up to Merissa, they might have been fooled into believing they really had something between them. They might have been tempted to move forward in a more physical way. She had made the smart choice.

Merissa turned at the sound of her voice. Billie thought she saw a fleeting hint of sadness or disappointment in her eyes, but it was gone in a flash, and Merissa's smile was bright and genuine. She looked more rested and happy than she had since Billie had met her—she had only known Merissa in a semi-exhausted state, but some of her baggage seemed to have been shed this morning. She was wearing a ratty navy hoodie from McGill and tight jeans, and she looked fresh and outdoorsy and beautiful.

Yeah. Billie was a fucking genius.

"You look good," she said. Her voice sounded a little breathless, even though she hadn't done anything more physical than walk down a flight of stairs.

"I slept great. I guess I've been kind of tense at night, with all the creaks and groans of a big empty house keeping me up, and it was nice to have someone in the other room."

"Mm-hmm. Nice," Billie said, although she wouldn't have chosen that word. She'd lain awake most of the night, too aware of Merissa only yards away in her warm bed. She'd been the composed one at the start of their relationship, and now they'd traded places. She felt worn-out and a little raw, and Merissa looked cool and relaxed.

"I have something to do today," she said, taking the bucket of feed from Merissa and carrying it to the stall Merissa pointed to. "I was going to cancel since we should stick together until the detectives figure out who was in your house, but if you'd like to get away from here for a change of pace, you're welcome to come with me."

Merissa winced when Billie mentioned the break-in, but otherwise she seemed to be handling it well. "What kind of thing?" she asked, and then she waved off her own question. "Doesn't matter. Yes, I'd like to get out of here for a while. This was supposed to be my safe place, but it isn't anymore."

Her voice cracked slightly, and Billie guessed she wasn't as tranquil as she appeared on the surface. "The afternoon will do you good, then. We can leave as soon as we finish feeding."

"Do I need to change?"

"No. Barn clothes are perfect." Billie closed the latch after feeding a tall bay gelding, and she returned to the feed room for the next bucket. They worked together and fed the entire row of horses. Billie had been convinced she was better off not getting close to Merissa, but for someone who was fighting hard to keep her personal life separate from her role as Merissa's protector, she seemed to touch her a lot. She couldn't help but let her fingers graze Merissa's when they exchanged buckets, and she always managed to bump against her when they walked through the feed room door. Her body pulled her toward Merissa. Her heart wasn't pulling her away, it was merely protecting itself. Billie was used to distance. The few times she'd gotten close to anyone she'd been scarred so thickly she didn't think another person would ever be able to see the wounds underneath.

Still, she was bringing Merissa to the one place where those wounds had been on display. She really had been planning to cancel her plans to volunteer today, but when she saw the chinks in Merissa's wall of serenity, she had decided a day working with the wounded soldier program would be good for both of them. She drove them over the bridge and north to Olympia while they made small talk about the weather and the scenery, and she was struck again by how Merissa made even the everyday activities like taking a drive and getting a cup of coffee seem momentous.

Billie shared normal moments with Mike's kids and occasionally with Don and Marie, but she usually was on her own when she wasn't at work. Even the few women she'd dated recently hadn't been allowed to infiltrate Billie's world. They went out to eat or to a movie, went home—usually not to Billie's place—and had sex, and then went their separate ways. Shopping and eating and taking care of her apartment were solitary events for Billie, and had been for most of her life. Merissa had wedged herself into these daily routines—not because she necessarily wanted to, but because they needed to stay close for safety—and her company only highlighted how empty Billie's life really had been. Part of her wished she could go back to the way she had been before, not really aware of how much another person could fill the regular parts of life. But mostly, she was happy to have had even these short days of togetherness, even though it had been forced on them.

Billie wound along side streets on the outskirts of Shelton until she reached the dusty little stables with a sign over the entrance announcing it as the home of the Bright Stars Therapeutic Riding Program. Billie parked under a huge, drooping fir tree and shut off the engine. A few horses lazed in dirt paddocks, and an outdoor arena to their right was filled with colorful props, ready for the next lesson.

Merissa took everything in before turning to Billie. "I've heard of Bright Stars," she said. "It's a program for soldiers, isn't it? Do you teach here?"

"No. I'm a volunteer. They work with soldiers in transition, mostly ones coming home from war with injuries or PTSD. This is…" She paused. Only her mounted team knew she'd ridden here, but they didn't know the details beyond the lessons. She could easily have canceled today and stayed at the farm with Merissa, but instead, she had brought her here. A few restless nights and an enjoyable shopping trip or two and she was ready to spill her secrets? *Yes.* "This is where I learned to ride."

Merissa looked at her with surprise clearly etched in her raised eyebrows and wide eyes. Was she more shocked that Billie had ridden here, or that she was sharing part of herself? For Billie, the latter was definitely the most unexpected. "When did you start?"

"About three years ago." Billie looked at the old white-gray mare who was in the paddock closest to them, swishing her tail at flies and resting with one hind leg cocked. Gambler. One of the first horses Billie had ever ridden. "I had been back from the Middle East for a few years, but I wasn't handling it well. I'd been injured, and was healing slowly. I'd…well, I lost someone close to me. He was my best friend and I missed him so much. I was floundering, and couldn't find the meaning in life I'd always known before."

Merissa remained quiet for a moment before speaking. "Did you find meaning here?"

"Yes. And peace." Billie toyed with the door handle as she spoke. The enclosed car added to the intimacy of the situation, and she swung back and forth between feeling stifled and trapped and feeling secure and close to Merissa. "At first I just sat in the saddle and barely moved while volunteers led me around, but eventually the horses broke through my pain and I started to actually ride. As soon as I heard about the new mounted unit, I applied for the job."

"I'm sorry about your friend," Merissa said softly. She silently offered support, too, by the small nudges and movements of her thigh and arm as she sought contact with Billie.

"Me, too. I'm still close to his wife, and his kids come to visit me sometimes. It's sort of like having a real family." Billie hesitated again. She wasn't used to this, and her words came out slowly and erratically, like an old machine coming to life again—sputtering and stalling, but gradually growing stronger and steadier.

"You asked about my family last night and I wasn't sure how to answer. I usually don't talk about them. I love my dad and my two sisters, but more because it's expected than because we're really close." Billie hated admitting her lack of genuine feelings for her family because she usually thought people would think she was cold and unfeeling when the opposite was really the truth. But after hearing Merissa talk about her own parents last night, Billie felt she was the one person who might understand her. "He fished off the coast of Alaska. It was dangerous work, but it paid well, and he thought he was doing something good for our family by earning extra money, but instead it pushed us apart."

Billie remembered the shame of being dropped on the doorstep of strangers whenever her dad had to go back to sea. In her mind, it was always winter, and her memories were punctuated by shivers and a stuttering chill. "He used to leave us with family members, but he was gone so often that the three of us wore out our welcome. Eventually, we worked our way through his close friends and soon were staying with people he barely knew."

She was caught in the past, wondering why she didn't feel as much resentment and embarrassment as she usually did when she traveled back in time, and it took her some time to realize Merissa was holding her hand. The touch had calmed Billie before she'd even registered it. The scent of Merissa permeated the car, just as it had lingered in the steam after Merissa's shower this morning, and Billie grew warm again.

"My older sisters each got married as soon as they turned eighteen, about a year apart. Probably more to finally have a home than because they were in love. I thought Jill—we're closest in age—might keep me with her when she moved in with her new husband, but she didn't." Billie's voice began to sound more controlled and less childlike to her own ears as Merissa's thumb stroked the side of her palm and sent tremors of heat through her body and gave her the strength she needed to tell Merissa about the worst night of all. "Dad had to leave again the day after her wedding, and I was foisted off on one of our neighbors. When I was lying in bed that night, completely alone for the first time and obviously unwanted, I promised myself I'd never be in that position again, at the mercy of someone else's decisions."

Merissa cleared her throat. "I remember the exact night when I knew my dream of having my parents follow me here wasn't going to come true. Mom called to check on me and said they were going on a tour of Italy. She said it was something they'd been wanting to do, but hadn't before because it was for adults only. I had thought they would miss me, but instead they were relieved I was gone and they had more freedom. Not that they were ever really tied down by the responsibilities of parenthood."

Billie felt the release of tension when she sighed and she realized she had been holding her breath. She had always thought something would be lost if she talked about her past. Her carefully cultivated aura of control, her well-hidden shame that maybe if she'd been a better daughter he might have stayed around. Instead, she'd given Merissa her pain and got understanding in return. She felt the web of connection grow between them as if it was a tangible thing.

"We both found the comfort we needed in horses," Merissa said with a smile, squeezing Billie's hand.

Merissa at her fancy barn with animals worth tens of thousands and a posse of grooms to take care of them, and Billie here, where the fences were sagging and the horses were mostly rescues—other people's cast-offs. But their experiences weren't nearly as different as Billie had originally thought. They both had been in pain and both had been healed by the gentle presence of the horses.

"Thank you for talking to me," Merissa said. She leaned over and gave Billie a kiss on the cheek. She pulled back a few inches and looked at her for a moment before she kissed her again, this time moving in a slow but steady trail to Billie's mouth.

The softness of her lips against Billie's skin was almost unbearable. She turned her head and their lips met and Billie thought she might explode from the sensations. How could something so gentle trigger a longing so intense? The kiss lingered but never moved beyond the initial tenderness. Merissa still held one hand, and Billie rested the other on Merissa's knee, needing to connect them by as many points of contact as possible. She wanted to taste Merissa with her tongue, to wrap her fingers in Merissa's hair and pull her closer, deeper, but she was too aware of being in a public place and of the tenuous connection they had made. The kiss honored what they'd shared, and Billie eventually pulled away, not trusting her willpower enough to keep it from moving to something more physical than emotional.

Merissa's cheeks and neck were flushed. "That was pretty damned wonderful," she said. She raised her voice. "It would have been even better if that old man wasn't staring through the window."

"I heard that," Don said.

Billie jumped at his voice, surprised he had managed to get so close to the car without her sensing someone near. She had thought she was still alert to what was going on, but Merissa's kiss had affected her more than she realized.

She rolled down the window. "Are you spying on us?"

"Jeez, no. I saw you drive in and came over to say hello. I didn't expect to find you making out in the car. Now I'm going to have to gouge out my eyeballs."

Merissa laughed. "Serves you right for interrupting a beautiful moment."

"Ugh. Next time I see the windows starting to steam up, I'm running the other way."

Billie pushed open her door and made Don step back out of its way. "I see the bodyguard duty is going well," he said. His grin faded and he spoke quietly as Merissa got out of the car on the other side. "I've never seen anyone get within a hundred yards of you without you knowing. I was at the car door before she saw me. When did you?"

Billie didn't answer the rhetorical question. She nodded to show she understood his worries about her attraction to Merissa putting them both in danger. She had let it happen once, and she wouldn't do it again.

"Are you here to volunteer?" he asked Merissa, returning to his normal, friendly self. He wouldn't mention her slip again, but she was grateful to him for the warning. What if he had been someone who wanted to hurt Merissa? She'd never have forgiven herself for being distracted by a kiss.

No matter how mind-blowing the kiss had been.

CHAPTER SIXTEEN

After filling out her volunteer forms and getting a quick training session from the coordinator, Merissa spent the next three hours leading horses around the arena and talking to the riders and sidewalkers on her team. Don was one of her partners during the first lesson, and he plied her with questions about Fancy and how she was settling in at Merissa's barn. Merissa had known Billie would be in sole charge of the horses until the other riders started coming for weekly training sessions during the second month of their stay, but she hadn't realized the others were being purposefully kept away. She decided it was Abby's way of giving her space to be a little sad or crazy after watching Dennis die, and giving her the privacy she needed to lean on Billie for support. Don obviously was going through some sort of withdrawal, though, and she knew she'd made a friend for life when she told him to come visit his little mare anytime.

Even more fun than hearing him gush about his pinto was watching him and Billie interact during the second lesson, when they were working together to support a young man who had injured his spine. They were an unlikely pair, but obviously a close one, and their jokes and playfulness helped their rider laugh and relax in the saddle. They never lost their focus on safety, though, and she admired the careful way they made sure he was secure and confident. Billie was obviously volunteering here as a way to give back to the program that had helped her heal. After piecing together snippets of his conversation, Merissa figured Don was here for the same reason—gratitude that these animals had helped Billie become whole again. He clearly cared about her. Billie might not have had a close family while growing up, but one had formed around her here and in her mounted unit.

Merissa had less chance to talk with the riders since her job was to concentrate on controlling the horse she was leading, but she felt herself loosening up as well while she worked. Her mind let go of her own problems and worries for minutes at a time, while she attended to the horses and riders in her care.

She was sorry when the lessons ended, but she was determined to stay involved with this group. She had a chance to see what good work they were doing after talking to Billie and the other riders about their experiences here. While they untacked and groomed the horses, she was mentally making lists of equipment she could donate, as well as a couple of her older horses she thought would enjoy the quiet work of carrying wounded riders.

After the last rider left, Merissa, Billie, and Don haltered three of the therapy horses and took them over to the driveway to munch on the unmown grass lining the road. Merissa leaned against her palomino's side and let the smell of horse and the crunching of his teeth relax her while Billie told Don about the latest events at the farm. She still felt queasy when she thought about some stranger creeping through her house and touching her personal belongings. Even worse was the knowledge that no one had seen or heard anything, and the intruder had so easily gotten through her door and into her home. What if she was there the next time?

Being here with Billie made the rest of the world, with all its questions and violence, recede for a short time. Merissa had turned to the animals for companionship when she was young, but along the way her riding time had become training time. Watching Billie work with her six charges for the simple joy of being with them, and now spending time here with riders who desperately needed the connection horses offered, made her reconnect with the childlike love she used to feel.

Billie had made her world better and brighter in other ways, as well. She'd helped Merissa deal with the most traumatic experiences she'd ever faced, and even though Merissa had at first resented how much Billie's strength showed her own weakness, she'd come to rely on her help each step of the way. When she looked back at the morning after Dennis had been shot, she realized that what she'd been annoyed with was actually the gift Billie had given her. She had let Merissa feel weak, had encouraged her to accept her emotions and not try to hide them or fight them or put on a brave, but fake, act.

Humility. That was the lesson Merissa had needed to learn. She had always prided herself on independence and strength, but she had been needy and frightened. And Billie let her know it was okay. Now she was ready to stand tall again and fight back against the invisible person who was attacking her world.

"We have two good suspects," Billie was saying to Don. "They're both contractors who might have had a reason to want Morgan killed. One because he never hired him, and the other might have known Dennis was possibly selling his company to Merissa with some clauses that wouldn't be in his favor."

"Don't forget Karen," Merissa said. She hated accusing Dennis's wife of murder, but she had to express her doubts about the woman's grief. "When I told her I had those files, I mentioned that I was meeting with Jeff and Edwin. She knew I would be away from home and could have put the photos in my room. She seems in a hurry to dump the firm."

"You also have to keep Carlyle in mind," Don said, holding up his hand as if to ward off Billie's protests before they even came. "Dennis Morgan was a public figure known for tearing down run-down properties and building high-rent condos and retail spaces in their place, and he might have been recognized nosing around the neighborhood. Carlyle would face eviction, and maybe he thought offing the man in charge would save his home."

Billie laid her hand on her gray mare's shoulder. "I'd have been homeless, too, if those plans had gone through. Want to add me to the list?"

"Nah. You had Beth's kids with you the night he was killed. They'd have blabbed to their mother by now if you'd taken them on a shooting spree."

Billie glared at him, and he sheepishly apologized.

"I'm sorry, Merissa. He was your friend and colleague, and I shouldn't be making jokes."

"It's okay," Merissa said. She knew he hadn't meant anything disrespectful and she liked the way his teasing flustered Billie. She was always so composed, and Merissa was happy to see she could be rattled out of it from time to time. She had a few ideas about how to shake Billie's stoic demeanor herself. "While we're at it, we should put me on the list of suspects. Maybe I wanted a quick promotion."

"You were on the other side of the car, so I think your alibi will hold up," Billie said. "We have four possibilities, then. Maybe more, because Carlyle might have been telling the truth, and his car was borrowed for use in the shooting. Percy's friend could have been another disgruntled neighbor, or someone hired by the top three."

Merissa sighed. Adding up the suspects was exhausting when there was no concrete evidence against any of them. "Who knows how many people have been displaced because of the firm's renovation projects, and maybe one of them wanted revenge. I never really thought about our plans for renewal being something worth killing over."

Don snorted. "On the contrary, in the case of Billie's apartment, you'd think there'd be dancing in the street, not shooting. Kudos on your effort to get rid of the place, by the way."

Merissa had to laugh at Billie's indignant frown. "Thank you. Although it's a shame to lose an historical landmark from the tar-papered roof period."

Billie held up her hand to stop them. "Hey. Homeless person here."

"Please. Get another place," Don said. "One that doesn't require a decontamination shower every time you leave."

"What made you choose to live there, anyway?" Merissa asked. She had a hard time picturing Billie—who seemed so at home in the barn and woods on her farm—living in urban squalor. "You're very tidy and seem to like the outdoors, plus you work on those streets all day, so it's like living in your office. I'd have pictured you in a little place on Vashon Island or Brown's Point where you'd be surrounded by green and open spaces."

Billie shook her head. "Those places are nice, Merissa, but—"

"She wants to be seen as an Average Joe," Don said. "Or Average Josephina, if you prefer."

"I don't prefer," Billie said with a shake of her head in his direction. She turned back to Merissa, whose gelding was pulling her toward a patch of clover. "I stay there because it's cheap and I have no commute. If I were the type to put down roots, I'd probably pick a place like you mentioned. But who knows when I'll move on again."

"I know, I know," Don said, stretching his hand high like an eager teacher's pet. "Never. You're the most settled person I know."

Merissa looked back and forth between them, following the conversation like a tennis match. Billie's expressions were priceless as she seemed completely shocked by Don's words. Don, on the other hand, knew Billie far better than Merissa did—yet—and he looked confident in his assessment of her character. Merissa didn't know if she wanted to believe him because it made sense to do so or because she felt a wrenching pain when Billie said she'd be moving on again soon.

"I'm a nomad. I never stay in the same place for long."

"You've been here almost a decade."

"Okay, I've stayed for a while. But only because I got the job with the mounted team. Before I joined the department I lived all over the world."

"Of course you did. You were in the army. Most members of the military do the same thing. After they get out, some of them settle down and some keep moving. As I said before, you're a settler."

Billie looked at Merissa, as if hoping for some help in her argument, but Merissa just shrugged. She had learned about Billie's childhood today, and she thought those experiences would have made her desire a real home, the way Merissa did. Maybe they had made Billie afraid to believe in any sort of stability instead. She didn't trust herself to speak because the thought of Billie leaving before they had a chance to find out what their relationship could be without murder and threats hanging over it made her mouth suddenly feel powdery dry.

"You even made that cozy little reading nook in the police barn."

Merissa, even though her heart was bruised by Billie's insistence on being a rover, had to laugh at Don's statement. "She made a *what*?"

"You should see it," he said. "She has a cute little tea table and a coffeepot and she always makes sure there's cookies or some snack for us."

"I put a couple of chairs in the tack room. What's the big deal?"

Both Merissa and Don waved off Billie's comment. "How sweet of her to make a place where you can relax when you're off duty," Merissa said. Billie swung the loose end of her horse's lead rope and thwacked Merissa on the thigh.

"She even puts out horse magazines and books with—get this—color-coded sticky notes marking sections she thinks we should read. Mine are blue, and they're usually about ways to be more flexible and smooth. If I can only get Fancy to read them, we'll make Billie proud."

Billie tried to get him with her lead rope, but he was faster than Merissa and stepped out of the way. "I'm just trying to help," she said. "Just because I leave a few magazines lying around doesn't mean I'm putting down roots."

"No, but it does mean you're after Rachel's job. You're on the next sergeant's list, and she's sure to make lieutenant soon. We all know you want to take her place, and we're all rooting for you."

Merissa watched Billie shrug. She seemed to be trying to look nonchalant, but her small grin showed she was pleased with what Don said. "I might stick around for a little longer, if I get a chance to lead the team."

"See?" Don asked Merissa, poking her in the ribs. "Settled."

Merissa smiled. Don had won the argument this afternoon, but Merissa wasn't sure how serious Billie was about winning the war and moving somewhere else eventually. And then somewhere else. Always searching. But for now, for today, Billie was going to stay.

CHAPTER SEVENTEEN

*B*illie squinted against the glaring sunlight. She saw Mike in the distance, a tiny version of himself, and he was calling to her. She had to get to him.

She tried to walk but stumbled and fell in the hot sand. She coughed as the fine dust settled in her nose and throat, making it difficult to breathe. Every inhale made her choke, every exhale felt like her last. She yelled at Mike to wait for her, she was coming, but he had stopped shouting at her and was now staring into the distance behind her. She stood, but her right leg wouldn't support her weight, and she fell again. This time she stayed down, crawling on her belly and dragging her useless leg behind her. Only a few inches of progress, and her other leg tingled and her muscles seemed to evaporate in the glimmering, stifling air. She had to get to him before her arms wasted away as well.

"Watch out, Beast!" he yelled, running toward her and growing larger faster than was natural. Billie couldn't figure out how far away he was anymore; she lost all perspective and shaded her eyes to separate Mike from the mirage of green grass and trees that filled her vision. She realized he was within yards of her too late. He jumped on top of her to shield her from harm, but she hadn't prepared, hadn't taken a breath. When he landed, they sank into the ground—suddenly turned into a deep lake—and water poured into her, at first welcomed as it washed away the grit and pain, but then suffocating her.

She pushed him off her, clawing at her neck and gasping for air...

"Billie! Wake up!"

Billie's surroundings slowly swam into focus. She was sitting up in a bed. Where? Where was the door? Over to her left. Yes, the barn apartment. The green glow of her alarm clock. The silhouette in the doorway.

"Merissa," she rasped, her tongue scratchy and her voice hoarse. She cleared her throat and tried again. "Merissa?"

Merissa disappeared from the doorway and reappeared a moment later with a glass of water. She crossed quickly to the bed and sat next to Billie, supporting her trembling hands as she hurriedly gulped down the cold water.

"Are you okay?" Merissa's voice quavered. She set the empty glass on the bedside table and pulled her knees to her chest. "I was going to come in and talk to you, but I heard you mumbling in your sleep. You started to thrash around."

Billie took slow breaths, counting to the rhythm until she was fully awake. "I'm sorry. I should have warned you I might have nightmares tonight. Sometimes after working at the therapy program, they get worse."

Merissa scooched up the bed and gathered Billie into her arms. Billie wanted to protest, to claim she was fine and not to make a fuss, but the tight squeeze of Merissa's arms felt too good. Merissa put one leg over Billie's and coiled herself around her, maximizing the contact of their bodies and doing more to relax Billie than any breathing exercises could do. Billie fought back a wave of claustrophobia, unaccustomed to being touched after having one of her suffocating dreams, but eventually she managed to curl into Merissa's embrace without wanting to claw her way out.

"Were you dreaming about the friend you lost?" Merissa asked, her breath puffing against Billie's hair and making her nerve endings crackle with an intensity out of proportion to the soft touch. "You were calling for Mike."

Billie nodded, rubbing her cheek against Merissa's collarbone. She was gradually moving through the stages of wakefulness, from pain to numbness to normal feeling. She straightened her legs, and Merissa slipped her own between them, shocking Billie's body back to the present and to an awareness of how close they were and how little clothes they wore.

"You said something about a beast, too. Were you being chased?"

Billie laughed, the sound feeling good when the vibration echoed through Merissa's body and back into hers. "That was his nickname for me. He called me that because I was such a beast in the field."

"Really?"

"Do I detect a note of skepticism?" Billie asked, tickling Merissa for doubting her fearsome presence.

Merissa grabbed Billie's hand and pinned it against the mattress. "Maybe a little. I don't picture you as a wild, rampaging bull. I'd have thought you'd be called something like Socrates. Wise and a little annoying."

"Yeah, every army unit has someone named after a Greek philosopher. You wouldn't believe how many Platos I've met." Billie pulled her arm free and wrapped it around Merissa's waist, resting her hand on Merissa's ribcage. She'd had Mike's kids wrestle her awake from nightmares, but she'd never had Merissa's kind of touch to bring her out of the pain. The shock of moving from horror to delight was overwhelming, but Billie craved even more. "Actually, the guys in my unit called me the Beast because I somehow managed to collect stray animals wherever we went. I even had a wild monkey for a while. He just showed up in my tent one day, and I carried him around on my shoulder for almost a week before he disappeared again."

"If you have pictures, I'd love to see them." Merissa rubbed her hand over Billie's hair and down her back, over and over. "Do you have these nightmares often?"

"Not as much anymore." Billie was distracted by the slow strokes of Merissa's fingers and she was surprised she was still able to string words together to form sentences. "Usually only when something triggers them. Talking about Mike, going to the therapy lessons, the photos on your dresser. I've been expecting them to get worse with everything that's been going on around here, but I don't usually cry out or talk." Billie paused. Not that she knew about, anyway. She usually didn't have someone around to wake her and tell her what she'd said and done. She usually got out of bed and huddled alone in the tub while cold water from the shower beat against her and woke her sensations to the present. The gentle pressure from Merissa's body was quite preferable.

"You said you were coming to talk to me about something," Billie said. "Were you going to ask me to switch beds with you?"

Merissa had asked to stay with Billie another night, but she had insisted on taking the couch this time and letting Billie have the bed. Billie hadn't minded the sofa, especially since she'd had plenty of experience with less comfortable sleeping arrangements in her past, but she felt Merissa starting to regain control of herself and her life after the flurry of fear and helplessness launched by Dennis's death. Choosing where to sleep was a small step, but one she had let Merissa make.

"Of course not. You handled it without complaining last night, and I can do the same. Although, now that I'm here comforting you, I realize just how supportive this mattress really is and I remember reading an article about how overly soft couches are much better than firm mattresses for those having nightmares. I wouldn't want to deprive you of the benefits of sofa sleeping."

"Very kind of you. But I remember reading an article stating the exact opposite premise."

"Says the woman who was flailing and yelling on the supportive mattress."

"Touché," Billie said with a laugh. "Fine, we can switch places."

She made no move to leave the haven of Merissa's arms, and Merissa didn't seem inclined to let her go, either.

"I've been out there thinking," Merissa said, her voice growing serious.

"Uh-oh. What about?"

"About what you and Don were saying about suspects. When we just consider Dennis and the work he does in the city, there's a long list of them. When we cut out everyone who wouldn't have known when it was safe to put the pictures in my frames, we're left with a much shorter list."

"Yes," Billie said, slowly drawing out the one-syllable word. "Lemaine, Kensington, and Karen."

"I might have a way we can find out who it was."

"No."

Merissa pulled back and looked in Billie's eyes. "You haven't even heard my plan yet. Maybe it's a good one."

"Whatever it is, my answer is no. We're not putting you in danger to draw out a killer, if the one who planted the photos and the one who shot Dennis are even the same person. We'll leave it to the detectives."

"Who haven't gotten any closer to solving this case. Just listen. Please?"

"All right," Billie said. "Go ahead and try to convince me."

"So, I'll call—"

"No."

Merissa playfully shoved Billie toward the other side of the bed. "Give me a chance."

Billie sat up against the headboard. The thought of someone sneaking through Merissa's room made her ill. She didn't want her anywhere near the creep who had followed her to the office and took pictures of them. Even more, she didn't want Merissa anywhere near the one who had shot Dennis and who could easily have hit Merissa by mistake. But she would hear her out. "Go ahead. I won't interrupt again."

"I'll call Karen and tell her I want to buy the firm and I'll ask for a meeting with her lawyers. That way I'll seem legitimate when I contact Lemaine and Kensington."

Merissa paused, and Billie took it as permission to ask a question. "Do you really want to buy the company? My advice would be to get the hell out of that place and find another job. I'm sure there are excellent opportunities in Seattle, or with another company in Tacoma."

"The Morgan Group was the best. But to answer your question, I'm really not sure what I want to do. I'd like to continue the company in the same way it was when Dennis was at the top of his game, but I hadn't realized how much he'd changed, and I don't know if I can bring the firm back to life. Mediocre buildings and complexes will be built over the next couple of years, and they might ruin the Morgan name. I don't really need to make a decision right now. I just want Karen to think I have."

"How will this meeting scare out the others?"

"That's the cool part," Merissa said, her eyes bright with excitement. Billie understood—Merissa had been made weak, had been beaten down and scared. She wanted to take back her power, and playing the potential suspects was a great way to do so. If no one cared about the dangerousness of messing with a potential murderer. Billie cared. Very much.

"I'll call Ed Lemaine and tell him I'm going to buy the firm, but I plan to make it my policy not to be exclusive to any one developer. I'll also call Jeff Kensington and tell *him* sorry, but I'm buying the firm and signing an exclusive contract with Lemaine. Then we sit back and wait for one of them to make another move."

Merissa rested her elbow on the bed and leaned her head in her hand, looking pleased with herself.

"I have so many objections, it's hard to pick my favorite," Billie said. "Oh, yeah. Let's start with the one about how you're messing with someone who might be prepared to kill for his business."

"But no one has tried to kill me," Merissa said. "The photos were placed when I was away from home. I wasn't even grazed by a bullet in the car. Whoever did this might actually want me in charge now, as long as I'm on the right side when it comes to choosing contractors or investors or whatever group the killer is in."

"No one has tried to kill you *yet*. Push these people too far, and who knows what will happen. Besides, I thought your prime suspect was Karen. How does she fit in this plan?"

Merissa shrugged. "I'll have to wing that part. At the very least, I'll have a chance to talk to her about Dennis. I can let her know I was aware of the decline in the quality of his work—she doesn't have to be told I figured this out because of the stolen files. I worked with him every day, and as far as she knows, I had access to this information all along. Maybe she'll share something about his health or whether they were having financial trouble."

"Or you can request an audit of all of Dennis's accounts," Billie said, without thinking. She clamped a hand over her mouth and mumbled around it. "Shit."

Merissa reached over and pulled Billie's hand away. "Spill. What good would it do?"

Billie sighed. She'd crossed the line and made the suggestion. She might as well give her reasons. "I was remembering Dennis's clause about independent audits. If she knew he was on the take, she'd fight it. Or, she might have been skimming off the top, and he found out. If she was as involved with the books as you seemed to think, this would be a good way to get to her."

"Meaning you like my plan."

Billie actually did. Ulterior motives aside, Merissa was interested in possibly buying the firm, and she had a right to call this meeting and to ask for an audit. The seeds of information and misinformation she would sow were only hearsay, and might really provoke the reactions she was hoping for. The main trouble was, this was Merissa and not some hypothetical person. She was alive and smiling and lying next to Billie in bed. Billie wasn't going to condone anything—no matter how reasonable or effective it might be—if it meant she'd be in danger.

"I like my plan better. Have nothing more to do with the Morgan Group. You are talented and you have a vision for the city. You can be successful elsewhere."

Merissa's smile faded. "Yes, I could find another job and another mentor. And I probably will. But Dennis gave me so much, and I owe him this. All I'll do is meet with Karen and call Jeff and Edwin. Afterward, I promise to follow all your rules and not go anywhere alone or trust anyone or have predictable patterns. We can see what happens, and immediately go to the police if any of them makes a move."

Billie shook her head. She wanted to give Merissa what she needed—a chance to find Dennis's killer. She just couldn't accept the risks involved with Merissa's plan. "What if I say no again?"

Merissa shrugged. "You have to sleep sometime. I'd rather do this with you watching my back than alone, though."

Billie shook her head again. She had no doubt Merissa would sneak out and do this on her own if she had to, because she truly thought she was doing what was right for Dennis and for justice. Billie couldn't let her do this alone, without anyone close to protect her. Merissa seemed to sense her starting to cave, and she shifted on the bed until she was straddling Billie's thighs and her face was only an inch from Billie's.

"I owe you one," she said, leaning forward for a kiss.

❖

Merissa meant her kiss to be one of gratitude because Billie had accepted her plan. Billie might not like it, or be convinced it would work, but she would be there for Merissa, and she had no doubt she could trust Billie with her life.

Like their first kiss, this one stayed chaste for a long time, although Merissa's reaction was anything but sweet and innocent. Her lips barely brushed Billie's, and she felt herself getting wet. Their noses bumped as she tilted her head and kissed the corners of Billie's mouth, and her belly clenched in anticipation. She had pushed Billie out of her comfort zone more than once since they met, but Billie was getting her revenge right now. Merissa's entire body was uncomfortable—in the best way possible.

She wanted to open her mouth, to use her teeth, to do whatever it took to drive Billie wild, but she held back and feathered kisses across Billie's cheekbones. Her hands were on Billie's shoulders, and she felt the residual tension from her nightmare. Merissa would wait until the only tightness left in Billie was a need to come, and then she would help her with that release as well.

Merissa returned her attention to Billie's mouth, and they drank each other in with a slow and delicate kiss. Merissa felt her own achingly taut muscles relaxing under Billie's hands as they kneaded her hips and pulled her closer. She wasn't being entirely selfless with her insistence on holding back their passion. She had been disturbed by Billie's nightmare, too. She'd had bad dreams in her life, of course, especially in these days following Dennis's murder, but she had never experienced anything like what she saw happening to Billie. Her flailing arms, trying to get some invisible object or person off her. Her rasping voice as she strangled her screams. Her vacant eyes staring blindly at something Merissa would never see. Merissa stretched out on top of her so their bodies pressed together from corner to corner and she turned her head to allow Billie better access to the sensitive skin on her neck. Billie's tongue traced a fiery trail, helping to erase the image of her in pain, unseeing, crying out for her friend.

Merissa gasped when Billie's teeth caught her earlobe with a gentle pinch. Billie still had her secrets, and Merissa had a feeling it would be years before she'd openly talk about her experiences in the army. She'd shared so much of herself with Merissa, though, parts of her childhood Merissa doubted anyone else knew. Merissa herself rarely told anyone about her past, but once she trusted someone with who she was, she gave herself completely. She wouldn't hold anything back from Billie right now. Could she accept something different from Billie?

She felt Billie sigh beneath her, as the tension from the dreams faded a bit more, replaced by an increased urgency in their movement together. "Thank you for holding me," Billie whispered, her tongue flicking against Merissa's ear and adding emphasis to her words. "These nightmares are usually hidden from everyone, but I'm glad you were here."

Merissa smiled and burrowed closer. Yes, she could live with the secrets that would eventually be told if she and Billie gave this attraction between them a chance to grow. Merissa had been feeling like a helpless pawn for a week now, pushed and pulled in different directions because of the murder, but Billie made her feel strong again. Necessary.

She opened Billie's legs with a firm nudge of her knee and settled between them, controlling and building the pace between them. Billie had only known her in this weakened state, bewildered by the unexpected and frightening events in her life, but Merissa wanted Billie to know her strength as well. Her demanding and stubborn sides, her determination and drive. All the dimensions that usually were part of her but had been missing lately, leaving her flat. Deflated.

Merissa thrust herself tightly against Billie and paused, feeling the heat and wetness building where they were joined, and then released the pressure and moved away. She heard Billie's response in her breath. A gasping inhale, a longing exhale. Billie tugged on her hips, urging her closer again, but Merissa got on her knees between Billie's legs and pulled her satiny nightshirt over her head. Billie followed, propping herself on her elbows and sucking Merissa's nipple into her mouth firmly and abruptly. Merissa's illusion that she was in control shattered, and her hips jerked in response as she nearly came from the exquisite sensation of Billie's warm mouth and teeth against her. She pushed Billie back against the bed and tugged her tank top up to her neck—not wanting to pause long enough to pull it all the way off—and lowered her head to Billie's breast. Her touch was as restrained as Billie's had been determined, and she teased and tickled with her tongue until Billie could no longer remain still.

Merissa shifted until she and Billie were looking directly at each other. She wanted to speak, to tell Billie how much she wanted and needed her, to whisper *yes* or *more* or the other words she used during sex to connect herself to the woman she was with, but she didn't need to say or ask for anything. The connection between them was undeniably there, not requiring talk or direction. When she wanted more pressure, Billie sensed it and responded. When Billie's eyes fluttered closed as she came close to orgasm, Merissa seemed to know the exact moment to drive against her and bring them both to climax. She shuddered in Billie's arms and was gripped tightly as their bodies settled back into a soft, pulsing rhythm.

Billie wrapped her arms around Merissa and rolled until she was on her side, their legs still entwined. As the intensity of sex abated, Merissa felt herself sink deeper into Billie's arms, closer to sleep. At the same time, she sensed Billie's agitation rising again. She moved until their bodies were apart and faced Billie, her head propped on her curved arm and her free hand lightly touching Billie's dark hair where it fell in a wave across the side of her face.

"What's wrong?"

"Nothing. You felt wonderful...*we* felt wonderful together." Billie glanced away, and then at Merissa again. "I wasn't expecting this, but I've wanted to feel you close to me for a long time now. I guess the effects of the nightmare take some time to dissipate all the way."

"Try again," Merissa said with a smile, tracing her fingers over the curves and hollows of Billie's cheek.

Billie sighed, and Merissa felt the movement arc through her hand and into her heart. Pain, worry, guilt. She knew the emotions must be part of Billie's dreams, but they were aggravated by the present. By Merissa. "Tell me what's wrong," she insisted.

Billie shook her head. "Yesterday at the stables, Don managed to get all the way to the car, and I didn't realize he was there. He told me he was surprised, that usually no one could get close without me sensing it, and he was right. I need to be alert, Merissa. To be aware of everything going on around us, not so wrapped up in you that the rest of the world, including people who want to hurt you, can slip inside my defenses. He warned me not to get so close I couldn't protect you. I wish we   "

Merissa put her fingers over Billie's mouth to stop the sentence, and then cupped her chin and kept Billie's eyes on her. "Don't regret this. Please. It meant something real to me to be here for you when you woke up. And it meant even more to feel connected like we did."

Billie put her hand on Merissa's waist and dragged her thumb over her lower ribs. "I don't regret it. And I want more of you, of us, but not now. Not until I know you're safe."

Merissa closed her eyes for a moment, letting her fingers continue their journey from Billie's chin to her neck and to the swell of her breasts. Billie was pulling away because she cared too much. Merissa didn't agree with Billie's decision, but she had to recognize the depth of emotion behind it. If Merissa didn't matter so much, Billie wouldn't have felt the need for distance and objectivity.

"I think you're wrong," Merissa said, using the work-roughened pads of her fingers to urge Billie's nipple to grow tight and erect. Billie's body strained toward her even as Billie's mind wanted to disconnect. "You care about your team, don't you? You've let them be part of your life. Do you think you wouldn't do whatever it took to keep them safe?"

"Of course," Billie said, her breath hitching when Merissa squeezed her taut nipple. "But you're different. If anything happened to you because I got careless..."

Merissa smoothed her hand across Billie's stomach, feeling the waves of reaction follow her touch. She barely brushed against delicate strands of hair before changing course and easing her hand down Billie's thigh.

"You really want us to take a step back?"

Billie hesitated. "Yes," she said finally, sounding as if it took tremendous effort to push the word out.

"Starting now? Or later?" Merissa slid a finger through Billie's wetness and used her palm to apply gentle pressure and keep Billie's hips still.

"Later." The word came out as a gasp, and Merissa swirled her finger around Billie's clit, increasing pressure until Billie arched against her and cried her name.

Merissa traced a line up Billie's abdomen and chest with a damp finger. "So," she said in a long breath. "Starting now?"

"Later," Billie repeated, flipping Merissa on her back with a suddenness that made her laugh. She lowered her mouth to Merissa's navel and licked a circle around it. She raised her head and looked at Merissa with a wicked grin. "Much, much later."

Chapter Eighteen

Merissa tapped on the open door to Dennis's office and waited until Karen looked up from her calculator and nodded for her to enter. Merissa sat in the chair opposite her, feeling a stab of sadness when she remembered how many times she had sat like this with Dennis, sharing ideas and arguments and mock insults across the dark walnut desk. No matter how boring his plans had become, in person he had been as vibrant and brilliant as always. She blinked away the heat of threatening tears.

"Hello, Merissa, dear. You're earlier than I expected, and my lawyer isn't here with the papers yet." Karen gave her a perfect small smile with the perfect little sigh as it faded away. The appropriately grieving widow. The act felt fake to Merissa, but she wondered if she was only searching desperately for someone to blame for Dennis's shooting. Her desire for justice was clouding her judgment, and everyone seemed like a potential murderer to her.

"Hi, Karen," she answered, matching her in tone and expression. "I guess I wanted to walk around the office for a while before we started. It feels so empty without Dennis in it, but at the same time I feel closest to him here." Actually, she had been hoping for another chance to snoop around, but Karen's presence had foiled that.

Karen gathered some loose papers and stuffed them in a folder. "I'm here for the same reason," she said. "I feel closer to him here, where he loved to be. Even more than in our home."

Merissa reached out and picked up a wood and brass toy gyroscope. She had given it to Dennis last Christmas, but she didn't feel comfortable asking to take it back. She spun the inner wheel. "I know he was trying to change that and spend more time with you. I'm sure the memories of having him around more lately must be a comfort to you."

Karen snorted, and Merissa looked at her in surprise. It was the first honest-feeling reaction she had heard from Karen so far.

"It might have been a comfort twenty years ago, dear, but not now. To tell you the truth, we spent most of the past few months arguing." Karen shook her head. "What an awful thing to admit," she said quietly, and Merissa felt like the rest of the room—including herself—receded, and Karen was talking to herself.

"Almost forty years of marriage. I spent most of them fighting with him to stop working so much." Her voice took on an exaggerated nagging tone. "*Spend time with me and the kids. Take me on dates, on vacations, out to dinner.* After a while, I gave up and was resigned to having an absent, workaholic husband. And eventually, I rediscovered myself. I found hobbies, new friends, a whole life I'd given up when I got married. And then he decides he wants to be around more."

Karen looked at Merissa as if surprised to see her there. She held out one hand in a beseeching manner. "Don't get me wrong. I've always loved him, but he had a life separate from me here at the office. It took me years to figure it out, but I made a life of my own, with him as only a small part of it. I adapted, and when he suddenly was around more, I was as resentful as he used to be when I'd plead with him to spend more time at home. I finally got what I had been asking for, and I didn't want it anymore. Do I sound like a horrible person?"

The last sentence was barely audible, and Merissa shook her head automatically. She wasn't sure if she was absolving Karen of her guilt or if she was just sad because of the story. She wondered if one of Karen's new hobbies had been a lover. Would she have killed Dennis to get him out of the way, while not giving up the monetary benefits of his workaholic lifestyle? Maybe the lover had decided he was done with being the man on the side and had wanted to step more fully into Karen's life. Getting rid of Dennis might have seemed like his only option.

"I understand how the two of you could have grown apart," Merissa said. She thought of Billie, who was likely pacing back and forth under the window behind Karen, ready to catch Merissa if she decided to jump again. As much as Merissa loved her job, she wouldn't sacrifice a relationship with someone like Billie for it. And she knew Billie would be the same. She had grown up as the sacrifice in her dad's attempt to earn more for his family. Merissa was certain she wouldn't want to be on either end of the deal ever again. Dennis had been different. When she had first started—and even during the past year—Dennis had always been here, whether she had come in early or stayed late. He never turned down an opportunity to go on one of their scouting trips, when they'd spend most of the day driving and talking and having lunch together. She could understand Karen's resentment and her gradual drift away from Dennis.

"We did grow apart." Karen fidgeted with the calculator while Merissa played with the gyroscope. Neither met the other's eyes. "And it was awkward when he tried to fit back into the life I'd made. Early in our marriage, I was the one who changed and compromised to fit in *his* life. Things changed when he wasn't looking. Still, I believe we would have grown closer again, somehow. Especially since he was talking about retiring."

"Retiring?" Merissa repeated. She had seen the papers and knew Dennis had been thinking of selling the firm, but she didn't realize he had shared the news with Karen.

Karen looked at her. "Yes. I tried to convince him to stay with the firm, maybe slow down and gradually taper off. He was too young and active to retire. He'd have been bored out of his mind, and not having this job would have driven him crazy."

Driven both of them crazy, Merissa decided. "Sounds like your marriage was his top priority. Unless there was another reason for him to want to retire. I'd noticed some of his designs were growing sort of, well, repetitious. Maybe he was feeling tired and stagnant at work. He seemed as sharp as usual when I saw him here, but was he having any health issues?"

Merissa didn't think Karen was a good enough actress to pull off the shocked expression she had on her face, from her raised eyebrows to her short-lived stutter as she answered Merissa.

"Dennis might have had some human failings as a husband, but as a designer he's never been anything but brilliant. Are you accusing him of being senile? Or just growing too stale to keep up with a young, up-and-coming urban planner like you, with the international diploma your grandfather bought you."

Whoa, time to back off. Merissa put her hands out flat, as if she was calming a nervous horse. "I'm not implying either one. If I'm going to buy the firm, I need as much information as possible about the present state of the company. Dennis didn't share the type of details I need with any of us who work here. I didn't even know he wanted to retire until you just told me."

Merissa wasn't sure what graduating from a school in Canada had to do with anything, and she had paid for her own tuition and expenses, never touching a penny of her grandfather's money. She kept her defensive reaction to Karen's words to herself, though, since getting into an argument wouldn't get her what she needed. Besides, if Billie heard raised voices from her post outside the office, she'd be sure to come barging through the window to Merissa's rescue.

"Dennis had a style that worked for him and for his investors," she continued while Karen visibly fought for control over her emotions. "It made sense for him to be consistent with his plans, and I only thought the repetition might have been boring for a designer with his immense talent and gift for innovation."

Merissa worried that she might be laying it on too thick, but Karen gave a little sniff and nodded, looking mollified.

"I don't know about the designs you're talking about, since I had so little to do with the company, but you're right—he was a genius in his field. I only hope you learned enough from him while you had the chance, and that you appreciated the knowledge he shared." Karen stood up and tossed the calculator onto the desk. "I'd hate to see this firm ever fold, ruining his good reputation and the years of hard work he put into making it a success. I hear my lawyers out in the lobby. Let's meet in the conference room."

Merissa fumed for a moment before she got up and followed Karen out of the office. She was tempted to call for backup after the unveiled insult and have Billie come in and punch Karen. Or maybe they could follow Karen's car after this meeting, until she committed some traffic infraction and Billie could give her a massive ticket. She wasn't convinced Billie would do either one, especially since Merissa wasn't in any real danger, but the imagined look on Karen's face made her smile.

Merissa walked down the familiar hallway toward the conference room. She still wasn't sure how truthful Karen was being. She honestly hadn't seemed aware of the downward spiral of Dennis's plans lately, but Merissa was sure Karen had more of a handle on the firm's accounts and business than she claimed. Her anger might be intended to cover up a decline in his health or to downplay her own relief that Dennis wasn't hanging around long enough to retire and drive her mad. She seemed oddly determined to preserve the company that had taken Dennis's time and energy away from her during the earlier stages of their marriage. Merissa could explain the discrepancy either by greed—Karen wanted to make a huge profit from selling the firm—or from a sense of vengeance. Did she want to squeeze as much money as possible out of the company, thereby getting her revenge for the years and love it seemed to have taken from her?

Either way, the audit would stall the negotiations enough to give her time to really decide what she wanted, while letting Karen and the legal team believe she was ready to buy. If she sounded like a window-shopper, she wouldn't get the info she and Billie needed, either from Karen or from Lemaine and Kensington.

She put her navy leather briefcase on the table next to her and shook hands with the lawyers when Karen introduced them. Mr. Kerslake and Mr. Ross of Kerslake, Ross, and Peters. Merissa couldn't help but wonder about the missing Mr. or Ms. Peters, but she saved her questions for the necessary, not the merely curious.

After an initial walk-through of the contract, Merissa paused and flipped through the pages once more to give herself time to collect herself. The price Karen was asking was huge, and Merissa wished she had her grandfather's skills in negotiating just for one day. She pursed her lips, trying to look thoughtful and unswayed by the figures they were tossing about so casually.

"I'll need to see the books for the past five years, so I can prepare my counteroffer," she said, implying there was no way in hell she was agreeing to this initial price tag. The tactic gave her time, as well, for her and Billie to look over Dennis's finances.

Karen and the two men carried on some sort of unspoken conversation, made up of vague nods and shakes of the head before one of them answered her.

"Of course, Ms. Karr. We'll make copies and have them messaged to you," said Mr. Kerslake.

"Thank you," Merissa said. She slid the single sheet of paper out of her folder. Dennis's handwritten clauses. "I'd also like to consult you about drafting a partnership agreement, incorporating the following clauses."

She cleared her throat and read the list a little too loudly, but once she started in her imperious tone she'd have felt even sillier switching to a more normal voice, so the entire list was read as if she was a town crier announcing the latest edict from the king. She finally got to the last clause and she set the paper down with a sigh of relief. She'd glanced at Karen after every item, trying to determine whether or not she'd been aware of Dennis's plans for the firm, but Karen watched her with a slightly puzzled expression. When she finished, there was another flurry of nonverbal communication among Karen and the lawyers.

"May I see the list?" Mr. Ross reached for it and reread it silently, his fingers steepled under his chin. "You do realize you'll be the sole owner of the firm, don't you, Ms. Karr?" he asked as he pushed the paper along the table to Mr. Kerslake. "You'll be able to choose contractors using any criteria you wish. You don't need us to put it into writing for you."

"True," Merissa said, lengthening the tiny word while she searched for some reasonable explanation to give him. *I wanted to see the grieving widow's reaction to them* sounded too callous. "But

Dennis's death suggests to me that a partnership may be the way to go. And I'd rather have these details worked out now."

The three seemed to reach a consensus. "Of course, we'll be glad to draft a document incorporating these clauses," Kerslake said. "We'll also need time to find a suitable auditor."

"Perfect," Merissa said. Time was exactly what she wanted. She thanked everyone and left the room, wishing she could hover outside the door and hear what they had to say about her partnership bombshell—especially Karen—but Dennis had made sure his conference rooms were soundproof and private. Even with her ear to the door, she wasn't able to hear anything.

"What are you doing?"

Merissa jumped at the sound of Billie's voice. "Eavesdropping," she said, without a hint of guilt.

Billie grinned. "Hear anything good?"

"Just you. The damned door is too thick. Why did you come inside?"

Billie grabbed her hand and led her outside. "You were taking so long, and I was getting nervous. I sent a text. Well, maybe a few texts."

"My phone was turned off." Merissa pulled it out of her briefcase as they walked up the hill toward Billie's car. "Time for part two of the plan."

She was about to enter Kensington's number when Billie closed her hand over Merissa's and stopped her. She used her other hand to sift through Merissa's hair and tuck it behind her ear. "You don't have to do this. I don't want you doing anything that might put you in danger. I'm sorry about Dennis, but I can't risk losing you on the off chance this little scheme of yours gets the wrong person angry."

"We need to find out the truth," Merissa said, although the thought of leaving all this pain and fear behind and letting herself see only a new future—one with Billie in it—was terribly appealing.

"The truth isn't worth your safety."

Merissa shook her head, not because she disagreed with Billie, but because she wasn't sure what she believed anymore. "I've gone this far. I'll call Lemaine and Kensington, and if nothing comes of it, then I'll back off."

Billie didn't say she approved, but she released Merissa's hand and let her dial.

Merissa called Lemaine first. She told him she was thinking of buying the business and hoped they would be able to work together, but that she would spread her business among other contractors as well. With Kensington, she said she was going to buy the firm and would follow Dennis's precedent and work solely with Lemaine.

She managed to get through the calls with only a slight shake in her voice. Billie's hand on her lower back—steadying, supporting, protecting—kept her calm enough to speak. She was accustomed to dealing directly and honestly with people after years of watching her grandfather manipulate and prevaricate. She didn't want to be like him, whether in business or in her personal life, but here she was, fibbing to Karen, her legal team, and these two men all in the space of an hour. She ended the call to Jeff and powered down her phone, glad to be back to the present with the frank and honest Billie.

"Well?" Billie asked as they started walking up the hill again. "Did you get a sense of their reactions? I couldn't tell anything from your side of the conversation."

Merissa sighed. "I learned disappointingly little. I guess I expected some concrete evidence to come out after all this planning and fuss. Maybe even an outraged admission of guilt," she admitted with a slight smile. "But they were both professional. If you could hear a shrug in someone's voice, I heard it in Lemaine's. I got the sense he thinks of me as an amateur and not worth his time, like his attention was shifting to the next order of business in his day even before he said good-bye."

Merissa attempted to keep her disappointment hidden, but the bump from Billie's shoulder made it clear she hadn't been successful. Aside from solving Dennis's murder, she had sort of been hoping for more reaction over the potential loss of her business, but why would either man really care? She didn't have Dennis's credentials or his experience. What she did have were a handful of design ideas and enough money to buy the firm. She shook off the sinking sense of self-worth. She grabbed Billie's hand and gave it a squeeze, anchoring herself in the here and now. She didn't have to judge herself by impossibly high standards just because she had been born into wealth.

She continued with her assessment of the calls. "Jeff Kensington sounded disappointed but resigned. I suppose Dennis led him on so many times he was relieved to hear me come right out and say I wouldn't ever work with him."

"It was worth a shot," Billie said. "And until we're sure neither one will retaliate, I'm going to stay so close you won't know where I end and you begin."

Merissa felt her face relax into a genuine and happy smile. "In that case, let's hurry home so you can take up your guard duty post in the bedroom."

CHAPTER NINETEEN

Billie was off the sofa bed and halfway across the room before she even noticed she was awake. She stood still in the darkness for a moment while she tried to recapture the details of the nightmare. She had been crouched on the dusty ground, covering her teammates as they crossed an open street in the twilight shadows. Her grip had been loose on her rifle, ready to tighten and aim if necessary but not so tense she might overcommit to a harmless stray sound or movement. Something had caught her attention, but she couldn't remember what it was. A silhouette glimpse of someone lying in wait? A snap of a twig or scuttle of a kicked pebble? The smell of foreign cigarette smoke?

Whatever it had been, it had signaled danger. A haunting one from her past, or a chilling one in the present? She quietly walked to the window and stood to one side while she looked across the pastures and outbuildings. She barely registered the flicker of movement on the path leading to the upper barns before she was pushing away from the wall and hurrying to the front door of the apartment.

She picked up her gun and boots and carefully shut the door behind her, not wanting to wake Merissa who was sleeping in the bedroom, and ran down the steps in bare feet. She paused briefly to pull on her boots at the bottom of the staircase. She had been tempted last night when Merissa had made it clear she'd have willingly shared the bed with Billie again, but Billie hadn't been able to say yes. She couldn't risk Merissa by letting her guard down. She had slept better the night before than she had for years—albeit not for long after their hours of lovemaking. Would she have been as sensitive to the danger outside the apartment if she'd been nestled in Merissa's arms? She focused on that aspect of her decision to sleep on the couch. If she managed to protect her own heart while protecting Merissa, it was only a bonus. She had gotten very close very fast, and she was already feeling a sort of dependence. She had been slow to fall asleep last night, and her nightmares had been bad. She couldn't rely on Merissa or anyone else for her sanity. She had let it happen for one night, and the lack of Merissa's touch had made the usual nighttime problems seem nearly unbearable.

The tangible proof of her need to stay detached was moving stealthily through the night ahead of her, although she wasn't sure why someone coming after Merissa would head away from the house and the barn apartment. She stopped for a moment and scanned the property behind her in case this was just a distraction, meant to lure her away from Merissa, but everything seemed still. She resumed her original course with her pistol held at her side. She hadn't been through these upper barns before tonight, but the moon lit her path well enough for her to move without making a sound. The person she followed either wasn't as skilled in stealth tactics, or didn't realize she was trailing behind. Either way, whoever it was moved without trying to stay hidden or remaining quiet.

She had nearly caught up to the intruder when the barn door opened in front of her and the person turned on the overhead lights. Billie recognized Jean-Yves as her eyes adjusted to the bright lights. She tucked her gun in the waistband of her sweatpants, ready to draw it if necessary, and stepped out of the dark shadows.

Jean-Yves nearly bumped into her as he was coming out of a feed room to her right, and he yelped and dropped the bandages he had in his arms.

"Where'd you come from?" he asked, bending down to pick up the bandages. "Were you following me?"

"Were you sneaking around in the middle of the night?" Billie countered. She retrieved one of the bandages that had rolled away from him. She wiped off the dirt from the floor and handed it to him. He didn't look like someone up to no good, unless his thermos was full of chloroform instead of coffee and the strips of cotton were meant to tie Merissa's wrists together.

"One of the horses up here has an injured leg, and I need to soak it every few hours." He turned away from her and walked down the aisle, but stopped a few yards away.

"I'm looking out for her, too, you know," he said without looking back at Billie.

She sighed and rubbed her eyes. "I know."

He continued walking and unlatched a stall door. "While you're here, you might as well help me."

She studied him for a moment. "Are you planning to club me over the head with your thermos once I'm inside the stall?"

"Maybe," he said with a shrug. "Are you planning to shoot me with your gun?"

Billie moved the pistol so it rested against her lower back, still comfortably close and accessible, but less visible. "Truce?"

"Truce."

She went after him into the stall and gasped when she saw the small bay horse huddled in the corner. Every bone seemed to be on display, and his coat was patchy and rough. All four legs were wrapped in colorful bandages like the ones Jean-Yves carried, but she could see swelling above and below the cotton on the horse's left foreleg.

She slowly approached the gelding and held out her hand for him to sniff. He didn't seem interested in making the effort, so she carefully rubbed his forehead and neck.

"What happened to him?"

"Neglect and starvation to name just two."

His voice sounded as angry as Billie felt inside. Merissa couldn't possibly be responsible for this. She turned to face Jean-Yves, and he held up his hands as if to fend off an attack. "Not here, so put your hackles down. All the animals in these upper barns are rescues."

He knelt next to the horse and started unwrapping one of its legs, and Billie did the same on the opposite side.

"Merissa runs an animal rescue here?" she asked as she unwound a long strip of flannel. She felt as if she had been constantly revising her opinion of Merissa since the moment they met. Every layer peeled away gave Billie a new idea of the woman behind the controlled and elegant exterior, just like she'd had to get past the extravagant and cool front rooms of the mansion to get to Merissa's hidden, cozy suite.

"A local group was about to fold because it couldn't afford operating costs anymore. These barns were empty, and Merissa offered them to the rescue. Rub his legs like this, to help with circulation." Jean-Yves massaged the horse's bare leg while he spoke, switching between instructions to Billie and comments about Merissa without pausing in between. "She doesn't actually run the rescue, but she's on the board and she pays for most of the bills, including vet care, feed, and boarding. Without her, who knows where these horses would be now."

Billie remained silent as she finished with the foreleg and followed Jean-Yves as he changed position to work on the horse's hind legs. She hadn't completely lost her doubts about his loyalty to Merissa and had still had him on her list of suspects...until she heard him speak just now. The same respect and admiration and concern for Merissa that Billie was feeling were apparent in Jean-Yves's voice. He was no more likely to have broken into her room and changed the photos than Billie was.

He rewrapped the horse with practiced skill and showed Billie through the barn, introducing her to the various residents. The horses here couldn't compete with Mariposa and the other highly bred polo ponies in Merissa's main barn, but Jean-Yves's pride in them was as clear as his devotion to Merissa. He described in detail the state each had been in when it arrived at the farm, and pointed out all the positive changes in coats, hooves, and general condition. Billie would gladly have followed him through the other barns as well, but she made herself thank him and say good night after touring just the first one. She felt a lingering tension after thinking an intruder had been on the farm, and she needed to get back to the apartment and Merissa.

She jogged down the sloping driveway, keeping on the grassy border where her footfalls were masked instead of on the noisy gravel even though the night's threat seemed to have been a false one. Her progress around the main barn areas was silent, and she froze at the sound of movement coming from inside the dark arena. She glanced over her shoulder and saw the light in the upper barn. Jean-Yves's form was just visible moving near the doorway, and she knew Merissa would approach her directly if she was out here. Billie crept forward, her breathing slow and even, until she came to the end of the arena's long wall.

Someone was definitely moving around inside the arena. She inched toward the large sliding doors and drew her gun in a fluid motion as she pulled open one side, hoping to use the element of surprise to her advantage.

Unfortunately, the horse inside the arena beat her to it. Billie got a glimpse of the tall liver chestnut coming at her before she tried to move out of its path. She wasn't quick enough, and the horse spun her around as it careened into her shoulder and out the door.

"Shit," she said, picking up her dropped gun and tucking it back into her waistband. The horse—she recognized it now as Agincourt, one of the young horses Merissa was training—had none of Billie's concern about moving quietly as he trotted along the gravel path to the sound of pebbles ringing against metal horseshoes. Billie sprinted after him, stopping just long enough to grab a halter from the nearest stall as they passed by the main barn.

Agincourt stopped for a mouthful of grass, but moved on again as soon as Billie got close enough to touch him. She cursed and followed him to the next tempting patch of greenery, trying to keep her demeanor calm and unthreatening.

"Hey, fella," she said in a sing-song voice. "I just want to pet you. Don't pay any attention to the halter I'm holding. Damn!"

She stomped after him as he moved away from her reaching hand and swerved toward the main house. She circled around and tried to herd him back toward the safety of the barn. The path to the main road was blocked by the closed iron gate, but he still had acres of land to use for evasive purposes. An easy leap over the gate on the path leading to the trails, and he'd have miles of forest in which to get lost or hurt. She finally got him heading down a dead-end path between two pastures, but he turned around and came toward her at a brisk trot. She tried to block his way, but he feinted right and then whipped past her to the left, using all his polo skills to make her look like a fool. Billie swore again and ran after him.

She lost count of how many times the horse let her get within grabbing distance before running off again. She stopped to catch her breath and push her sweaty bangs out of her eyes when she heard the swish of grain in a bucket. She looked behind her and saw Merissa standing there with a rubber feed tub in her hands.

Billie's frustration melted away at the sight of Merissa so close to her. She was wearing a short robe made of a silky lavender material, belted at the waist and with a deep V in the front, through which the lacy top edge of a camisole was visible. The robe stopped midthigh, and the memory of those slender but muscular legs wrapped around Billie's hips made her sweat more than the exertion of chasing the horse had.

Merissa's hair was wild and sleep tousled, and a pair of tall work boots covered her calves. The combination of delicate satiny beauty with the mud-encrusted rubber of her boots was more stunning than either look could have been on its own. Ethereally gorgeous and exquisitely sexy. Practical and down to earth. A dreamer and a hard worker. Merissa was all of them at once. While talking to Jean-Yves in the upper barns, Billie had been thinking she had found Merissa's true nature the deeper she got—whether in her home or on her farm—but each layer only added to the one before and didn't cancel it out. Merissa was everything at once.

Billie took an automatic step back. She wasn't really afraid of getting to know Merissa so deeply, or of discovering how her attraction grew stronger with every new thing she learned about her. What scared Billie most was her desire to let Merissa see all the different sides and angles of her as well. To show Merissa all her contradictory, muddled, mixed-up emotions and traits.

Billie took another step away as the damned horse trotted directly to Merissa and stuck his nose in the grain bucket.

"What's going on?" Merissa asked as she easily looped a lead rope around the horse's neck. "I was worried when I noticed you weren't in the apartment and I came looking for you."

"I needed some exercise, so I was out here for a midnight jog. I guess Agincourt had the same idea."

Merissa gave an exasperated sounding sigh, and Billie stopped joking around. "Fine. I saw someone moving around the property and I came out to investigate. I followed him to the upper barn before I realized it was Jean-Yves."

"He has some horses that need to be cared for every few hours," Merissa said, resting her hand on the chestnut's neck.

"I know. I saw them. I think what you're doing for the rescue horses is wonderful."

Merissa waved off her compliment. "So how did Aggie get out?"

"What was he doing in the arena overnight?" Billie countered, crossing her arms over her chest and hugging herself as she finally noticed the cold night air seeping through her thin shirt. Even though neither threat had panned out as a real one, she had still experienced surges of adrenaline and the tension of being on high alert. Now that both incidents were over, she was dropping fast.

"I didn't want him cooped up in a stall all night before his first polo match, so I let him stay in there where he could move around if he wanted to. But let's get the two of you into the barn before you freeze. I think he's worked out most of his kinks by now."

Billie followed Merissa into the barn. She felt a little silly about her inability to catch Agincourt—why hadn't she thought to run into the feed room for some tempting grain?—and she wondered how much of their antics Merissa had seen before she stepped in and caught the horse. At least the sight of Merissa's rear end, barely covered by the flimsy robe, was enough to distract her from her embarrassment, and she focused all her attention there while they walked. She was barely functioning as the fatigue of assuaged worry overwhelmed her and she leaned against the wall while Merissa shut the horse into an empty stall with the remaining grain.

Merissa came over to her and gently pried the halter Billie had been holding out of her tight grip. She brushed her fingertips over Billie's face, tracing her cheekbone and jawline.

"You look exhausted," she said. "I don't want you to wear yourself out worrying about me."

"I'm fine. Just tired," Billie said. She was barely able to string words into sentences, but she needed to explain what had happened. "When I was coming back from the upper barn, I heard a noise coming from the arena. I opened the door to investigate, and Agincourt ran out."

Merissa shook her head. "Were you having one of your nightmares before you went outside? Is that why you panicked when you saw Jean-Yves?"

"I didn't panic," Billie said with a flash of indignation, although she had been rash in both instances. She should have recognized Jean-Yves sooner. And she should have realized the noises she heard in the arena were equine and not human. "I just want to keep you safe. I *need* to keep you safe."

"I know. But you have to take care of yourself as well and not let your nightmares and your memories make you see danger where there's none."

Billie sighed and leaned into Merissa's touch. The sound of swishing tails and horses shifting in their stalls and the woody scent of clean shavings were familiar and comforting as she became more aware of her surroundings. Merissa's hand was familiar, too, even after such a short time knowing her. Coursing with life and roughened by work and riding, Merissa's palm cradled Billie's head and gave her strength. Merissa was right. Billie usually needed time to recover after her dreams, slowly disentangling the past from the present. Most days, the pull backward in time was strong, but now her need to protect Merissa was even stronger. Billie had been catapulted to the present, but she hadn't been able to separate the fear and danger she felt in her nightmares from her perception of what was happening in real life.

Merissa rubbed her hands briskly over Billie's arms. "Let's get upstairs where it's warm," she said, taking Billie's hand and pulling her toward the staircase. She paused on the landing and kicked off her muddy boots before leading Billie into the bedroom, bypassing the sofa bed. Billie put her gun on the dresser across the room and dropped onto the bed. Merissa took off her robe and scooted against Billie's back, wrapping her arms around Billie's waist and pulling her close.

Billie moved away just long enough to peel off her sweats and T-shirt. She slid back into Merissa's embrace, reveling in the whisper of satin and bare skin against her back and legs. Exhaustion battled arousal, but Billie knew both sleep and sex were the easy ways to end the night. Instead of opting for either one, she began to talk instead.

"The nightmares are usually about the day my best friend Mike died," she said. She felt Merissa's arms tighten around her, and she was certain Merissa understood what it meant for Billie to talk about this. She'd never told anyone else, not even Beth or her therapists. "Dream-versions of the day, with weird elements added in. Different every time. But some parts are real and the same each time. The layer of grit on my teeth from dust and sand, the smell of cheap cigarette smoke, the explosion, the pain. We were in an alley after a mission, heading back to the landing zone where a chopper was supposed to pick us up…"

Billie talked in fits and starts, pushing herself to get the words out. Merissa held her and stroked her hair as she struggled to give voice to gruesome sights and sounds and sensations she would never be able to forget. She'd always thought that talking about what happened that day would make it worse—more real, if that was even possible—but she felt her body relax as she spoke. Not with the adrenaline-drop exhaustion she was accustomed to feeling after a bad night, but with a soft slide toward sleep. She got to the end of her story, and instead of despair and hurt she felt only a sense of being emptied out.

Merissa kissed her temple when Billie fell silent. "Thank you," she whispered. "Both for telling me, and for trying to save me tonight."

"I will always try to save you," Billie said, barely floating through consciousness on her way to a hopefully dreamless sleep. "And thank you for listening to me."

CHAPTER TWENTY

Billie woke with the sun, tangled in the sheets and with Merissa. She'd only had a few hours of sleep after her nighttime recon adventures and she'd worn herself out talking to Merissa about her past, but she felt more refreshed than she had in ages. She was awake and present, not ragged from being torn out of her nightmares.

Merissa stirred against her, sending shivers of pleasure through Billie's body. She wanted to wake Merissa with more than the chaste kiss she gave her, but the day was going to be a full one, and they had polo ponies to groom and haul to the match. Billie kissed Merissa again, and then burrowed her face into the space where Merissa's neck and shoulder met as she felt her stretch and sigh.

"Mmm. Good morning," Merissa said. She propped herself up on one elbow, her hair spilling onto Billie's chest, and smiled at her. "How did you sleep?"

"Great," Billie said with a smile. "Better than I have for a long time."

"I'm glad." Merissa leaned over and kissed her quickly on the mouth. "I'd love to stay in bed all day with you, but we have a long list of things to do this morning."

Billie got out of bed, relieved Merissa hadn't mentioned much about last night. She had found it difficult enough to talk about such intensely personal feelings in the dark, without actually looking at Merissa. She wasn't ready to face her confessions in the light of day. She pulled on a pair of old jeans and layered a sweatshirt and light jacket over a T-shirt. The day would be a chilly one, but she'd be working hard enough to need to shed some clothing later on. She turned around and watched a topless Merissa shimmy into a pair of skintight white breeches. Maybe Cal wouldn't mind if Merissa showed up for the match a little late. Billie was about to toss Merissa back onto the bed and kiss her gorgeous breasts, but Merissa caught her staring and hurriedly put on a sports bra and collared shirt.

"Don't you dare," she said, as if reading Billie's mind.

"Don't dare what?" Billie asked innocently as she walked over and caught Merissa behind the knees, flipping her gently onto the bed and stretching out on top of her.

"Don't you dare make us late," Merissa said, but she giggled as Billie covered her neck with a series of playful, nipping kisses and wrapped her fingers in Billie's hair.

Billie let herself enjoy the feel of Merissa squirming underneath her for a few more moments, and then she got to her feet and pulled Merissa along with her. She caught her in a tight hug, saying thank you the best way she could right now.

"Go feed your horses," she said. "I'll make us some coffee, and then I'll come down and load the van."

Merissa left the apartment door open when she left, and Billie heard the horses neighing for their breakfast while she made a pot of coffee. She tossed a few granola bars in a bag and poured the brewed coffee into a thermos. The horses would eat better than she and Merissa would this morning.

The next two hours were spent grooming horses and braiding their manes and tails, polishing Merissa's tack, and stuffing everything they might need during the day into several large navy blue trunks with Merissa's initials in white block letters. Billie worked alongside Jean-Yves, and she was surprised to find the day untainted by the events of last night. Usually the residue of nightmares colored her waking hours, but today she didn't feel any lingering doubts about Jean-Yves or fear another intruder was lurking in the shadows. She wouldn't let her guard down and risk

Merissa's safety, but the unwarranted and uncontrollable anxiety she had been feeling when she was outside in the dark had faded.

Once they had four horses and as many trunks and saddles loaded onto the van, Jean-Yves caught her arm and pulled her aside. "Protect her," he said.

"With my life," Billie promised, meaning it without hesitation. He nodded and let her go, and she got in the driver's seat of the van. Merissa got in beside her and poured each of them a cup of coffee as soon as Billie navigated the winding driveway and they were on the main road.

Billie followed Merissa's directions south on I-5 and west on Highway 101. They exited and drove through some lush forested areas, dense with fir trees and ferns, before the huge farm where the polo matches would be held opened up in front of them. The grounds were already bustling with people leading, riding, and trailering horses, and Billie slowly drove to the edge of the parking lot where they'd have room to unload the horses and equipment. She and Merissa had just lowered the ramp when Cal came over to greet them.

"Thanks for filling in today, Merissa," she said, peering around her and into the trailer. "It's nice to see you both. Oh, wow. She's even more beautiful than I expected."

"I have a feeling she only asked me here today because she wanted to see my horse," Merissa said to Billie with an exaggerated sigh. "I feel used."

"Nonsense," Cal said as she walked up the ramp to see the mare. "You'll be a valuable member of our team. Oh, did I forget to mention that we're all supposed to trade horses every chukker? I guess I'll have to ride one of yours…maybe this black one."

"Not a chance," Billie said as she moved past Cal and untied Mariposa's lead rope. "I'm bodyguard for both of them today."

Merissa followed her with a gray mare, and Billie looked over her shoulder and smiled when she saw Cal visibly sigh as she unhooked Agincourt and brought him down the ramp. Cal's two grooms came with them on the second and third trips as they unloaded horses and tack and stowed everything in the temporary stabling.

"Great timing, Sarge," Billie said when Rachel finally appeared in the stall where she was grooming Mariposa. "We just got all the heavy trunks unloaded."

Rachel grinned without a shred of guilt. "I know. I was watching from around the corner in case you tried to rope me into helping."

"We'll let you do all the loading when we're done, then." Billie ran a soft finishing cloth over the mare's black coat and brought out even more shine than she'd had before.

Rachel stepped inside and ran her hand over the horse's neck. "This is the one Cal wants, isn't she? I have a feeling she'll be planning a trip to Argentina soon, even though she has so many horses we're about to run out of stalls."

Rachel couldn't hide her fond smile as she spoke, and Billie knew she'd relent even if Cal wanted to buy the entire country's supply of polo ponies. "And you'll go along as what, her conscience? Translator? Girlfriend who lies on the beach?"

"All three, possibly." Rachel stooped down and felt the joints and tendons in the mare's front leg. "Or maybe I'll buy one like her for myself. Can you picture me in dress uniform, riding a horse like this in parades and at state functions? I'd be irresistible."

"Yeah, you'll be the next cover model for *Mounted Police Weekly*." Billie dropped a protective boot on the ground by Rachel's feet. "Make yourself useful while you're down there and put this on her."

Rachel strapped the leather snugly over the mare's delicate cannon bone, and then she stood up. "I walked through the parking lots and the other barns," she said, switching from her joking self to her police sergeant persona without skipping a beat. "I didn't see anything suspicious, but there are so many people here, it's hard to tell who belongs and who doesn't. Stay as close to Merissa as you can today. Cal's grooms will help you with her horses, and I'll keep an eye on her if you need to leave the field and bring one back here to the barn."

"I don't need a babysitter," Merissa called from the stall next door. The walls were made of thin canvas and didn't seem to be soundproof. "I'm not a child."

"I'm not your babysitter," Billie said. "I'm your bodyguard, like you're a movie star."

"She's your groom," Rachel countered. "Who will just happen to be everywhere you are."

"Much better," Merissa said, appearing in the doorway with Agincourt's reins in her hand. "Hey, groom, I'm going to the practice arena now. Mind giving me a leg up?"

Billie rolled her eyes and she and Rachel left Mariposa's stall. "Sure thing, *boss*. Wouldn't want you to strain a precious muscle by getting on the horse by yourself."

Merissa just smiled sweetly at her and bent her knee. Billie took hold of it and gave her a firm lift off the ground, nearly catapulting her across Aggie's back and off the other side. Merissa grabbed his neck and righted herself, laughing and kicking playfully at Billie. "Fine. I'll call you bodyguard from now on."

"Thank you," Billie said, pulling a rag out of her back pocket and dusting Merissa's tall brown boots. "All I want is a little respect."

Cal came over to the group leading her first mount, and Rachel lifted her smoothly into the saddle. The two of them followed the riders as they walked toward the arena, and Billie couldn't keep her eyes off Merissa's seat. She swayed gently in the saddle, keeping time with Agincourt's swinging stride.

"Ah, polo," Rachel said, as if she could read Billie's mind. "The ultimate spectator sport."

Billie couldn't agree more. She leaned her elbows on a fence rail and watched Merissa ride the dark chestnut gelding around the practice ring. She moved fluidly through the crowds of other riders, handling her horse with a nearly invisible touch that only years of hard work and practice combined with natural skill could produce. She was as elegant and graceful in the saddle as she was out of it, and Billie had to remind herself to stop staring at her every once in a while, and scan the other onlookers. There were several teams riding during the day, and each one had brought a number of grooms and supporters, but Billie gradually was able to sort them out in her mind. Everyone seemed to belong, and she hoped the day would prove to be uneventful except for the excitement of the matches.

Rachel had set some folding chairs and a cooler full of drinks and snacks in the shade of an oak tree, and Billie joined her there after giving Merissa some bottled water and a good luck pat on the leg—not that Merissa looked like she needed any luck. Her skills and determination would surely make her the star of the match. Billie uncapped her own water and leaned back in the chair, lifting the collar of her jacket to keep her neck warm. She hadn't noticed the chill in the air when she was working with the horses, but once she was sitting still it was pronounced. Still, a little sunshine streamed around the clouds, and no rain was forecast to make the polo fields miserable and slick.

After a few minutes of the first chukker, Billie forgot about her water and about the cold day. She sat forward with her elbows on her knees and watched Merissa transform on the polo field. Not in a good way. Granted, the team was new to her, but she was an experienced player and should be quick to adapt. Instead, she seemed to play outside the team. She wasn't hogging the ball and trying to make all the spectacular plays by herself, but she also wasn't helping the other players when they had control of the ball. She tended to stay out of their way and she seemed surprised when one of them tried to assist her when she was moving down the field toward the goal. Except for the times when Cal called out instructions to her, she seemed to be playing individual polo instead of a team sport.

"You should get her second horse now," Rachel suggested. "I'll take guard duty while you're gone."

Rachel was frowning as she watched the match, and Billie was sure the same expression was on her own face. She jogged across the pasture and quickly put Mariposa's saddle and bridle on her. She ran back to the field with the mare easily trotting alongside her. Maybe Agincourt's youth and inexperience were keeping Merissa from playing more aggressively as part of a team. Mariposa was bred and trained to be the ultimate polo mount, and Billie was sure Merissa would come to life while riding her.

"He was a good boy," Merissa said with a smile as she handed Agincourt's reins to Billie.

Billie held him with one hand while she gave Merissa a boost onto the mare—more gently this time—with the other. Merissa didn't seem to think there had been anything wrong with her performance in the chukker, and she looked stunning enough for people to stop and gape at her when she rode in the practice arena on Mariposa, so Billie pushed her confusion away and concentrated on getting Aggie untacked and back in his stall and herself back to the arena. She dropped into the folding chair with a tired sigh, but forgot about how hard being a groom really was once she saw Merissa change into a stiffer, less beautiful rider once she was back in the game.

Billie wondered why Merissa's connection and comfort disappeared when she rode the few yards from the practice ring to the performance one, but she kept silent on the subject until she and Merissa were alone in a corner of the field with Aggie during the break after the third period of play.

"You've been quiet today," Merissa said. "Are you still worried something might happen while we're here?"

Billie shrugged. "It seems safe enough, but we can't get complacent. I guess I'm just confused about something."

"What is it?" Merissa asked, pulling off her helmet and fluffing out her sweaty blond hair.

Billie tamped down her desire to help by running her fingers through those silky locks. "You seem to change when you ride onto the field." She hesitated. "Remember when you rode Ranger at our practice session? You were trying to be the leader and have him be the horse, instead of working as a team. You do the same thing with the other riders."

"What are you saying? That I'm bossing them around?"

"No, not at all." Billie frowned at the angry tone in Merissa's voice. "I just think you're used to being independent. In everything you do, whether it's on the polo field or at work or in your personal life. You don't seem to trust anyone else on the field, whether it's your horse or your teammates. You look like you're on a third team of one during the game."

Merissa raised her eyebrows in surprise, and Billie saw hurt and shock in her expression. "Thanks for the riding lesson, but I do just fine when I play polo. I'm new to this team, so maybe I don't appear to belong with them as easily as Cal does. You might have more experience with your police horses than I do, but I've been playing this sport since I was a child. If I want advice on improving my game, I'll hire a professional."

Merissa swung onto Agincourt's back without asking for help. Billie stood for a moment and watched her trot away. She'd made a huge mess of the day by trying to tell Merissa how to ride, and she wasn't sure whether Merissa would forgive her for insulting the way she played polo. Billie rubbed her hand across her eyes. Had she been trying to push Merissa away, like she had when she told her how to ride Ranger? Or had she really been trying to help? Either way, her main duty was to keep Merissa safe. Billie grabbed the gloves Merissa had dropped in her haste to get away and ran across the field after her.

CHAPTER TWENTY-ONE

Merissa rode Aggie into the arena for the next chukker without gloves and with a tight hold on the reins. The gelding shook his head in frustration as she sent him down the field after Cal and the polo ball without loosening her grip.

"Sorry, boy," she whispered, getting control of herself and softening the reins so he had more freedom to move. Damn Billie, getting her upset right before she had to ride. What did she know anyway? How many polo matches had she been in during her short riding career?

Merissa galloped aimlessly up and down the field for a few more minutes, following the ball in play but not actually doing much to help either her teammates or herself make a goal. Billie's advice slowly seeped into her brain, and Aggie's fast canter soothed her agitated thoughts. She missed an easy pass from Cal and mouthed yet another apology as the tumbling mass of players and horses rushed past her.

If she were to be completely honest, she'd always been envious of the way Cal's team seemed to click intuitively with one another. Her own team, while each player was excellent in her own right, had never been able to find the same rhythm she witnessed when watching Cal and her group ride. Merissa had blamed their personalities and their lack of time to spend hours practicing together and becoming friends off the field, but maybe she just hadn't tried hard enough.

Merissa swung her mallet and blocked an opponent's shot, but the impact made her jolt in the saddle. She'd never be this stiff in the practice ring, but she usually felt a little less secure in the saddle when she rode in a match. Performance anxiety, she had told herself. Everyone was a little less flexible and relaxed when they're competing.

Billie had seen the difference in her match riding as something abnormal, though. Merissa glanced over at her as she and Aggie careened by. Billie's hands were clasped between her knees, and there was clearly tension in her shoulders and posture. Merissa had no doubt Billie would never tell her something about her riding out of spite or meanness. Merissa returned her focus to the game playing out around her. She hadn't contributed much this chukker, but instead of rushing into the fray and trying to make up for lost time, she remained a little on the outskirts of play, observing the others.

Cal was obviously the leader, in her spot as number 1. She called out encouragement and advice, and she was always on hand to block an opponent or pass the ball to a free player. She had made two of the team's four goals so far, but that was because she was a better shot than the others and made more of her attempts than they did and not because she monopolized the play. Amy and Laura were less experienced, but they were constantly watching out for each other and for Merissa and Cal, too.

As Merissa watched them connect on the field, she realized that more than half of their play was devoted to assisting another player. She shook her head as the bell rang and the scoreless chukker ended. Her own style of play was much different—when she wasn't controlling or chasing the ball herself, she tended to fade into the background. She had always thought it was because she didn't want to interfere with other players, but maybe she was trying to protect herself from being interfered *with*.

She slid off Aggie's back and handed his reins to Billie, who wordlessly gave her Mariposa's in return. Merissa only had a few seconds to apologize, so she started talking right away.

"I'm not a team player," she said. "That sucks, and it was hard to hear. But I shouldn't have gotten angry with you because you told me the truth. I'm sorry, Billie."

Billie gave Merissa's shoulder a squeeze. Even the brief contact reached Merissa deep inside. Billie's words made sense to her now, but she learned more about connecting to someone through Billie's touch than anything she might say. Billie's hand on her shoulder held residual memories of Billie catching her when she fell out of Dennis's window, comforting her the morning after his shooting, sliding down her belly in the dark night...Sex and saving and sharing. Becoming a team of two.

"You're used to taking care of yourself," Billie continued, letting go of Merissa and straightening the cheek piece of Mariposa's bridle. "Whether you're on horseback or not. It's great to be strong and independent, but sometimes it's better to need other people. To rely on a team."

"Yeah, you're one to talk," Merissa said with a grin as Billie lifted her onto Mariposa's back. Billie was right about her, and not just when it came to polo—even when she had tried to learn more about Dennis's killer, she had felt an undeniable urge to make her own decisions and go off in secret. Trusting someone else to have her back wasn't natural for her. Her grandfather had taught her not to trust anyone, and her parents hadn't been there for her when she needed them to fight for her. She had confidence in her horses and in Jean-Yves, but no one else. Until Billie.

Billie kept her hand on Merissa's thigh after she was in the saddle. "I agree. I have a hard time trusting other people and believing they'll be around when I need them. But I'm learning. With my unit and my friends. With you."

"Maybe change is possible," Merissa said with a hopeful lift of her shoulder. She covered Billie's hand where it lay against her leg and pressed it tightly against her thigh, feeling her flooding response to Billie's touch. Even when her mind was reflecting and spinning with information, her body's connection to Billie managed to override everything else. Instead of fighting against it, she let her body absorb Billie's strength and let her sizzling nerve endings energize her. "I'll give it a try."

"You're a beautiful rider on your own, and you're on a stunning horse. With Cal and her team on your side, you'll be unbeatable."

Merissa grinned. "You are the best groom ever," she said as she leaned down and kissed Billie on the mouth. She meant to give her a quick thank you—to be continued later, of course—but she lingered for a moment, gliding her tongue along the corner of Billie's mouth. She sat straight in the saddle again, pleased to see the flush on Billie's cheeks and neck before she turned away and rode back onto the field for the fifth period.

"Bodyguard," Billie called after her in a husky voice. Merissa's smile widened but she didn't turn around.

With Billie's compliments ringing in her mind, Merissa attacked the fifth chukker with the intention of being part of the team, not necessarily winning or scoring any goals. Mariposa was a dream to ride, never shying away from close contact or rough play and faster than most of the other horses. Merissa found herself in control of the ball early in the chukker, and instead of following her own path toward the goal, she veered toward Laura and let her clear the way for Merissa to score the tying goal. In the final seconds, Cal got the ball but was heavily guarded as she galloped to the goal line. Merissa and Mariposa squeezed between the line of the ball and the defending player, neatly pushing her off course and out of Cal's way.

"Excellent job," Cal said as they rode off the field together when the bell rang. "You finally rode well enough to deserve that amazing horse of yours."

She smiled in a teasing way as she spoke, but Merissa knew the words were true. She hopped off the mare and was rewarded with a kiss on the mouth from Billie.

"Amazing," Billie said. "You made everyone on the team better because you were there. I'm proud of you."

Merissa was speechless as she got on her dark gray mare for the final chukker. Cal's words had meant a lot to her, and she had certainly heard enough praise about her riding to last a lifetime from instructors and trainers who were always hoping to please the daughter of a multimillionaire, but Billie's simple statements were heartfelt and deeply meaningful.

"You make me better because you're here," she said, meeting Billie's eyes and hoping Billie could see how seriously she meant those words. They stood close for a moment, not needing touch to feel connected, before Merissa turned Misty toward the field.

The mare was her most experienced horse, although not her most spectacular. She'd never be as agile and fast as Mariposa, but she knew the game inside and out, and she gave Merissa every opportunity to try out her new team player philosophy. No one scored in the final chukker—giving Cal's team the victory by a narrow margin—but Merissa had more fun playing polo than she had since college.

The newfound camaraderie lasted as they brought their horses back to the barn and got ready to leave. She and her regular team usually packed quickly and in silence before heading back to their busy lives, but today she enjoyed lingering with Billie, Rachel, and Cal. Especially Billie. She was hoping to have a few moments alone with her to properly thank her for the kick in the breeches, and when she saw Billie walk Misty around the corner of the barn and toward the van, she grabbed Mariposa's lead rope and hurried after her. Rachel and Cal were in the next stall, playfully arguing about a trip to South America, as Merissa left.

She got to the van, but Billie was nowhere in sight. Merissa led Mariposa up the ramp. She'd tie the mare in her stall and then search for Billie. She had only taken a few steps toward the back of the trailer when the door slammed behind her, most likely blown shut by the increasing wind. She turned around and pushed on the door, needing the light from outside to help her secure Mariposa properly, but it was locked.

"Very funny, Cal," she called, assuming she was the prankster. She jiggled the door again, but instead of hearing Cal's laughter and the rasp of the metal opening up again, she heard the ramp slam against the back of the trailer and the bolt lock into place.

Merissa ran to the side window, pulling Mariposa after her, and tried to see who was outside the trailer. She slammed her fists against the sidewall and screamed for Billie, for Rachel or Cal, for anyone to help her. The van's engine started with a loud roar, and Merissa was thrown to the floor as it jolted forward. One of her friends might teasingly lock her inside for a brief time, but they would never take a joke so far and endanger her or her horse.

Mariposa whinnied and danced across the floor, her metal shoes thudding on the rubber mat dangerously close to Merissa's head. She grabbed the loose lead rope and got to her feet again, bracing herself with legs far apart as the van took a steep turn and drove off the farm's property.

The van accelerated quickly once it came to the paved road, and Mariposa shied again, throwing Merissa against a steel partition. She grunted in pain and staggered back a few steps to stay out of the frightened mare's way. Her stomach turned as shadows of fir trees flashed past the windows at what felt like dizzying speed.

The mare called out again, and Merissa coaxed her slowly toward the front of the van where she managed to enclose her in one of the stalls. As soon as she was confined in the familiar space, Mariposa settled down. Merissa's stomach wasn't nearly as cooperative, and she fought off waves of nausea as she tried to imagine how to escape. She groped along the wall again, searching for handholds to help her remain steady, and came to one of the windows. She might be able to squeeze through it if the van slowed enough, but the latches were on the outside of the trailer to keep the horses from accidentally opening them. Aluminum bars covered them as well, meant to keep the animals from dangling their heads outside where they could get hurt. The back door was out of the question, and the tack room was only accessible from outside the van.

Merissa slowly sank to the floor and wrapped her arms around her bent knees. She'd just made steps to trust other people to help her today, and now she was all alone. She hadn't been trying to go off on her own when everyone was working hard to protect her. She had just wanted to follow Billie. She rested her forehead on her knees and gulped for breath. All she got was a lungful of diesel fumes. She choked back a sob. She was helpless and alone. Too sick to think clearly. At the mercy of whoever was driving the van.

Mariposa stomped her foot, and Merissa lifted her head. Was she really alone? She had her horse here, an animal that was relying on her for protection and safety. She had Cal in her mind telling her to get her head out of her ass and do something. Most of all, she had

Billie inside, pleading with her to make a plan, gather information, and do her best to escape back to the safety of her bodyguard's arms.

She pulled herself to her feet again and peered through the mesh covering the windows. She saw farmland and cows and another lane of traffic. She banged on the window and waved as a car passed them, but no one even looked in her direction. Where were they? She finally saw one of the few and far between signs: I-101, just a few miles outside of Shelton, heading west toward the ocean beaches. She was tearing at the thick mesh with one of her short nails when the van slowed and turned off the highway at an exit where there was nothing more than a gas station and an out-of-business diner. Within minutes, they were on an isolated road leading to nowhere.

Merissa choked back a retching cough when the van swung off the macadam and onto an unpaved road, the gravel pinging off the undercarriage like gunshots. They must be nearing their destination, and she didn't want to stick around and find out what was in store for her there. She untied Mariposa and looped the lead rope around the horse's neck as makeshift reins. As soon as she was outside of the van's stall, the mare got edgy again, probably picking up on Merissa's fear. Merissa fought to control her emotions and transmit only calm, confident feelings to her horse, but the battle wasn't an easy one. She gasped out loud when the van jerked to a stop, and she twisted her fingers tightly in Mariposa's mane. She'd have one shot at this, and she had to make it work.

She heard the footsteps crunch on the gravel, heard the ramp's hinges squeak as it was lowered. As soon as she saw a sliver of daylight at the door, she swung herself onto Mariposa's bare back and urged her forward. The mare's polo training told her exactly what needed to be done—she barreled forward and a push from her shoulder swung the door open and sent the man who was standing outside it flying off the ramp. Merissa caught a glimpse of a slender guy in a ski mask, but she didn't stick around to notice any identifying features. She kicked Mariposa forward and they galloped down the gravel road, back the way they'd come.

Merissa was tempted to veer off the open road where they could be followed by the van or shot at if the kidnapper had a weapon, but she didn't want to risk a fall in the dense undergrowth. After they had run for about a mile she slowed the mare enough to look behind her. No cloud of dust to signal the van's approach. No sound of pursuing footsteps or vehicles. When she turned to the road ahead again, she saw a flash of white streak by her in the woods. A sign, on one of the trees. She'd have to take a chance and stop long enough to read it in the hopes that it would give her a clue about where she was and how to contact help.

She pulled Mariposa to a halt and stared down the road for a long moment. She hated the thought of heading back toward the van and captivity, but she trotted back to the sign.

Play. Written in bold black letters. Given the amount of rainfall in the Northwest and the potholed, dusty condition of the road, any sign out here would soon be dirty and torn. Merissa faced away from the van again and noticed another sign almost a quarter of a mile away. She jogged toward it.

The. Her hands shook as she grabbed a fistful of Mariposa's black mane and cantered her to the next rectangle of white.

Game.

It's a game, Merissa, and you have to learn how to play it, Lemaine had said to her.

A shudder ran through her. Had he arranged for her to be kidnapped and brought here? To be frightened like a chained animal, and then allowed to escape only to be given this message? The idea of being led through this charade like a puppet made her feel furious and weak at the same time. He obviously wasn't afraid of letting her know who was behind all this, and when faced with his gutsy move, she felt the sense of power her escape had given her fizzle away in an instant. He must be so far removed from the abduction that he was confident she'd never be able to blame him for it. She had no proof, except for the words she had heard him say when they were alone. She wiped angrily at the tears on her cheeks, and then she aimed Mariposa toward the main road again and jogged slowly along it until she got to the run-down gas station.

Chapter Twenty-two

Billie left Merissa in the stabling area with Cal and Rachel while she took Misty to the van. Instead of going directly across the parking lot, she took a detour around the barn and down a different aisle, keeping an eye out for anyone suspicious or out of place. The day had gone smoothly so far, except for her short-lived spat with Merissa, but Billie figured the chaotic time after the matches would be ideal for any troublemakers.

She was leading the gray mare back from her recon trip when she saw Merissa and Mariposa pass by the end of the barn alone, heading toward the van. She clucked to Misty and walked faster. Merissa must have seen her leave and was following her, without realizing Billie had veered off course.

She pulled Misty to a halt when a horse in front of them shied away from a water hose and stepped into their path, but they moved on again as soon as the way was clear. They turned the corner at the end of the aisle just in time for Billie to see Merissa's van pulling away from its parking place and heading toward the exit. She hurried Misty into a jog and they ran toward the departing van.

Billie didn't panic at first. Maybe Merissa was moving the van closer to their stalls to make loading equipment and horses easier. But then she caught a glimpse of the driver in the van's rearview mirror. It definitely wasn't Merissa. Billie couldn't make out the guy's features under his low-slung baseball cap, and she ran faster to try to catch up and see some identifying characteristic. She glanced from side to side as she and Misty ran across the lot, hoping to see

Merissa standing somewhere, as perplexed as Billie was to see her van driving away.

The van drove through the exit and turned left. Merissa was obviously not in the parking lot. The two facts rolled through Billie's mind like a wave of seasickness, and she turned Misty in a tight circle and hurried back to the stalls.

"Merissa?" she called as she came down the barn aisle. "Merissa, where are you? Rachel, Cal, I need you."

Rachel and Cal rushed out of two adjoining stalls. "What's going on?" Rachel asked. "I thought Merissa was with you."

"She was heading toward the van." Billie gasped for breath. "By the time I got to the parking lot, it was pulling out. Driven by a guy in a red baseball cap. I need to follow them, try to find her."

Rachel pulled out her phone and snapped out orders. "Billie, take my truck, and Cal take the car. Try to find the van. I'll have the exits closed until I can talk to everyone here, find out if anyone saw what happened."

Billie locked Misty in a stall and grabbed Rachel's keys from her. The three of them scattered, and Billie dashed back to the parking lot and jumped in Rachel's pickup. Rachel was already at the gate talking to the attendant, and they motioned for her to drive on the grass and around the cars and trailers waiting in line to go home. Billie turned left and drove in the direction the van had taken, but she wasn't sure where to go once her street intersected with the highway. She followed a hunch and turned west, driving as fast as she could make the old truck go, scanning every side road and exit for a sign of the van.

This was hopeless. Her hands were shaking, and she gripped the steering wheel tighter to try to control them. Her mind swung between hopeful scenarios and horrific ones. Maybe Merissa had run into a friend and stopped to talk. She could be back at the barn right now, wondering where Billie was and why there was such a fuss at the gate.

Or maybe whoever had killed Dennis had come after Merissa, too. And had waited for the one moment today when no one else was with her.

Billie drove a few miles before her second thoughts grew too insistent to ignore. She should have gotten onto I-5. But going north or south? She pulled off the road and sat on the shoulder, slowing her breath because she felt close to hyperventilating. The physical sensations were similar to the ones she experienced in her nightmares, but this wasn't a bad dream. This was real and happening right now. Merissa was gone.

Her phone buzzed and she dropped it on the floor of the truck when her shaking fingers tried to answer. She leaned over and picked it up again.

"Hello? Merissa? Rachel?"

"Hey, Billie."

Merissa's soft voice was at once wonderful to hear and terrifying. "Merissa. Where the hell are you? What happened?"

"I'm at a gas station with Mariposa. Please come get me. I'll explain everything once you're here."

The exit number Merissa gave her was two more miles down the road. Billie called Rachel while she drove, letting her know Merissa was all right. She pulled into the station and put the truck in park before she jumped out of the cab and ran over to where Merissa stood with her black mare.

She grabbed Merissa in a tight hug and held her without speaking for a long time. Her whole body trembled with relief as she held Merissa in her embrace, but a separate part of her seemed to back away and watch from the outside. The effort to find closure after Mike's death had taken just about every ounce of her strength and sanity. She still suffered from nightmares and sadness. Living mere minutes with the realization that Merissa might have been harmed or worse had been all Billie could bear. What would she ever do if something really did happen to Merissa? She wouldn't survive it.

She stepped away. "What happened? How did you and Mariposa get here?"

Merissa sagged against her horse and told Billie the entire story, from her ride in the van, to her escape, to the signs along her escape route. Once she finished, Billie had to make an effort to relax her clenched fists. She wanted to kill Edwin Lemaine for putting Merissa through this. She wanted to arrest him and let him rot in prison. Do something. But his brazen way of abducting Merissa and letting her know who he was and how much power he had made her feel sick with dread. He was confident. Overly so, or had he kept his own hands so clean he knew Dennis's murder and Merissa's kidnapping would never be tied to him?

"Take me where this happened," Billie said. Merissa frowned, obviously not comfortable returning to the crime scene, but she gave a brief nod. They loaded Mariposa into Cal's trailer and drove away from the highway. Billie called Rachel again with the details Merissa had given her, and then she tucked her phone in her pocket and took Merissa's hand, holding it tightly.

"I saw you leave the barn aisle," Merissa said quietly, looking out the window as she spoke. "I wanted to find you, not to go off on my own."

"I know, Merissa," Billie said, squeezing her hand. "I went the long way out there because I was looking for suspicious people. I didn't know one was waiting for you at the van. I was supposed to be protecting you and I failed."

"No," Merissa said, turning to face Billie. "I did. I was alone, even though you told me not to be."

Billie sighed. "Lemaine had obviously prepared for this show of power and he wouldn't have left your kidnapping to chance. The guy who abducted you might have taken advantage of you being alone, but he probably had another plan in place in case we were together every second. I feel guilty about it, but it might have happened no matter how careful we were."

She didn't add her suspicion that Lemaine's plan for the abduction might have included more physical force that had proved unnecessary since Merissa walked into the van on her own. Maybe they were lucky things happened the way they did. He'd likely already killed at least once. Another body on the way to getting his message across to Merissa might not have bothered him.

Billie parked on the opposite side of the road when they came to the gravel road where Merissa had raced Mariposa to safety. She didn't want to destroy any possible evidence by driving over tracks and footprints, but she doubted forensics would turn up anything useful. Lemaine seemed too careful and too far removed from his own crimes to leave clues behind.

She and Merissa waited in silence for the detectives to arrive. Merissa seemed to have collapsed inward, and Billie couldn't blame her. The trauma she'd experienced wouldn't just disappear, especially since she was still recovering from being a witness to Dennis's death. Billie was doing her best to deal with one thing at a time, as each step presented itself. Step one, talk to the detective. Step two, walk down the road with Merissa to see where the signs had been posted, and discover they were—unsurprisingly—no longer there. Step three, wait while Merissa gave her statement. Step four, call Don. Step five, drive her back to her farm.

Billie was reminded of the first day she had met Merissa. She had found her in the precinct, hunched in the uncomfortable chair, looking diminished somehow because of the ordeal she had been through. Merissa wore the same expression now, but Billie wasn't fooled into believing that Merissa was either weak or defeated. She had simply been through too many difficult things to bear. So had Billie.

Just as Merissa slid back into her role of victim for the moment, Billie once again became the person who could calm and distract scared people. She talked about the polo match, reliving certain shots and fouls, until Merissa joined in. Merissa seemed to spark to life a little bit while they talked about her sport and the day's game.

As soon as they drove up to the barn at Merissa's place, Jean Yves came out to hug her and to lead Mariposa into the barn. Billie and Merissa were alone, for the moment.

Billie took both of Merissa's hands in hers and faced her. "Cal will take your other horses to her barn for the night. You should be able to pick up your van by the afternoon, and you can get the horses whenever you're ready. Lieutenant Hargrove will be by to talk to you tomorrow morning."

Merissa nodded. "Okay. Why are you telling me all of this now?"

Billie sighed and leaned her forehead against Merissa's. "Because I won't be here tomorrow. I'm going back to my place tonight."

Merissa gave her a confused frown. "Do you think I'm safe? After all this time being guarded and nothing happening, why are you leaving me alone the moment something does go wrong?"

"Because I'm too close." Billie looked over her shoulder and saw a car coming up the driveway. "I'm not keeping you safe like I should. You need someone who will focus on your safety, not on *you*."

"But you said Lemaine might have made this happen even if we hadn't been apart for those few minutes." She gripped Billie's hands tightly.

"Maybe." Billie shifted uncomfortably and pulled her hands away. "I guess the real problem is me. I can't handle the thought of something bad happening to you. I almost lost it today, and I can't go through this kind of loss again. Not after Mike. Not after getting so close to you."

Merissa opened her mouth to speak, but the car Billie had seen parked next to them, and Don got out.

"Did I hear that someone needs a bodyguard?" he asked, pulling a small suitcase off the backseat.

"Hey, Don. Thank you for coming. Merissa, Don will be watching you until Hargrove comes by tomorrow. She'll make whatever arrangements need to be done. I'll grab my stuff out of the apartment and get out of here so the two of you can get some sleep."

CHAPTER TWENTY-THREE

Merissa was tired of waiting for Billie to come to her senses and come back to her. The first day after her abduction had been spent talking to detectives and settling her horses back in their stalls after Jean-Yves collected them from Cal's farm. Hargrove told her they hadn't found any evidence of foul play in the van or along the trail. The threatening signs had either been taped in place or attached with thin nails that left no mark as proof of their existence. For all the police had discovered, there was nothing to prove that Merissa hadn't driven the van away from the farm herself, and then claimed she had been kidnapped. Hargrove had seemed to believe her story, but she warned Merissa that without a shred of evidence, her charges against Lemaine wouldn't amount to anything.

The following two days had been spent with Don as a constant shadow. He had proved to be a dutiful bodyguard, staying within ten feet of her at all times. He followed her around the barn, into her kitchen, out on the trails. She had moved back to the main house the night Billie left, and he took up residence on her couch. He was sympathetic to her cause, but repeated what Hargrove had said. Without anything besides her statement, no one would convict Lemaine of foul play.

Like Hargrove and Cal, Don seemed to believe that Merissa's frustration was due to the stalled investigation. She was angry that he'd get away with what he had done to her, but she was more upset about Billie leaving than anything to do with Edwin Lemaine. She was angry because Billie had given up on her when things got too hard to handle. She was even more upset with herself because she had been admittedly relieved the first night. She was exhausted by this whole ordeal, and part of her wanted to give up on her job and her quest to find Dennis's killer and to go back to the way life had been before. Easy. Simple.

Lonely.

As much as she wanted to reset her life and be comfortably alone on her farm with her horses once again, she found herself aching for Billie. For her touch and her laughter. For her annoying way of giving advice and her bad habit of usually being right. Merissa had once believed that her most important goals were to figure out who had shot Dennis and to continue his original and excellent work in urban renewal. Now, she wasn't as convinced about those goals. Maybe Billie was worth her time and energy in a way nothing else was.

Once she decided to go to her, she had to find a way to get past the ever-vigilant Don. She knew the key to distracting him was his pinto mare, Fancy. She arranged to take the pair on a trail ride, and she had Aggie towering over little Fancy in the grooming area. Don was currying her and singing some sort of lullaby under his breath. Merissa went into the tack room—about as far away as Don let her go without coming to hunt her down—and she kicked over a stool with a loud crash.

Don was at the door before she had a chance to leave the room. "What happened? Are you okay?"

"I climbed on the stool to reach that storage container and fell," Merissa said. She limped across the room and winced. "I can't ride like this. I'll need to soak my foot before it starts to swell."

"I'll put the horses away and help you back to the house," Don said. "We'll have our trail ride another time."

"No," Merissa protested a little too firmly. "I mean, I hate to have you miss out on a ride because of me. You haven't had a chance to take Fancy out since you got here, and I'm sure you're dying to exercise her. I have Epsom salts and a bucket right here, and Jean-Yves is cleaning stalls in the next aisle. I'll stay here and soak my ankle while you go on a short trail ride."

Don looked at Fancy, obviously tempted by the offer. Too easy, Merissa thought.

"You promise you'll stay here?"

"I'll be safe," Merissa said with a vague nod. She wasn't really lying. She'd be safest when she was with Billie again.

Don sighed. "Half hour. That's all. Let me help you get over to a chair. You're sure—"

Merissa waved him off. "I'm sure. Just enjoy your ride."

She waited in the tack room until she heard him lead Fancy out the back door of the barn. She felt only a little guilty as she jumped up and scampered back to the house and got in her car. She couldn't see Fancy near the trailhead, so she and Don must already be on their way. She put her car in gear and drove up to the main road and back to Tacoma.

Merissa felt uneasy as she parked around the corner from where Dennis had been shot. She had felt brave at home, but now she was anxious to reach the safety of Billie's apartment. She stepped out of her car and shut the door as a silver car pulled up behind her. She looked at the driver and halted in surprise. Don. He gave her a wink and motioned for her to hurry into the apartment building. She stared at him for a moment longer, and then walked quickly to the door. She had underestimated him, and he had obviously let her think she was sneaking out. She smiled as she hurried up the stairs. She clearly had his approval as the right person for Billie. Now to convince Billie herself...

She paused on the second floor landing to let a tall dark-haired guy pass her, but he stopped next to her instead of continuing on. She stood her ground, even though she wanted to back away from him.

"I saw you in the paper," he said. "The shooting a few weeks ago. You were in the car, weren't you."

Merissa nodded slowly.

"You told the cops it was my car."

Shit. Merissa debated whether to run up to Billie or down to Don. Neither one seemed to be a viable option since the guy in front of her was blocking her way.

"I didn't see who—"

"I didn't do it. I'm real sorry about your friend, and I'm sorry if it was my car. But I didn't shoot him."

Merissa's throat was dry, but she managed another nod. "Okay. Well, thank you." She cleared her throat.

"Name's Carlyle," the man said. "You here to see Billie?"

"Yes," Merissa said.

"I've been worried about her. She isn't the same since she got back." He narrowed his eyes and stared at her. "Do you know somethin' about that?"

"What's wrong with her?"

"She's quiet. Sad. Not our normal Billie." He stepped aside to let her pass. "You go on and cheer her up."

"I'll do my best," Merissa said, slipping past him and walking down the hallway. Her hands were shaking and she wiped her sweaty palms on her jeans. Would she always be expecting guns and violence now? She hated how watching Dennis get shot had turned her into someone filled with fear. She had to face down her fear right now, though, and get Billie to come back to her. She knocked loudly on the door and heard the creak of floorboards through the paper-thin walls as someone walked toward her.

Billie answered the door, and the flash of expression on Billie's face gave Merissa hope. Billie was happy to see her, no matter how much she tried to hide her pleasure behind a mask of indifference.

"Merissa."

"Can I come in?"

Billie nodded and moved out of the way. She looked down the hall as Merissa came inside. "Where's Don? He's supposed to be guarding you."

"He's outside the building," Merissa said. "I tried to trick him into going on a trail ride so I could come here and see you, but he saw through my plan and followed me here."

Billie smiled briefly. "He looks easy to fool, but he isn't. What are you doing here, Merissa?"

"I came to see you." Merissa took a deep breath and stepped toward Billie. "I miss you."

Billie closed her eyes. "I miss you, too. But it's—"

"I know," Merissa said. "It's too hard. You can't face loss again. You want to protect yourself. But you've got it all wrong, Billie. What we had together was easy and natural and comfortable. The hard parts came when we tried to push each other away."

Billie didn't answer, and Merissa pressed on. "We each have learned to be self-sufficient and detached from other people, and being that way might mean less chance of loss, but it also means one hundred percent chance of loneliness. I'd rather have you than the security of all those barriers I've put around me."

Billie reached out and cupped Merissa's cheek. "I felt so helpless when you were kidnapped. I can't stand the thought of you being in danger when I'm unable to help."

Merissa covered Billie's hand with her own. "Then I'll quit all this. I'll give up searching for answers about the shooting. I won't buy the firm."

Billie pulled Merissa into a tight hug, and Merissa felt relief seep through her body as it curved to fit against Billie's.

"No," Billie said, her hand tangling in Merissa's hair as she held her close. She pushed them apart with her hands on Merissa's shoulders. "If we're going to make it together, we both have to stop hiding from challenges. You are the kind of person who wants answers and who needs to find justice for Dennis. You're also damned good at your job and deserve to be able to work where and how you want. No more running away."

"You promise? It hurt to have you leave me." Merissa rested her hands on Billie's hips, wanting to trust even though she'd been hurt by her.

"I promise," Billie said.

She leaned forward and kissed Merissa, sliding her tongue gently across Merissa's lower lip. Merissa had lived a lifetime without Billie, but after a few short weeks, even three days without her had been profoundly lonely. She opened her mouth in an invitation to deepen the kiss, and Billie seemed more than happy to oblige. Merissa tightened her grip and nestled Billie's hips snugly against her own.

"Want the grand tour of the apartment?" Billie asked. Merissa gasped as the words were breathed against her ear. The softness of Billie's whispers sent shockwaves down Merissa's body, reaching everyplace where their bodies were in contact. "We can start with the bedroom."

"Hmm," Merissa said, moaning as Billie nibbled the side of her neck. "I guess it depends. When Don mentioned your bedbug problem, was he kidding?"

Billie stopped the progress her mouth was making and looked thoughtful, although her hands refused to remain still. She slid them over Merissa's ribcage and brushed her thumbs across Merissa's breasts. "I really don't see a problem. As long as I call them pets and not pests, a few bedbugs here and there aren't bad."

Merissa arched closer as Billie continued to tease her nipples through the rough wool of her sweater. She didn't think she could stand much more of this before she tore their clothes off and connected them skin to skin. "Let's take that tour," she said. "I'll take my chances with the bedbugs."

CHAPTER TWENTY-FOUR

B illie poured four cups of coffee and put them on a tray with cream and sugar. She carried it out to the group assembled in her living room, pausing in the doorway to admire how easily Merissa had adapted to the apartment. She was curled on the love seat with her bare feet tucked under her, wearing a thin pale-green sweater and khakis. Her hair was loose and framing her face, and Billie nearly dropped the tray of hot coffee when she remembered the night they'd spent together.

She set the tray on the coffee table and handed Merissa coffee with a splash of cream. Clark drank his black, but Don dosed his with cream and sugar.

"So, what did you guys find out?" Billie asked as she sat down close to Merissa. Once she and Merissa had decided to see the search for Dennis's killer through to the end, they realized they couldn't bring Lemaine to justice on their own. Billie had called in reinforcements.

"It took hours, but we went through a ton of traffic camera footage from the week before Dennis Morgan was killed," Clark said. "We found Percy and followed him around the city."

Don nodded. "He dealt with a lot of different people on the streets, but we were able to narrow the possible shooters to four men."

Clark pulled several still photos from a folder and placed them on the table, tapping one of them. "This guy—Will Jones—seems to be our most likely suspect. He never spoke to Percy face-to-face, but they left cash and drugs for each other in Percy's mailbox. The night before the murder, just after Carlyle said Percy took his keys, Percy left a package in the box. An hour later, Will was there. The next day, they did the same thing in reverse."

"What do you think, Merissa?" Billie asked. She handed her the photo. "Could this be the guy who kidnapped you, too?"

Billie put her hand on Merissa's thigh while Merissa examined the picture. Billie still hated to be reminded of the day Merissa had been abducted. It hadn't even been a week, and the fear and rawness were still present.

"The height and weight seem about right," Merissa said. "But I never got a look at his face. It was covered up the whole time I saw him."

"I got a better look since he couldn't really wear a ski mask in the farm's parking lot and on the way out the gate," Billie said. "The hair color and the shape of his face are similar."

Billie got up to answer a knock at the door, and Rachel and Cal joined the group. Billie had mentioned their plan to Hargrove, but Abby had covered her ears and repeated, *I don't want to know*, until Billie finally walked away. Don and Clark repeated their information to Rachel and Cal while Billie got more coffee from her kitchen.

"What about you two?" Don asked.

"I did some digging into Lemaine's finances and subsidiaries," Rachel said, sitting on one of the folding chairs Billie had set out for them. "He follows the same predictable pattern with everything he gets his hands on. Apartment buildings, restaurants, strip malls. Take the strip malls, for instance. Once he gets involved, all the unique stores and smaller businesses are out. By the time he's done, they have more than eighty percent of shops or restaurants in common. He serves on a ton of advisory boards, and even when he doesn't seem to have real power on paper, his influence is easy to see once you start looking for it."

Merissa stirred her coffee. "He has a lot of power, but little imagination," she said. "The same thing happened when he got his hooks into Dennis. Lemaine didn't want different designs and creative options. He wanted a series of cookie-cutter blueprints backed by the firm's reputation."

Rachel nudged Cal's leg with her foot. "Tell them about the investors."

Billie had asked Cal to use her family's connections in the business world to check into the stable of investors Lemaine used most regularly. She wasn't sure how any of this information would help them take him down, but at least it was giving them more of a picture of the man and his influence.

"They were pretty evasive," Cal said with a shrug. "But when they act like that, they tend to tell you what you wanted to know in a roundabout way. Everyone I talked to denied letting Lemaine influence their decisions, but they all told me stories about *friends* who tried to cross Lemaine and suffered for it. Investors are supposed to make their own decisions, choose the projects or people or products they want to back, but the ones who work with Lemaine can't do that."

Cal pulled out a stack of spreadsheets and handed them around. "I snooped around through public records and talked to assistants and secretaries, and I got a clear picture of the type of investment each investor favored." She pointed at the string of words across the bottom of each page. "Rachel cross-referenced these and found the criteria most often used by each investor. Some like projects with a philanthropic angle, some prefer small and safe investments over high-cost, high-risk ones. Some support the arts, others focus on projects benefiting children."

Cal flipped through the stack of papers. "Anyway, once you look for it, it's easy to see the criteria an investor uses to make decisions. The projects that deviate from their usual ones stand out clearly. In almost every instance, those standouts are Lemaine's projects. He somehow has enough influence to control what his investors do and what they back."

Merissa shook her head as she looked over one of Cal's spreadsheets. "He has control all over the city. He has the ability to decide how these wealthy and influential people will invest their money. What could we possibly do to intimidate him enough to get a confession out of him? I'm guessing the people he controls will lie, cheat, and steal to protect him, maybe because they're scared of him or have been threatened by him. They would be too scared to stand up against him."

Billie had an idea brewing, but she was tempted to keep it quiet because it involved Merissa. She didn't want Merissa to have any dealings with this man, but he had to be stopped before he got control over the entire city. Urban renewal projects with individual character and housing options for middle- and working-class citizens would be severely limited. Pretty soon Tacoma would be nothing more than a series of the same strip malls, bowling alleys, and restaurants.

Even beyond Lemaine's goals for the city, Billie felt she had to give Merissa a chance to best him because Billie understood the pain of losing someone. If she had the chance to find justice for Mike, she'd definitely take it. She didn't, but she could offer the opportunity to Merissa.

"I have an idea," she said. "It involves Merissa and Carlyle…"

Merissa stood on the front porch of the tan-colored house and looked at the view. From this vantage point in one of the more prestigious neighborhoods on Browns Point, she could see Mount Rainier to her far left and the city of Tacoma sprawling beneath her. The ferry to Vashon Island slowly churned its way across the Sound. The houses in this neighborhood were huge, but all fairly similar in shape and style. They were also packed tightly together. If she'd had to make a choice, she'd have opted for a less fancy house with more space, but the developer had certainly been trying to make the most of these view properties.

She turned away from the city and toward the door, ringing the bell and clasping and unclasping her hands while she waited. She was about to rush down the stairs and away from the house in relief because no one was home when the door opened and Edwin Lemaine stood in front of her. He was as smooth and put together as usual, with a high-necked black sweater and pressed gray pants. He was clearly surprised to see her, but the expression didn't last long and was quickly replaced by his controlled smile.

"Merissa, dear. I wasn't expecting you. At my house. Come in."

He stood back, and Merissa walked in, wincing at the sound of the door clicking shut. She wished she were better at hiding her distaste for and fear of the man, but she realized those very emotions were ones he would expect to see in her. He had bullied her, he had kidnapped her, and he knew he held all the cards.

He shut the door without locking it, and as soon as he turned away, Merissa unlatched it quietly and left it slightly ajar. He led the way into his study. No warm woods and warmth here, just a sleek modern style with uncomfortable and expensive black leather chairs. Merissa perched on the edge of one and spoke before Edwin could ask her why she was there.

"I got your message."

"Ah. Clever girl to escape as easily as you did. I thought you might be too carsick to function."

A shiver ran through her at his mention of something so personal. What else had he learned about her? And how had he found out about her getting carsick? From Dennis?

"I think I did exactly what you wanted me to."

"And in the future?"

Merissa wanted to gag. "I'll do exactly what you want me to do. I want to play the game, Mr. Lemaine. The Morgan Group offers money and prestige, and I want both of those things. I'll do what it takes to make the firm as successful as Dennis did."

Lemaine leaned back in his chair with a smile. "Excellent, my dear. I believe we're going to get along just fine, as long as you agree to work exclusively with me. First thing Monday, we'll meet with—"

Both he and Merissa jumped to their feet when the front door burst open. Edwin was halfway to the study door when Carlyle ran in with a gun in his hand and a crazed look on his face. Merissa yelped and backed away along with Edwin, who held his hands up either in a gesture of surrender or an attempt to calm his assailant.

"I need the name," Carlyle said with a slur in his voice. "I know you were behind this, you and Percy, using my car and settin' me up. Give me the name of the guy who shot that dude, or you'll be next."

"I have no idea what you're talking about," Edwin said, inching back toward his desk. Merissa wondered if he had a gun hidden in there.

"And you," Carlyle continued, turning toward her with a snarl. "I recognize you. You're the lady that told the cops on me. Turned in my car and had me locked up for days. Damned cops think I did it 'cause of you."

Merissa's heart was beating so loudly she was certain everyone in the room could hear the thudding.

"I didn't see you in the car, I just told the police I saw one like it," Merissa said, her voice coming out thin and flute-like. "What do you want from me?"

"Nothing. It's him who's got something I want. The name of the guy who shot your friend. Tell me and I leave."

Merissa looked at Edwin, pleading with her eyes for him to talk. He was still on the front side of the desk and wouldn't be able to make it to any of the drawers before Carlyle shot him.

"Fine," he snapped, as if the word was painful to say. "He was just some disgusting street trash like you. Name's Al Brown. Hangs out near the train station. Now get out of my house. You've got what you want."

"Liar," Carlyle said with a hiss. He grabbed Merissa and held her with his left arm wrapped around her throat, his gloved right holding the gun to her temple. "Tell me, or she dies."

"Please, Edwin," Merissa pleaded. "You know who shot Dennis, so let whoever it was take the fall. Please."

"Her first, you next," said Carlyle.

"Will Jones," Edwin spat out. "His name was Will Jones. Now let her go and get the hell out of my house."

"Sound right to you?" Carlyle asked Merissa. He let go of the grip he'd had on her.

"I do believe it does," she said, straightening up and facing Lemaine. He seemed to realize they had worked together to trick him, and he dove for his desk drawer. Carlyle tossed the gun he had been holding onto the desk.

"Looking for this?" he asked. "I borrowed it, but you can have it back now."

Lemaine grabbed the gun and raised it. Carlyle didn't flinch when Edwin pulled the trigger and there was only the sound of an empty round clicking into place. "Except for the bullets. I seem to have misplaced those."

Merissa stepped back as Lieutenant Hargrove and several other officers came through the door and into the house. Billie was right on their heels, and she grabbed Merissa into a tight hug.

"You're okay?" she asked, holding Merissa at arm's length as if to make certain she was still in one piece. "I was so scared."

"I'm fine," Merissa said. "Just a little shaky."

"I'm good, too, thanks for asking," Carlyle said.

Billie rolled her eyes at him and led them both out of the house to where Rachel and the rest of the mounted team were waiting. Carlyle proceeded to give them a rundown of what happened, including an only slightly exaggerated version of his own part in the ruse. Merissa led Billie a few yards away.

"I think my career as an undercover cop starts and ends today," she said, brushing Billie's dark bangs out of her eyes. "I'm going to concentrate instead on my own career, not Dennis's anymore."

"You're not going to buy the firm?" Billie asked, tucking Merissa's hair behind her car and tracing its curve until Merissa felt her breath become as shallow as it had been in Lemaine's house, but for a very different   and much better—reason. "What made you decide?"

Merissa turned her head and kissed Billie's hand. "Dennis had a great reputation, but it's tainted now. I don't want to inherit his bad decisions, but I'll always remember the conversations we had and what I learned from him. I'll keep his good ideas alive in a way, but it's time to focus on my own vision. After being so up close and personal with a sleaze like Lemaine, I know I have to try to make it work. This business of urban planning needs someone with morals." She glanced over at Carlyle who seemed to be mimicking

Edwin's attempt to shoot him as he told his version of the story to anyone who would listen. "And someone who cares about the people who live in the city. I think I can do something good with my own company."

"I have no doubt," Billie said. "You already have done something great for Tacoma. And for me." She pulled Merissa to her and kissed her softly. "I love you, Merissa."

"I love you, too, Billie. Bedbugs and all."

Chapter Twenty-five

As Billie guided her mount Misty onto the polo field on the warm spring day, she mentally checked every possible exit route. Don was in place near the gate and he gave her a thumbs-up when she glanced his way. She had personally locked the gate leading to the trails this morning.

Billie halted next to Merissa and Aggie, across from Cal and Rachel. They were supposedly going to play a fun match against each other, but Billie wasn't going to let her guard down for a moment because she knew the threat of a kidnapping was a very real one today. She glared at Cal and mouthed the words, *I'm watching you.*

Cal's grin only widened, and she reached down to pat Mariposa's glossy black neck with a wicked look on her face.

"I don't think this was a good idea," Billie murmured to Merissa. "She's a flight risk."

Merissa's laughter washed over Billie like a wave. She would never get tired of hearing the sound, whether they were joking around in the grocery store, tangled together in bed at night, or spending time with friends. Before she had met Merissa, Billie had been starting to get closer to her teammates and to Beth, but she was still holding back. Merissa had settled her, given her a place to call home, and Billie trusted her with everything she was. She hadn't expected to have her love for Merissa expand out to other people, but in the months they had spent together, Billie's world had exploded into a series of relationships. Connections that had been tentative in the past were strong and vibrant now, blossoming from gray to full color.

"Don can catch her if she bolts through the gate," Billie continued, nudging Misty closer to Merissa. "But we know how well Mariposa jumps. What if Cal tries to take her over the fence?"

Merissa kept her smile in place, and she spoke out of the corner of her mouth in an exaggerated whisper loud enough for Cal and Rachel to hear. "Who do you think sent Jean-Yves to ride in the outdoor arena? He's under orders to lasso anyone who gallops his way."

"Good, because I think they came here in Cal's sports car to throw us off the scent. What do you want to bet Rachel's truck and a horse trailer are parked just around the bend?"

"Like I'd help her steal your mare just to save thousands of dollars and keep Cal from going to Argentina and buying twenty horses," Rachel said with a snort. "Now are we going to play polo, or are you two conspiracy theorists going to stand there fretting all day?"

"Polo," Merissa said. She tossed the practice ball between the two rows of horses with a flick of her wrist and ran after it before anyone else was ready to move.

"Damn," Rachel said as Cal and Mariposa took off after Merissa. "She's been playing polo with Cal too much."

Rachel bolted after the others, but Billie cantered slowly on a parallel path. Merissa caught her eye and swiftly sent the ball across the field. Billie scored before the other team had a chance to regroup and rush over to her.

"Good plan," Billie said when Merissa trotted back to her side. They had discussed strategy the night before, as if they had been preparing for war, and Merissa's horse figurines had cantered across an imaginary polo field on the bedroom rug while Merissa and Billie plotted how to beat their opponents.

"You were right about Cal," Merissa said. "She's so excited to be riding Mariposa that she's going to gallop full speed everywhere she goes." She put her reins and mallet handle in one hand and reached over to lace her fingers briefly with Billie's. They seemed to share the need to touch each other whenever possible. For Billie it was a matter of survival. She needed Merissa's skin next to hers as much as she needed air or food.

"And Rachel will do whatever it takes to stay close to her. Brilliant idea to put her on your slowest polo pony."

Merissa smiled. "We make an excellent team," she said. She bridged the gap between them and kissed Billie. "In more ways than one."

For a moment, all their carefully laid plans flew out of Billie's head as she breathed in Merissa's scent of lavender, combined with the earthier elements of horse and saddle soap. The combination was intoxicating, and Billie was about to cede the match and drag Merissa back to the house when Cal and Rachel rode by.

"We won't have any trouble beating them now," Cal said to Rachel. "Billie will be so flustered she won't know which goal is theirs."

"I'd worry about my own riding if I were you," Merissa said. She slowly disengaged her hand from Billie's, letting her fingertips remain in contact for a long moment before she trailed after Cal, taunting her. "I've never seen Mariposa canter so slowly on the polo field. Were you holding her back on purpose?"

Billie laughed at Merissa's obvious tactics. Luckily, Cal was so competitive she would likely take the bait and become even more reckless in her play. Merissa had quickly become an expert negotiator in the months after opening her design firm. Billie would never say it out loud, but she had a feeling Merissa had learned more from watching her grandfather than she realized. She was putting her skills to use in a positive way, though, as she created her visionary plans and refused to compromise when it came to the citizens of Tacoma. She and Billie were committed to protecting them, in very different ways.

Billie stopped in the middle of the field and watched her friends bickering good-naturedly about who was going to throw the ball to start the next skirmish. Loud pounding and occasional shouts from the main house punctuated the idyllic peace of the farm, but they were welcome noises to Billie. She had moved into the nanny wing with Merissa, but they had decided to renovate the main part of the house for them to use as a fresh start.

Billie had expected Merissa—with her training and talent—to take control of the project, but she had left most of the design work to Billie. She had protested at first, but then she had become engrossed in the plans. She had endured Don's earlier teasing about being settled in her seedy apartment and about the reading nook she had created in the police barn, but now she realized he had been right about her. She was a settler at heart, and she was discovering a real joy in planning a space where she and Merissa would live.

Merissa. She was the reason Billie was willing to settle down. A fancy home was nice. Living on the farm was wonderful. But Billie would gladly have stayed in her bedbuggy apartment if it meant Merissa would be with her. She filled Billie's life with unexpected pleasure and gave her the sense of belonging Billie had always wanted but never had. She had watched Merissa with pride over the past months as she put her heart and soul into her new firm, and she had seen what must have been the same look of pleasure on Merissa's face when Billie looked up from sketching a plan for one of their rooms and caught her staring. They brought out something in each other—something better and brighter than either could produce on her own.

Billie knew Merissa had given her something even more profound than a newfound love of decorating. She had smoothed the edges of the past, helping Billie through her nightmares and easing the pain with frantic sex, soft touches, space. Merissa seemed to understand what Billie needed even when she couldn't articulate it. She wasn't forgetting the past, but she was now able to focus on some of the better aspects of it. Her friendship with Mike, the times when her dad was home between fishing trips. Billie could see other sides beyond the pain and trauma now.

Billie watched Merissa twist in her saddle, keeping the ball just out of Cal's grasping reach. Her polo shirt skimmed up, revealing a glimpse of her slender waist and a clear view of her gorgeous rear. Sexy and playful. Billie couldn't keep her distance any longer, and she aimed toward Merissa as if her skin was magnetized and Billie couldn't resist its pull.

"Are you ready?" Merissa asked, tossing the white polo ball in her right hand as Billie once again walked to her side.

Billie grinned and gave her a wink. Was she ready for life with Merissa, with all the twists and turns and joy it would bring? "You bet," she said.

As usual, Merissa seemed to know when Billie was talking about something beyond the surface of mere words. She stopped juggling the ball and focused her attention on Billie. "Me, too, love of my life."

"Oh, gag," said Cal. "Just throw the damned ball."

Merissa smiled at Billie, promising a lifetime of fun and love, before she tossed the ball into play.

About the Author

Karis Walsh relocated from the Pacific Northwest and now works in a library in Texas. When she isn't reading or writing, she enjoys spending time outside with her animals, playing the viola, and hiking through the state park.

Books Available from Bold Strokes Books

Amounting to Nothing by Karis Walsh. When mounted police officer Billie Mitchell steps in to save beautiful murder witness Mcrissa Karr, worlds collide on the rough city streets of Tacoma, Washington. (978-1-62639-728-6)

Becoming You by Michelle Grubb. Airlie Porter has a secret. A deep, dark, destructive secret that threatens to engulf her if she can't find the courage to face who she really is and who she really wants to be with. (978-1-62639-811-5)

Birthright by Missouri Vaun. When spies bring news that a swordswoman imprisoned in a neighboring kingdom bears the Royal mark, Princess Kathryn sets out to rescue Aiden, true heir to the Belstaff throne. (978-1-62639-485-8)

Crescent City Confidential by Aurora Rey. When romance and danger are in the air, writer Sam Torres learns the Big Easy is anything but. (978-1-62639-764-4)

Love Down Under by MJ Williamz. Wylie loves Amarina, but if Amarina isn't out, can their relationship last? (978-1-62639-726-2)

Privacy Glass by Missouri Vaun. Things heat up when Nash Wiley commandeers a limo and her best friend for a late drive out to the beach: Champagne on ice, seat belts optional, and privacy glass a must. (978-1-62639-705-7)

The Impasse by Franci McMahon. A horse packing excursion into the Montana Wilderness becomes an adventure of terrifying proportions for Miles and ten women on an outfitter led trip. (978-1-62639-781-1)

The Right Kind of Wrong by PJ Trebelhorn. Bartender Quinn Burke is happy with her life as a playgirl until she realizes she can't fight her feelings any longer for her best friend, bookstore owner Grace Everett. (978-1-62639-771-2)

Wishing on a Dream by Julie Cannon. Can two women change everything for the chance at love? (978-1-62639-762-0)

A Quiet Death by Cari Hunter. When the body of a young Pakistani girl is found out on the moors, the investigation leaves Detective Sanne Jensen facing an ordeal she may not survive. (978-1-62639-815-3)

Buried Heart by Laydin Michaels. When Drew Chambliss meets Cicely Jones, her buried past finds its way to the surface—will they survive its discovery or will their chance at love turn to dust? (978-1-62639-801-6)

Escape: Exodus Book Three by Gun Brooke. Aboard the Exodus ship *Pathfinder*, President Thea Tylio still holds Caya Lindemay, a clairvoyant changer, in protective custody, which has devastating consequences endangering their relationship and the entire Exodus mission. (978-1-62639-635-7)

Genuine Gold by Ann Aptaker. New York, 1952. Outlaw Cantor Gold is thrown back into her honky-tonk Coney Island past, where crime and passion simmer in a neon glare. (978-1-62639-730-9)

Into Thin Air by Jeannie Levig. When her girlfriend disappears, Hannah Lewis discovers her world isn't as orderly as she thought it was. (978-1-62639-722-4)

Night Voice by CF Frizzell. When talk show host Sable finally acknowledges her risqué radio relationship with a mysterious caller, she welcomes a *real* relationship with local tradeswoman Riley Burke. (978-1-62639-813-9)

Raging at the Stars by Lesley Davis. When the unbelievable theories start revealing themselves as truths, can you trust in the ones who have conspired against you from the start? (978-1-62639-720-0)

She Wolf by Sheri Lewis Wohl. When the hunter becomes the hunted, more than love might be lost. (978-1-62639-741-5)

Smothered and Covered by Missouri Vaun. The last person Nash Wiley expects to bump into over a two a.m. breakfast at Waffle House is her college crush, decked out in a curve-hugging law enforcement uniform. (978-1-62639-704-0)

The Butterfly Whisperer by Lisa Moreau. Reunited after ten years, can Jordan and Sophie heal the past and rediscover love or will differing desires keep them apart? (978-1-62639-791-0)

The Devil's Due by Ali Vali. Cain and Emma Casey are awaiting the birth of their third child, but as always in Cain's world, there are new and old enemies to face in post Katrina-ravaged New Orleans. (978-1-62639-591-6)

Widows of the Sun-Moon by Barbara Ann Wright. With immortality now out of their grasp, the gods of Calamity fight amongst themselves, egged on by the mad goddess they thought they'd left behind. (978-1-62639-777-4)

18 Months by Samantha Boyette. Alissa Reeves has only had two girlfriends and they've both gone missing. Now it's up to her to find out why. (978-1-62639-804-7)

Arrested Hearts by Holly Stratimore. A reckless cop with a secret death wish and a health nut who is afraid to die might be a perfect combination for love. (978-1-62639-809-2)

Capturing Jessica by Jane Hardee. Hyperrealist sculptor Michael tries desperately to conceal the love she holds for best friend, Jess, unaware Jess's feelings for her are changing. (978-1-62639-836-8)

Counting to Zero by AJ Quinn. NSA agent Emma Thorpe and computer hacker Paxton James must learn to trust each other as they work to stop a threat clock that's rapidly counting down to zero. (978-1-62639-783-5)

Courageous Love by KC Richardson. Two women fight a devastating disease, and their own demons, while trying to fall in love. (978-1-62639-797-2)

Pathogen by Jessica L. Webb. Can Dr. Kate Morrison navigate a deadly virus and the threat of bioterrorism, as well as her new relationship with Sergeant Andy Wyles and her own troubled past? (978-1-62639-833-7)

Rainbow Gap by Lee Lynch. Jaudon Vickers and Berry Garland, polar opposites, dream and love in this tale of lesbian lives set in Central Florida against the tapestry of societal change and the Vietnam War. (978-1-62639-799-6)

Steel and Promise by Alexa Black. Lady Nivrai's cruel desires and modified body make most of the galaxy fear her, but courtesan Cailyn Derys soon discovers the real monsters are the ones without the claws. (978-1-62639-805-4)

Swelter by D. Jackson Leigh. Teal Giovanni's mistake shines an unwanted spotlight on a small Texas ranch where August Reese is secluded until she can testify against a powerful drug kingpin. (978-1-62639-795-8)

Without Justice by Carsen Taite. Cade Kelly and Emily Sinclair must battle each other in the pursuit of justice, but can they fight their undeniable attraction outside the walls of the courtroom? (978-1-62639-560-2)

21 Questions by Mason Dixon. To find love, start by asking the right questions. (978-1-62639-724-8)

A Palette for Love by Charlotte Greene. When newly minted Ph.D. Chloé Devereaux returns to New Orleans, she doesn't expect her new job, and her powerful employer—Amelia Winters—to be so appealing. (978-1-62639-758-3)

By the Dark of Her Eyes by Cameron MacElvee. When Brenna Taylor inherits a decrepit property haunted by tormented ghosts, Alejandra Santana must not only restore Brenna's house and property but also save her soul. (978-1-62639-834-4)

Cash Braddock by Ashley Bartlett. Cash Braddock just wants to hang with her cat, fall in love, and deal drugs. What's the problem with that? (978-1-62639-706-4)